Needing Her

Also by Molly McAdams

Needing Her

A NOVELLA

MOLLY MCADAMS

WILLIAM MORROW IMPULSE
An Imprint of HarperCollinsPublishers

Excerpt from *From Ashes* copyright © 2012 by Molly Jester.
Excerpt from *Forgiving Lies* copyright © 2013 by Molly Jester.

EPub Edition JANUARY 2014 ISBN: 9780062300119
Print Edition ISBN: 9780062300126

10 9 8 7 6 5 4 3 2 1

Needing Her

Chapter One

Maci

AMBER SLAPPED A hand over her mouth and had to work at swallowing her coffee before she burst out laughing. "Oh, I would have paid to have been there! Stupid night shifts at the hospital getting in my way of all the fun stuff."

"You should've seen the look on Shelby's face when Bryce pulled me in for a long kiss in front of her." I grinned against my cup and drained the rest of it. "It really was priceless."

"I would have even suffered through being near Bryce if it meant watching that skank get put in her place."

I rolled my eyes. Amber had never been one to hide her hate for Bryce, and even though I'd never understood why she didn't like him in the first place, it was becoming more of a running joke for us rather than her actually hating him. Besides, she couldn't hate him: he'd inadvertently brought us together a couple years ago and we'd been best friends since.

It had been my twenty-first birthday, and somehow over the course of the night filled with barhopping and Bryce being . . . well, Bryce, he'd ended up with a concussion and we'd spent the rest of my birthday in the ER. Amber had been one of his main nurses when we'd finally gotten him into a room, and not more than twenty minutes later, my night filled with drinking and not much food decided to make a reappearance all over my shoes. In my still-drunk mind, I hadn't even been upset about puking everywhere. I'd started crying because my favorite shoes were ruined and "favorite shoes can't be ruined on my birthday." Amber and another nurse had cleaned everything while I sat there crying like a three-year-old over my shoes, and when they were done, a pair of sequined Uggs were placed in front of me. Amber had told me at the time they were her favorites and I could borrow them so I could finish out my birthday wearing a pair of "favorites." It'd been a lasting insta-friendship, even though she still wouldn't let me live that night down.

She groaned and tossed her phone roughly onto the table. "I swear this guy is a machine. He never stops. I mean, *never*. If it weren't for the fact that we have jobs, I don't think he'd ever let me leave the bed."

"Is this still Aaron? You said you two still sneak

into the closets at the hospital . . ." I drifted off, my accusation sounding more like a question.

"Yeah, exactly. Machine. Let's just hope we're busy tonight, I need at least a twelve-hour break from that man before we go back to one of our apartments, or he's going to break me."

I shook my head sadly at her and almost chickened out of asking my question twice before finally blurting, "Do you actually enjoy having sex?"

"Is that a trick question? Of course I do, who doesn't?"

"I just—I don't know. In the books I read, these women have amazing partners and I know what I'm reading is fantasy . . . I mean, seriously, I get that. But I don't enjoy sex with Bryce at all. It has nothing to do with wishing it was like what I read, it's just really, *really* bad."

Amber eyed me with a confused look. "Then why are you still seeing him? Maci, you're hot, it's not like you wouldn't have a chance with anyone else. You don't have to settle for him."

"I'm not. He's not even my boyfriend, you can't settle for someone you aren't technically dating."

"Exactly! But you're still not getting out there either because he's *always* with you and stops anyone from coming near you."

I sighed and twirled my empty coffee cup between my fingers. "I know."

"You just need to drop him. And since you two

only have this friends-with-benefits thing going on, it shouldn't be a big deal to end it."

"We're not *together* because my brothers would flip if they knew I was dating anyone."

"No, you just *think* your brothers would flip," Amber argued. "There's a difference."

My jaw dropped and I looked at her like she was delusional. "Max Bertrand asked me on a date right before college started and canceled via text the day of. I saw him the next day and he turned and literally *ran* the other way, Amber. He had tape on his nose and huge bruises under his eyes!"

She shrugged. "Maybe he didn't want you to see him looking like that."

"He *still* runs away from me, you've seen him do it! Besides, my brothers fessed up to it."

"Huh"—she looked like she was trying to find something to support her argument before finally throwing her hands up in the air—"okay, fine. They're a little protective."

"Or *a lot* protective." I rolled my eyes and snorted. "Anyway, Bryce knows all that and is completely fine with staying how we are. Eh, well, for now."

I knew Bryce figured we would be a legitimate couple eventually, but he was expecting me to change in that time; and there wasn't a chance in hell of that happening. I was positive the only reason he was okay staying "just friends" for now is because he and I both knew his family wouldn't approve of the way

I looked. I didn't fit in with their perfect country-club multimillion-dollar house, and I was more than okay with that. I had grown up in a loving home, and my mom always encouraged each of us to find who we are and be that person.

And that person wasn't a back-to-her-blonde-roots, polo-wearing, club-for-brunch-on-Sunday kind of girl. It's not like I was goth or grunge, or even some peace-pushing, tree-hugging hippy. I was just Maci. I'd dyed my hair a vibrant red years ago and never gone back. My nose was pierced with a small hoop in it, I have a few tattoos, and I cussed too much from growing up with older brothers—something that Bryce was always reminding me he hated—if that was enough of a reason for Bryce to keep me hidden from his family, then so be it. It just helped with the arrangement I needed in hiding him from my brothers.

"Tell me something," Amber said suddenly. "What don't you like about sex with Bryce?"

"The whole thing?" Amber's expression deadpanned, and after looking around to make sure we were alone outside the café, I sat up straight. "Okay, fine. Well, first, he seriously lasts forever but however he's doing it doesn't feel good. Like, it's almost painful. Second, I've never had an orgasm with him. Ever. I always have to finish myself when I go home or after he leaves. And, third, there's never any foreplay—it almost seems like a business transaction. Take your clothes off, let him thrust for a while put your clothes back on and part ways. It's the most awkward part of our relationship . . . friendship, gah, whatever-the-fuck it's called."

Amber was cracking up by now, and though she was covering her mouth to try to quiet it, her entire body was shaking and her face was turning red.

"Why are you laughing, this isn't funny!"

"Seriously." She snorted and her laughs got louder. "Oh my God, I'm sorry. Whew!" She fanned at her watering eyes. "Oh that just makes me hate him more. And to think, Shelby can't stand you because you're 'with' Bryce Anderson? If only she knew . . . if only she knew."

I dropped my head into my hands and groaned. "I want a guy who pays attention to me for once. It doesn't have to be this amazing, mind-blowing, the-world-stops-turning experience; I just want to enjoy it. Just once. That's all I want."

"Nope, I'm not letting you settle for anything less than your . . . whatever-the-hell experience you just said. We need to find a man who will give that to you."

"Sure . . . yeah. Not even counting the fact that guy is probably only found in fiction; that would involve me sleeping with numerous guys until I find one who will give me that experience. Not only do I not want to be labeled a slut like some best friends I know . . ." I cleared my throat and gave her a pointed look. "But that also sounds like the biggest headache."

"I won't take offense to that because I love you, but we've got to get you away from Bryce." She took a long drink from her cup and slapped her hand down on the table a few times. "Oh! Oh, what about your neighbor! That cop guy—"

"Detective."

"Same difference. He's all quiet, and intense, and . . . mmm. I bet he'd be good."

I bet he would be too. I'd had the biggest crush on him since I was twelve and he'd starred in practically every fantasy I'd ever had. "Yeah, that's not about to happen."

"Why not? Is he married?"

"Uh, no, he's not. But he's Dylan and Dakota's best friend. They all grew up together."

Amber's eyes glazed over, and a grin I knew too well crossed her face. "God your brothers are—wait! How did I not know he was their friend? Where have I been?"

"Not allowed near my brothers . . . ?"

"Yeah, but he's your neighbor! I didn't know you actually knew him. And you can't hide them from me forever. They're the only two of your brothers left who are available, and they're identical twins. It's every girl's fantasy."

"And this is where I throw up. Or pour bleach on my brain. Anything to forget you talking about fantasies and Dumb and Dumber in the same hour, let alone sentence."

She snorted and rolled her eyes. "You have to admit your brothers are good-looking."

I made a gagging noise the same moment my phone

went off. Reaching for it on the table, I saw Bryce's name and showed Amber. "Speak of the devil."

"Let me guess, he's lonely?" I made some sort of affirmative noise and she grabbed her purse as she stood to leave. "Tell him your vagina is no longer available. We're officially starting our manhunt for Mister Awesome, and he can't be in the running."

"God, Amber, you're ridiculous. We're not starting anything and I'm not going to end . . . whatever it is I have going on with Bryce right now." My lips pursed when I read his message.

Bryce A: Hey babe can I come over? Long day
at work need to unwind

"He's in the way of you finding anyone else," she argued.

"I don't want to find anyone else."

Her eyes narrowed and she pointed at my cell. "I'm finding you someone else. Anyone would be better than him. I'm going to come over tomorrow with the first guy that shows up in the ER tonight just to prove my point."

I laughed and shook my head. "Have fun at your shift."

"We still on for getting our apartments all Christmas-ed out this weekend?"

"How is that even a question? Of course."

"Just making sure! I'm going to have to warn Aaron my body won't be available for an entire day."

"That poor guy," I said in a monotone voice. "How will he ever live?"

She laughed and blew me a kiss. "Later, sweetie!"

Looking back at my phone, I tapped out a response as I stood and headed to my car.

Sure. I'm on my way back, come over in 30?

Despite the complaints I'd just shared about him, I really liked Bryce. We'd been close like this for a while now, and good friends for years before. He could be sweet when he wanted to, and was protective almost to a fault when it came to me. I needed to stay "single" to protect guys from my four older brothers, but it still felt good to have a constant in my life, and to be wanted by someone.

Connor

"Wait, you're leaving?"

My arms froze with the shirt partially over my head, and when they started moving again, my movements were careful as I finished pulling the shirt over my chest. With a deep breath in, I turned to look at the pissed-off girl. "That's how this works, sweetheart."

She pulled the sheet up on her chest as she used her other arm to sit up. "Then tell me what your definition of *this* is, because apparently it's different from mine."

Letting my hand slide to the back of my neck, I left

it there as I shrugged. "I picked you up at a bar. I'd met you not even an hour before we left; I don't know what else you could expect from that."

"Yeah, you're right," she scoffed. Her face scrunched together in anger, but even in the dark room I could see the wetness gathering in her eyes. "What else would I expect from some prick who picks up women in a fucking bar?"

I focused on her eyes a moment longer, willing myself to feel something for making her cry. Regardless of not remembering her name, it should bother me to see a woman cry—especially if I'd been the reason behind those tears.

But there was nothing.

There'd been nothing since I'd returned from my trip to Texas six months ago. Just countless, nameless women who never filled a void that shouldn't have even been there. Turning around, I slapped my hand over my phone and wallet resting on the chair, and walked toward the hall.

"For the record, douche, it's called a one-night stand. One. Night! Not one hour," her voice broke as she continued to scream insults as I left her apartment.

As soon as I was in my car, I pulled up the texts on my phone and tapped out the same message I did every night.

I need to know you're okay Cassidy. Please call.

My thumb hovered over the SEND button for a few seconds before going up and hitting CANCEL instead. I dropped the phone into one of the cup holders and scrubbed my hands down my face before cranking the engine and starting home.

She'd briefly come back into my life more than six months ago, and was only there for a little more than a week. But that week had fucking wrecked me.

My partner and I had gotten the call six months ago about a house fire that looked suspicious—and later ended up revealing the bodies of Cassidy's mom and stepdad—early that morning. And when Cassidy had shown up hours later, I couldn't take my eyes off her. I don't know if it'd been the obvious black eye she had, or if somehow, even during all the craziness of interviewing neighbors, I'd known that I recognized her—but she was all I could see that day. Days later, when I remembered her from a family-disturbance call I'd gone on years before, the completely innocent girl started haunting my every thought.

She was on my mind constantly. Knowing I'd made the wrong decision in not following up on that call killed me more than I'd ever be able to explain. With my past, and what my father had done to my sister and me, I hated knowing I'd let her live through years of abuse. And then she walked into the coffee shop that morning, and everything changed.

I hadn't been big on relationships before officially meeting Cassidy—for shit's sake, I was only twenty-five years old and had been career focused most my life. I'd had girls, and claimed a few as mine for a while, but something about actually settling down had always scared the living hell out of me. Not with Cassidy, though. With her, I would have done anything to make her stay in California with me instead of going back to her boyfriend in Texas.

It wasn't just that she had a past like mine . . . that she knew what it was like to grow up being physically abused by a parent. It wasn't just that she would understand my fears of turning into my father. And it wasn't just the fact that she was the strongest person I'd ever met, emotionally—and in a way, physically. It was all of that, added to something that was just Cassidy. Something that the small and deceivingly fragile-looking girl exuded from deep down that drew me to her. That within minutes had me ready to make her the center of my world.

When she'd left for Texas, I went out of my mind worrying about her with her boyfriend. He'd been the cause of her black eye, and no matter what she'd said about it being an accident as she tried to break up a fight, I couldn't get the sight of her sporting it out of my head. I'd gone after her, intent on bringing her back with me, and positive I'd find her looking much like she had when she'd come to California the morning of the fire. What I hadn't been ready for was her telling me to leave, or how she'd relaxed into him when he came near her, like he was a safe place for her.

But I hadn't stopped worrying about her, and no

matter how many girls there were, and how many nights I'd tried to wash away thoughts of her with drinks . . . she was always there. Her honey-colored eyes and soft smile still haunted me, and it was a daily battle to not contact her even though I was dying to know she was okay.

I pulled into my spot and slowly made my way up to my apartment. I'd been so lost in my thoughts of a girl over a thousand miles away, I didn't notice the one right in front of me until her voice filled the otherwise silent hall.

"Hey there, super-mysterious neighbor. You've been gone a lot lately."

"Maci," I grunted by way of acknowledgment.

"Where've you been?"

"Is that your business?"

"Wait, wait! Don't tell me." She stopped trying to unlock her door, raised one dark eyebrow, and pointed at me. "I can smell you from here . . . was her name Sweetheart? Or maybe it was Sweetheart."

"Hilarious," I said without emotion.

"Well I thought it was."

I rolled my eyes and walked past her to my door. "Good night, Maci."

"Yeah, whatever. Good seeing you too, Connor," she mumbled to herself as she went back to her door. "Don't ask how I've been, it's cool. Asshole."

"Maci."

"Yes, douchebag?"

My eyes narrowed and I watched as she fought

her smile. "You think you can try keeping it down tonight?"

Her smile instantly fell and her head jerked back as confusion settled over her face.

"I'm tired of being kept awake from your headboard hitting the wall." When her gray eyes flashed, I unlocked my door and glanced at her again. "And you really need to work at faking it. You sound pathetic even from my bed."

"You are such an asshole, Connor Green!"

"So you've said." I stepped into my apartment and locked the door behind me seconds before I heard her door slam.

Heading back to my bedroom, I stripped out of my clothes and went straight into the bathroom for a hot shower. The girl I'd gone home with tonight had taken a bath in her perfume, and I could feel it seeping into my skin, causing a headache to form that had nothing to do with what I'd drunk earlier. Pressing my hands against the wall, I dropped my head and let the water pour over me as the tightened muscles in my body started relaxing. As soon as I reached behind me for the shampoo, the water turned ice cold and I jumped away from the spray, slipping in the process and barely catching myself on the edge of the tub before hitting the bottom. I scrambled to get out of the shower and when I continued to slip, grabbed the handle and shut the water off instead.

On the other side of the thin wall, I heard the water

running, and loudly cursed Maci when I heard the distinct sound of her laughter filling her bathroom.

I slapped my hand on the wall connecting our apartments and shouted, "You sure you want to play this game, sweetheart?"

More laughs came from her side before I heard, "Hope you didn't bust your ass too hard!"

"Turn the damn water off, Maci!"

"Enjoy your night," she said in a singsong voice and then there was nothing but the running water from her shower.

Payback is about to be one hell of a bitch, Maci Price.

Chapter Two

Maci

TURNING THE WATER on in my shower, I waited for a good five minutes before stepping in, afraid that Connor would give me the same treatment I'd given him the night before. When I didn't hear movement from his bathroom, I jumped in and stayed tense as I washed my hair and body, ready to get out at a moment's notice if his water kicked on. When nothing had happened by the time I started shaving my legs, my body relaxed and I wondered again what was going on with him.

The Connor I'd grown up with was completely different from the one who had been hiding out next door for the last half year. He'd never been a very outgoing guy, but he also wouldn't have let that prank last night go. Amber nailed it when she called him quiet and intense yesterday. Connor exuded this intensity that was somehow demanding and still managed to make you feel safe near him, which was probably why he had been such a good police officer, and now detective. But Connor's way of dealing with most things was silently. The most I'd ever heard him talk was when he was with my brothers, but even then he was still the quiet and mature one. Almost like he'd lived a dozen lifetimes before and was simply going through the motions of this one.

But *this* Connor? The one I'd been trying to get a reaction out of last night was nothing like that. Over the last six months or so, Connor was no longer quiet and intense . . . he was gone. Physically and emotionally. I used to see him almost on a daily basis. He would always come into my apartment to use my Keurig because he forgot to start his coffeepot or was just coming in from a long investigation. I could count on both hands how many times I'd seen him in the last six months, and last night had been the first time he'd even said anything in months. He'd always been discreet about his home life, and shut down whenever anyone mentioned his older sister, Amy, but this was unlike anything I'd ever seen from him.

Shutting off the water, I stepped out of the shower and toweled off my hair and body before wrapping the towel around me and heading out to the kitchen for some much-needed caffeine. As soon as I rounded the corner into my living room, a scream burst from my chest and I clutched the towel around me as I tripped over myself from trying to back away too quickly. I landed with a thud on the hardwood floor and scrambled backward before turning and crawling back into my hallway.

My breathing was rapid and I covered my mouth in case the intruder could hear me. Not like he wouldn't have heard my scream, or seen me crawl away; but at the moment, quieting my breathing was much more important. When I'd calmed enough to remove my hand without screaming again, I shakily peeked around the corner and a terrified cry escaped as I jerked back to hide from the demon in my living room.

All my worst nightmares are coming to life!

Do I scream for help? Call 911? Oh my God, my phone is in my kitchen! Good God, get a freaking grip, Maci. It's not even real.

I slowly turned and eyed the offensive, life-sized blow-up toy standing in my living room, and tried not to start crying when I saw the white face, red hair, nose, cheeks, and lips. Forcing myself to stand and walk over to the object, I failed at calming my shaking arm as I reached out for the note taped to its chest. A whimper still left me when I touched it.

I hate clowns with a passion.

My blood boiled when I read the words on the page. I was going to kill him. Like honest to God, I was about to go down for murder.

Don't forget I still have a key to your apartment, Maci,
and I've known you most your life. I remember all of
your biggest fears.

This guy is for the shower, have fun finding my
payback for the headboard banging last night.

I really do feel bad for the poor bastard that has to
put up with that.

Connor

By the way, you're out of your little coffee-cup things.

I am so not out of coffee! I just went to the store a few
days ago. Swear to God if that man took all of them, I
wasn't just going to kill him. I was going to kill him,
then bring him back so I could junk-punch him.

I began storming into the kitchen, but when I remembered his words about another payback, I froze,
letting only my eyes move around to find any other
threats around me. Tiptoeing the rest of the way to
the kitchen, I opened the cupboard that held all the
K-cups and found two unopened boxes as well as one
opened. I hadn't moved them, Connor knew where
they were, so why would he say they were missing? I
reached up to grab one and immediately brought my
arm back before investigating for anything suspicious.
When it all appeared normal, I brought down a K-cup
and put it in the Keurig before going through the same
process in the mug cabinet.

Grabbing the handle of the mug closest to me, I
took a deep breath in and pulled it out quickly, pre-

pared for something to be behind it. Nothing.

I bet there is nothing else and he just said that to make me paranoid about my entire apartment. With a heavy sigh I started to slide the mug into the slot on the machine when I saw it, and a scream that rivaled the one I'd had for the clown filled my apartment as the mug went crashing down onto the floor. A giant piece broke off and the tarantula spilled out.

"Not okay. Not okay. Connor!" I screamed as I jumped onto my counter and kept pointing at it on the ground. "Connor help me!"

When a few minutes had passed and Connor hadn't come in, and the ginormous spider hadn't moved, I slid off the counter and opened up a drawer closest to me. Grabbing the tongs, I walked closer and had to try three times before I could make my arm go far enough to touch the now obviously plastic tarantula.

This meant war.

Running to my pantry, I grabbed a trash bag and opened it up before using the tongs to deposit the disgusting eight-legged beast in there, along with the two pieces of what had been my favorite mug. When the rest of the micro-shards were swept up and thrown out, I went to my knife block and took out the massive chef's knife before creeping back to my living room. An icy chill ran down my spine seeing the back of the clown, and I just knew that little bitch was about to come to life any second and turn around on me. With two deep breaths in and out, I mentally pumped myself up for what I knew I had to do and charged it with a war cry, slashing furiously until it deflated into a pile on my floor.

After I returned the knife to the block, I grabbed the tongs and put Bozo the heart-attack-inducing clown in the trash bag too.

Still in my towel, I stormed over to Connor's apartment with my key ring in hand. As soon as I saw that bastard, I was going to punch him in the throat, throw the trash bag at him, and then run back to the safety of my apartment. But there was another note on his door with my name on the front.

1. No, I won't help you with the big ugly spider.

2. If you made it this far without dying, I'm proud of you.

3. Did you really think I am stupid enough to stick around and suffer the wrath of Maci?

Yes. Yes, I did. And I'd lied about him being the mature one. I went back to my apartment completely defeated and exhausted even though I'd only been awake for an hour. And there was no way in hell I was about to check the rest of my coffee mugs to see if they were safe.

Grabbing my phone, I dialed the number at my office and waited until someone answered.

"Yep?"

"You know, if I can't answer the phone with a *yep* then you shouldn't be able to either."

There was a beat of silence. "Are you on your way in?"

"Pfft. No, I have things I need to get done today," I said as I grabbed underwear and a pair of jeans, and put them on.

"Like what? We need you here answering the phone, Maci."

"Dakota, you did just fine answering it this time, and hardly anyone ever calls the office phone anyway. They all call our cell phones." I put my phone on speaker and placed it down on my dresser as I grabbed a bra and angrily clasped it on. "I already told you I have things I need to do. So I'm not coming in to just sit there and play solitaire and Minesweeper."

"This is Dylan, and what's so important that you can't come in?"

I stood up quickly from grabbing the shirt that I'd just dropped on the floor and glared at my phone as I thought back through our conversation. *That little bastard.* "If I wanted you to know what I was doing, I would have already told you. Just tell Dad I'm cramping or something, he won't want to hear anything else. And don't bullshit me, Dakota. Dylan only calls me 'Mini,' you're losing your touch, bro."

"Maybe I call you both. You don't know me . . . you don't know what's in my head. Maybe I'll call you Mack tomorrow."

And this is why I never understood anyone's attraction to my brothers. Rolling my eyes, I grabbed my phone off the dresser and spoke over him as he continued to ramble. "Good-bye, Dakota!"

After rushing through putting on deodorant and brushing my teeth, I threw my wet hair up in a messy bun, and didn't even bother with makeup before heading out. There was no time for that. I had shit I needed to get done.

First things first . . . I needed to stop at a Starbucks, like, ten minutes ago.

Connor

THE NOTE WAS still taped to my front door when I got home later that night, but that wasn't saying much. Maci had keys to my place too. I was surprised that my door didn't have holes in it, though.

Cracking open my door cautiously, I inspected the small gap, looking for any kind of line or thread, and when I didn't find any, I flung the door open and stepped back.

Nothing.

What the hell? Doors are Maci's signature move . . . well, other than freezing my ass in the shower. I took silent and careful steps in as I looked around, inspecting every part of my apartment as I made my way to my bedroom. Going so far as to lift up the sofa cushions, and looking under the bed. But there was nothing.

Had the clown and spider scared her *that* bad? It

wasn't like she didn't deserve it, and, hell, I'd been saving those for almost a year now since I'd played my last prank on her. If I hadn't made sure her car was gone before I came back, I would have wondered if I'd actually given her a heart attack.

I'd just stripped out of my clothes and was walking into my bathroom when I heard a door shut. It could have been any of our neighbors, but knowing that it *could* be Maci, I jumped in the shower, turned on the water, and had the shampoo bottle in my hand within seconds. There was no way she was ruining two showers in a row.

The water didn't start right away like I'd been expecting, and it made a weird noise before it sprayed out on me; but by then, I'd already turned around to inspect it. A string of expletives left me, and it took me a few seconds before I reached for the handle to turn off the water . . . but a few seconds was still too late. I had green, sticky water all over me. Grabbing for the showerhead, I twisted it off and brought it down to inspect it. There were green chunks in the base and after a few sniffs I yelled and slammed my fist against the wall.

"Kool-aid, Maci? Fucking Kool-Aid? This stuff stains—oh shit!"

I turned the water back on and lifted the lever so the bath faucet ran instead. When I had as much of the leftover Kool-Aid powder out of the showerhead as possible, I screwed it back on and turned the shower on. Reaching for my body wash, I flipped open the top and tipped it over to pour some into my hand.

"What . . . the hell . . . is this? Maci Price!" I yelled and threw the bottle—of what was supposed to be my body wash—out of the shower and turned to wash off the massive amount of liquid gold glitter that was now in my hand.

My body was still stained with green streaks, the water still had a light green tint to it, and while most of the glitter had gone down the drain, there was now a filmy layer on my hand that wasn't going away.

I was going to ruin her.

Grabbing the bar of soap, I immediately began running it over my arms, chest, and stomach . . . but nothing was happening. There were no suds, it wasn't lathering at all, it was working about as well as a plastic bar of soap. I stepped out of the shower, water dripping off me and threw the useless bar into the trash before searching through the cupboard, but, of course, the extra bars were missing.

Gritting my teeth, I grabbed a washcloth and stepped back into the shower and attempted to get everything off using that and the water. When I gave up minutes later, I grabbed my shampoo bottle again, but hesitated. Unscrewing the cap, I took a hesitant sniff and had to bite down on the inside of my cheek when a very distinct smell hit me. I turned the bottle over and watched as my shampoo laced with vinegar poured steadily out.

"Maci!" I yelled and shut off the water.

Not bothering with a towel, I stalked into my bedroom, slipped on a pair of drawstring sweats, and made my way to her place. I didn't even knock, I just let myself in.

"You know . . ." Her calm voice reached me, and I stopped walking when I saw her on the couch. Leg up on the cushion as she sat there steadily painting her toenails. "Clear nail polish on bars of soap works wonders. Well, for my purposes, anyway."

"Maci, look at me," I bit out. When she didn't look up, I snapped. Stalking over to her, I grabbed the bottle of clear polish and threw it across the room.

"Connor!"

"I said fucking look at me!"

Her eyes widened and she leaned back into the couch as I crowded over her.

"This isn't funny. I have a job . . . a *real* job, something you would know nothing about, but I can't go to work with a green fucking face, Maci!"

"Okay, it was—"

"I don't care what it was," I said, cutting her off. "You better hope like hell that this comes off and that you have replacements for everything that was in my shower. And when I say "have" . . . I mean *now*."

She licked her full lips and her eyes darted away before coming back to me. "Yeah, all right, I'll go get them," she said, her voice breathy as her eyes held mine.

When she didn't make an attempt to get up, I leaned even closer and curled my lip. "Now."

"I need you to move first."

Shoving off the back of the sofa, I crossed my arms over my bare, stained chest and kept my glare on her as she hurried to the back of her apartment. She came back with a bag of all the extras that had been in my cupboards and I snatched it quickly away from her.

"You're such a damn child, Maci. Grow the hell up."

She visibly started and floundered for something to say as I walked to the door. "*I'm* the child? Are you kidding me? Like you had no part in this?"

"I scared you, that's completely different than what you just did. If I get suspension for showing up tomorrow like this, you can be sure your brothers will be informed about your boyfriend."

"You know what? Screw you, Connor! At least this morning you showed a part of the Connor I knew growing up . . . and at least you're showing *some* kind of emotion right now. Even if you are being an asshole! Whoever you've been the last however many months is not you. You've been a fucking zombie. No feelings, nothing. So at least there's something tonight. Glad to know you're still human."

What she said was hitting me hard. The fact that she noticed that much. The fact that she was right and this was the first time I could remember feeling anything, even if it was annoyance and anger.

Clearing my throat, I brushed away the realization that Maci could make me feel anything at all, and looked right into her gray eyes. "I'm the one with green skin, and you're pissed off? Real classy." With another deep breath, I left her apartment and went back to my shower for take two.

Maci

MY LEGS GAVE out and I collapsed onto the couch as soon as I heard his door shut. Jesus, was it ridiculous that I was still completely turned on from what had just happened? What am I saying; of course it was ridiculous . . . it was ridiculous to get turned on in the first place.

The way he'd more or less charged into my apartment and leaned into me so much that I'd had to lean into the couch had been what set it off. His throwing the nail polish that I'd used on his bar of soap across the room hadn't even stopped me from noticing the way he looked in those loose, plaid-flannel pajama pants that were hanging so low that I'd had a view to die for of his muscled V. Even in his anger, and the way he'd bitten out each word, I'd been completely lost in everything that was Connor Green. His intensity had filled my entire apartment . . . and it had been so. Incredibly. Hot.

But I hated the way he'd belittled me. I didn't know if it was part of this new Connor, or if he'd just been trying to hurt me because he was upset; but he'd never treated me like that before. That had been the one thing to snap me out of my hormone-driven haze that had my mind on a one-way path that led to us in my bed.

If it hadn't been for the way his face had fallen right before he'd left—if it hadn't been for the smallest glimpse of the old Connor . . . I wouldn't be playing back every second of those few minutes again and again. His blue eyes spearing mine, the way the muscles in his arms contracted when he was using them to keep himself up on the sofa, and his demanding air that'd had my entire body heating.

God I needed a cold shower. And judging from the length of his first one, and the fact that his water had just shut off again, I knew that was exactly what I would get if I tried to shower now. But I knew just how bad Kool-Aid stained skin, and I was positive he'd still have faded green streaks all over his skin. So instead of cooling down and trying to forget about the way he'd just made me feel . . . I did something worse.

I grabbed a box of baking soda and walked next door.

He glowered at me when he opened the door, and though his breathing was rough from trying to control his anger, he spoke in a deceivingly calm tone. "I'm still green, Maci."

Trying to force my eyes off the towel he was clutching to his hips, and the drops of water that were racing down his skin, I dropped my head to stare at the floor and held up the box of baking soda. "I came to help."

He huffed softly, his voice now holding a hint of a teasing tone. "I think you've done enough."

"It will come off, you just need—" I cut off when

his fingers grasped my chin and forced my head back to look at him.

"I'm sorry I yelled at you." His blue eyes searched my face, an unreadable emotion crossing his own. "You have no idea how much I hate that I scared you enough that you can't even look at me now."

I wasn't looking at him because I was afraid I wouldn't be able to stop myself from touching him. "You didn't scare me, Connor."

A sad smirk tugged at his lips, and he took the box from me with his free hand. "I know what to do with this. Go to sleep. I'll come by tomorrow morning to clean up the polish."

"But you—"

"Please, Maci," he said, cutting me off. "Go back to your apartment."

I stood there staring at the door long after he'd shut it in my face. That had gone completely different from the way I'd thought it would. I'd pictured Connor sitting on the edge of the tub, me between his legs as I helped get the stain off his face, shoulders, and chest. Which, of course, turned into my hands running other places, and Connor picking me up and depositing me on the bathroom counter. I'd pictured my head falling back as he repeatedly slammed into me, me crying out his name—

Jesus, my sex life was pathetic. I needed to stop reading so many romance novels.

"Don't even try it, sweetie. He's taken tonight."

My head whipped to the right when I heard the

sultry voice fill the hall, and my eyebrows shot up when I saw her. For fuck's sake, she looked like a whore. I'd put on my skimpy pajamas in preparation for Connor getting pissed and coming over tonight, and I was more covered than she was.

"W-what?"

She pulled her phone up to her ear and eyed me with a satisfied smirk on her face. "It's cute that you're trying to get his attention, but he needs a real woman to please him."

I eyed her fake breasts that were one more bounce from falling out of her shirt and had the urge to cover my small ones.

"I'm here," she said into the phone before dropping it in her purse. Watching the door expectantly next to me, she finally looked over to me again, one eyebrow raised. "You can leave now."

I shook my head to clear the confused, and self-doubted haze I'd just been in, and started backing away when the door opened.

"Maci? What are you doing out here?"

I looked up to see Connor in a pair of low-slung jeans with the button undone. His chest bare and red from where he'd officially de-greenified himself. "Uh . . ."

The whore pushed by me and into Connor's apartment before turning to look at me. "She was staring at your door, trying to get the courage to knock on it. It was kind of cute . . . in a puppy-looking-to-get-its-head-scratched sort of way."

Connor's head shot back to look at me, his eyebrows bunching together as he studied me.

"No, I just . . . I just needed my baking soda back." Oh my God . . . someone shoot me. How long had I stood there daydreaming about Connor? *I'm such a creeper!*

Whorey McWhore-Slut choked out a laugh and grabbed Connor's arm. His eyes had still been locked with mine, but at her touch he looked back to her and sighed. "I told you to go to sleep. I'll bring it by tomorrow."

"Aww, is it past the little girl's bedtime?"

"Don't talk to her like that, Sadie," he growled. "Go wait for me inside."

Sadie rolled her eyes and huffed. "Whatever."

I knew tomorrow I was going to look back on this and wish I'd said something to her. But at the moment, I felt unreasonably mortified by this entire thing. Dressing for him, playing out scenes in my head with him, standing outside his door for who knows how long as I played them all out . . . again. And then seeing the type of girl he does go after. Tons of makeup, perfectly curled hair that I'd bet would light up like a dry Christmas tree. Tall, fake body, little clothing, and an award-winning bitch-tude. The complete opposite of me. Eh, maybe except for the attitude.

Finally remembering how to move, I turned and walked toward my door, ignoring the first time Connor called my name.

"Maci, stop," he demanded and grabbed my arm as I opened my door. "Look at me."

Locking my jaw, I fought back the tightness in my throat and wondered why the hell I was about to cry as I turned to face him. And I really regretted giving him the baking soda. Maybe if he still had a green face, Sadie wouldn't be in his apartment right now.

"Are you okay?"

I nodded my head, afraid of how my voice would shake if I tried to talk. *I need to focus on something other than my humiliation. Be pissed that she's in there and acting like she's better than I am . . . yeah . . . oh, no. Angry tears. Nope. No. Bad idea.*

"Tell me why you were outside my door."

"I did," I managed to choke out without sounding like a strangled cat.

"Mace . . . did you . . . did you ever go back into your apartment?"

I hated that he had me completely figured out. I hated that his voice had gotten soft and low in a way that had my daydreams flooding back into my mind. And I freaking hated that even though I had been with Bryce just the night before, I was ready to cry over the fact that he was about to sleep with the slut in his apartment.

"Of course I did," I hissed and tried to jerk my arm back, but he didn't let go.

He sighed as he studied me, before finally asking, "Do you need the baking soda right now, or can it wait until tomorrow?"

"Tomorrow's fine."

The corner of his mouth slowly tilted up into a smirk and he squeezed my arm. "Then I'll see you in the morning, Mini."

And that was the final, crushing blow. Every last ounce of air left my body as I launched myself into my apartment and shut the door. *Mini. He fucking called me Mini.* I couldn't figure out if I wanted to laugh for being stupid enough to think that after years of wanting this man, something was finally about to happen. Or if I wanted to finally start crying over the fact that he liked women like Sadie and called me Mini. Like he was my brother or something.

When I was finally breathing again without feeling like there was a weight crushing my chest, I dragged myself to my bedroom and fell face-first onto the bed. Not five minutes later, I got intimately familiar with Sadie's voice, and I had no doubt she was being that loud because she knew I was right next door.

Grabbing my phone, I texted Bryce and went around collecting clothes for tomorrow. Not bothering with what I was wearing—since I'm sure at least Bryce would appreciate it—I threw a sweatshirt on over my camisole and slid into my flip-flops before running out of my apartment and to my car.

Chapter Three

Maci

"WELL, WELL, LOOK who it is . . . here all bright and early like she actually has a job or something."

I glanced at the clock and raised an eyebrow without ever looking up at him. "Screw off, Dylan."

"I'm Dakota."

Forcing my eyes to remain on my computer screen instead of looking up to confirm I was correct, I scoffed and kept clicking furiously on my mouse. "Dakota already tried that on me yesterday. You forget I've known you both my whole life . . . and you're twenty-five. Aren't you both old enough that you could stop trying to get people all confused?"

He sat down with a huff on my desk and brought his feet up to the arm of my chair. "But I did confuse you, right, Mini?"

"Didn't. And speaking of bright and early, I've been here for four hours. Where were you until just now?"

"Not your business. At least I still showed up, you didn't come at all yesterday."

"I told Dakota I was cramping."

He kicked my chair back so I wheeled away from the desk, taking my wireless mouse with me.

"Excuse you. I was about to beat my fastest time."

"You used the cramping excuse last week."

"Shit." I bit down on my lip and looked toward the back of the office. "Did Dad still buy it?"

"Yeah, he did that thing where he looks like you're about to throw snakes on him."

I laughed when Dylan tried to re-create the way Dad would jump back and alternate throwing his hands up to his ears like he didn't want to hear it, and throwing them back at you, as if to push you away from him.

"So where were you?" Dylan asked when he sat back on the desk.

"I've been here all morning, where were you?"

His expression went blank for a few seconds before he kicked his foot at me again, connecting with my knee. "I meant yesterday, Mini."

"Shit, that hurt!" I sat there holding my knee, breathing in and out dramatically through my teeth like Peter from *Family Guy* for a minute before glaring up at him. "I'll tell you if you tell me."

"I've been in meetings with clients since nine, so I didn't stop by here first. Now. Spill."

"Oh . . . huh." I'd been kind of hoping it would be something that I could tease him about. "I had cramps," I said as I scooted my chair back to the desk so I could start another game.

Dylan grabbed the arm of my chair and wheeled me back before hopping off the desk and grabbing each arm, caging me in. "You better tell me the truth before I get the others and we find every guy in your phone and beat their ass."

And this is why I can't have a boyfriend. I sighed and pushed on his chest until he moved away. "No need. I went shopping."

"Shopping."

"Yes, Dylan, shopping. Now go away."

"You ditched work on a Thursday to go shopping? What was so important that it couldn't wait two damn days, Mini? Was there a special on training bras?"

"I didn't go to the mall, asshole," I said as I scooted back toward the desk again.

"Then where were you?"

Turning to look at him, I flung out the hand that was still holding the mouse. "Why are you so interested in knowing my life all of a sudden?"

"Because we all agree you're being sketchy lately, and I'm about to go pound some dude's face in for touching my sister! Who is he, Mini?"

Shitfuck. "Who is *who*?"

"The guy I'm about to kill, who are you fuckin' around with?"

"You have a boyfriend, Maci?" Dakota asked as

he rounded the corner into my office. "Oh, fuck this. Who is he?"

I groaned into my hands and stared down at my desk. "I don't have a boyfriend. Dylan is being paranoid because I didn't come in yesterday."

"Yeah, where were you?" Dakota asked, but before I could answer, he leaned over me and paged the back office from my desk phone. "Maci has a boyfriend," he stated. Not five seconds later, I heard my oldest brothers, Craig and Sam, running down the hall.

"Who is he?" Craig, the oldest, asked.

"No one, I don't have a—"

"Where's her phone?"

I looked over to see Sam rummaging through my purse, so I pulled my phone out of my pocket before handing it to him. I wasn't worried about them finding anything, because I had a password that would take them forever to figure out.

Sam looked at my phone in his hand before handing it back to me. "She doesn't have a boyfriend, dumbasses. She wouldn't give up her phone like that if she did."

Ha. Win.

"Ask her where she was yesterday," Dylan prompted, and both Sam and Craig gave me a suspicious glare.

"Where were you?" Craig asked.

"I went shopping."

"Yeah," Dylan interjected, "but she wasn't at the mall, and won't say where she was."

Sam snatched the phone back out of my hand, and

Craig caged me in the way Dylan had earlier. "Who are you hiding from us?"

"What's your password?"

"Screw all of you! I'm not giving you my password. I told you what I was doing yesterday, and I don't have a boyfriend!"

"You know we're going to find out, Maci, you might as well just tell us now so we can get this over with."

"Craig, there's nothing to tell!"

"Either we give your boyfriend the message now, or he lives in fear of when we find him. Your choice."

"Jesus Christ! There's no boyfriend, no message needs to be delivered." *God!* How long had I been hooking up with Bryce and I'd never had to deal with this, but one day of pranking Connor, and all hell breaks loose with my brothers.

"Maci—"

"Daddy!" I yelled, and let a slow, coy smile spread across my face when all four of my brothers froze. "That's right, bitches. I just used the 'daddy' card."

They all stood and crossed their arms over their chests as they waited for what would come next. Four pairs of gray eyes were plotting another intervention, or my "boyfriend's" death. A couple seconds later, loud thuds could be heard coming down the hall until my dad appeared in my office.

"Boys, what in the hell is going on in here?" his deep voice boomed, and I couldn't help but smile when all four of them subtly flinched.

"Maci has a boyfriend," Craig answered for them.

Dad raised a graying eyebrow; but before he could respond, I pointed at Craig and said, "Now that's a damn dirty lie. They're harassing me because they *think* I have a boyfriend."

"But you don't?"

"Nope."

He studied me for a second before turning around to go back to the hall. "If she says she doesn't have one, then she doesn't. In my office, boys."

The boys all stood there glaring at me until Dad's footsteps could no longer be heard. One by one, they all turned and began leaving. When only Dylan was left, he grabbed a box of paper clips off my desk, opened it up, and threw the contents at me.

"Are you serious?"

"I'm gonna figure out who it is, brat," he called over his shoulder as he retreated down the hall.

I shook out my shirt and listened as more paper clips hit the floor. "Real mature."

Looking at the mess on the ground and under my desk, I sighed and lazily fell out of my chair to the floor to begin picking them all up. Crawling on my hands and knees under the desk to grab the dozens that had scattered there, I was just leaning back when I heard a soft laugh and froze.

"Do I want to know why you're down there?"

I jolted up and back, but misjudged the distance and ended up smacking my head on the corner of the desk. My hands flew up to hold my head, causing me to drop all the paper clips I'd just spent minutes on picking up. When I went to sit back on my heels, I rocked back too far and kept going, falling into my chair, which rolled to the side, leaving me to hit my head on the wall as I fell back.

"Son of a bitch, that fucking hurt! Ow, ow, ow! Shit," I hissed when I was fully, and safely, on the ground. "You don't scare someone who's under a desk, you motherfucker."

"I've always loved that mouth of yours."

My eyes shot open at the admission, and I found intense, blue eyes directly above my face. I'd officially stopped breathing. What'd he say?

Connor's face fell before he backed up and sat next to me. "Jesus, you hit your head that hard? I meant the way you can't finish a sentence without swearing."

And let's bring back the insecurities from last night. There's nothing about me that Connor Green finds appealing. Well, except the fact that I have lady bits. The anger and humiliation I'd felt last night came flooding back and I glared up at the ceiling.

"You okay?"

"Fine," I bit out. "Why are you here?"

He breathed heavily through his nose and drummed his fingers on the floor. "I came to check on you."

"Well . . . looks like you did a helluva lot of good with the checkup."

"It's not my fault you're prone to hurt yourself on every surface available and enjoy being on your back . . ." he trailed off.

"Fuck off, Connor. I don't need your shit today."

"Where were you when I came over this morning?"

"Not in my apartment . . . ?"

A low growl built up in the back of his throat as he leaned back over me. "You knew I was coming over. I thought you were sleeping, so I let you sleep until I was done cleaning that shit up. By then, you should've been getting ready to leave for work. I went to wake you up, and surprise, surprise . . . no Maci. Where were you?"

"Oh, so I'm back to being Maci again?" When Connor just looked at me confused, I rolled my eyes and looked past his head at the ceiling. "Thought I was Mini last night."

"Stop acting like a child. You knew I was coming over this morning and you weren't there. No note, nothing. I called you and you didn't answer, I was worried about you."

A short, humorless laugh bubbled out of my chest. "I can see were really worried. It took you almost five hours to come check where I work from when you last cal—" I cut off quickly and internally cursed for giving myself away.

His blue eyes narrowed. "I drove over here at eight, I saw your car here so I knew you were okay. Now. Tell me why you weren't there this morning, and why you weren't answering my calls, since apparently you knew I was calling."

"That's really none of your business, and I don't know why it's such a big deal that I wasn't there. All you needed to do was clean up the polish—that doesn't require me being there, right?"

"It does, because I wanted to talk to you."

Part of me was dying to know what he wanted to talk to me about. The other was remembering him calling me Mini, and balking at the idea of me thinking he liked my mouth. "Well I don't want to talk to you. So if you could leave now, I'd appreciate it."

Those intense blue eyes widened and he stared at me for a handful of seconds before shifting back and standing up. I scrambled awkwardly until I was vertical again, and fell into my chair. Trying not to show how much my head was still throbbing, I refused to grab my head again until he left.

"Why were you outside my door last night when Sadie came over?" he asked when he reached the door to leave. His back had been to me as he asked the question, but he turned to face me as he waited for my answer.

"I already told you la—"

"I'm not buying that."

"I don't care if you are or aren't. I told you why I was there, and you're just trying to make it out to be something different than it was."

He took three large steps until he was on the other side of my desk, and bent down to rest his hands on the wood. "I saw the way you looked, you can't keep tell—"

"Did you remember to pay Sweetheart before she left? Oh, wait, I forgot. You actually remembered this one's name. Did you remember to pay *Sadie*?"

Connor's head jerked back and his eyebrows slammed down. When he spoke, his voice was dark and sent chills through my body. "Come again?"

But he and I both knew there was no need to repeat the question. I glanced at his clothes, and noticed that he was in slacks and a button-down with a tie. His badge, gun, and handcuffs were all attached to his belt. *Damn, I've always loved the way he looked in his detective getup.* Forcing my eyes away from him, I woke up my computer and pretended to start a new game.

"Sorry you felt the need to come all the way over here to check on me, but you should probably go back to work, Detective Green."

"Watch yourself, Maci," he said in warning. "You're starting to look jealous."

I didn't look back at him as he walked out of the office. As soon as the door shut, I let out the breath I'd been holding and dropped my head onto my desk.

"Don't act like you're asleep, Mini, I just heard you talking. Who was here?"

I glared up at Dylan and rubbed at the back of my tender head. "Connor."

Dylan walked over and opened the door, looking out into the parking lot. "Well why'd he leave before talking to us, did he get a call?"

"He didn't come to see you two," I replied immediately, not realizing what I'd said until Dylan's expression turned murderous. Trying to keep calm, I thought quickly and rolled my eyes. "Oh God, come on, Dylan. Not like that, he was apologizing for the sounds his skank was making last night. Our walls are really thin."

It was beyond stupid that my heart was racing, and I was terrified of my brothers finding out about this unreciprocated crush I had on their best friend. But when they'd taken my phone, which had conversations between Bryce and me, I hadn't flinched.

"Lucky bastard." Dylan shook his head and smacked his hand on my desk, causing me to jump, before walking down the hall again.

"Yeah," I mumbled softly and failed at ignoring the pain spreading in my chest. *He views you like a sister, Maci. Nothing more.* "Lucky bastard."

Connor

"WHAT THE HELL, what the hell, what the hell?" I pulled my car into a strip-mall parking lot, threw it into park and groaned into my hands. "What. The. Hell?"

I didn't know why I'd gone there. I didn't know why I'd been worried about her in the first place. She spent nights away all the time, but she'd known I was coming over this morning. There was no way she hadn't heard

Sadie, because she'd been fucking obnoxious before I'd finally kicked her out. And for some damn reason, I'd spent the rest of the night wondering why Maci had still been outside my door, why she looked like she was trying to keep herself together . . . and why the fuck I'd had to picture her to get off.

This was Maci. *Maci.* I knew I couldn't think about her like this; and I knew that to continuously entertain the thoughts that had been playing in my mind since the night before would be dangerous. But even in the office, the only thing that had kept my mind clear enough to stop me from covering her body with mine and claiming her mouth was the fact that her brothers and dad were all in the back.

That mouth. Jesus, that mouth was perfect. How had I never noticed that? I loved that Maci swore just the same as her brothers did. It was just . . . so . . . Maci. But the way those full lips fell into her natural pout in the office had had me straining against my pants.

"Fuck!" I growled and slammed a hand down on the steering wheel before raking both hands through my hair.

I can't think about her like this!

And yet, I couldn't *stop* thinking about her like that. Her wild, vibrant red hair on my pillow with her body underneath me. That raspy voice of hers breathing out my name. Those full lips wrapped around my cock. All of it. All of her . . . was continuously playing through my mind.

Like a bucket of ice-cold water had been thrown on me, my phone rang, displaying Dylan's name.

"Yeah?" I answered cautiously.

"Mini said you stopped by. What? No love for me and Kota?"

"Had to get back to work. Sorry."

He grunted. "Have a question for you about Mini. Is she seeing someone?"

I muted the relieved breath that left my lungs, and didn't even have to think about my answer. Maci would kill me if she found out I told them about the douchebag who came over. "No, she's not."

"You're sure?"

"Yeah, Dylan, I'm sure."

He spoke away from the phone, telling what I'm guessing were the rest of the brothers what I had said. "Okay, well, hey. Let's all get together this weekend, grab some food and beers."

"Okay, I'm off after today, so just let me know."

"And, Connor."

"Hmm?"

"My sister doesn't need to hear your women screaming. Try to get them to keep it down, all right?"

So she had heard. Why is that bothering me so much?

"Connor."

"Yeah, I got you. It won't happen again. I'll make sure Maci's gone, or I'll go to their place . . . something."

"Appreciate it, bro. I'll call you later, we'll set something up for tomorrow night."

"All right. Later."

As soon as we were off the phone. I pulled up Maci's name and sent her a message.

I'm sorry about last night

Maci Price: I'm not sorry I made your face
green ;)

Which reminded me . . . hope she didn't have any plans for the evening.

Chapter Four

Maci

"Amber, if you don't let me get off the phone, then I'm never going to get ready. I love you, I'll see you in an hour."

"Ugh. Fine. Get ready, but we're picking up this conversation later. I'm not letting Bryce ruin your chances of meeting someone else tonight."

I eyed Bryce sitting on my couch and suppressed a sigh. "Whatever you say."

"I'm serious!"

"Uh-huh. I got it. Getting ready now. Bye."

Running into my bathroom, I took the towel off my head and threw it onto the floor before hastily running my brush through my hair. I was so behind on getting ready, and Bryce was one of those guys who got annoyed if we were late. Since Connor had confirmed there wasn't a chance in hell for anything between us, I really didn't want to start off a night with Bryce already bitching. And despite Amber still insisting on finding me someone . . . *anyone* other than Bryce . . . I wasn't willing to go through the process. I couldn't see the point in it. Not when we had a perfectly good—

"Son of a bitch! What the fuck?"

I shut off the blow dryer and threw it onto the bathroom countertop as I spit out what had gotten in my mouth when I'd been freaking out, and rubbed at my eyes so I could look in the mirror. My entire head was covered in white powder. I was going to shank the bastard.

"You okay?" Bryce's voice filled my hallway seconds before he appeared behind me. "What the hell happened to you?"

"I swear to God I'm going to kill that motherfucker!" I screeched as I pushed past Bryce and stomped down my hallway.

And I mean *stomped.* I looked like a little kid getting ready to throw a fit over not getting any ice cream.

"Language, Maci, and where are you going?"

"Probably to jail."

"What? Wait, stop walking!" Bryce grabbed my arm and turned me toward him. His eyes bouncing over my head and shoulders with confusion. "Who did this? What is all this, baby powder?"

I scratched at my head and neck and shook his

hand off as I turned back to open my apartment door. "Probably."

"I said stop!"

"I just need to kill him, Bryce. I'll be back in five seconds!"

"Maci!"

I flung open Connor's door and stormed over to where he was standing in the kitchen. Arms crossed over his chest, smirk on that stupid pretty face.

"You should really lay off all the coke," he said. "Or I can get you help, if you need it."

"I will fucking murder you, you stupid piece of shit!"

"That's the sweetest thing you've said to me all day."

"Maci!" Bryce barked and I turned to look at him. "I said stop, and I mean now. Get back in your apartment, don't make me say it again."

My head jerked back. I'd never seen Bryce like this. Usually he was carefree, ready to have a good time ... his only problem was his incessant need to be on time and to suck up to his incredibly rude parents. This was the first time I'd seen him look and act just like his dad. I couldn't move or say anything; I just stood there staring at him with my mouth wide open.

"I think you need to leave." Connor's voice was no longer teasing. It was dark, terrifying—and if I was being honest with myself—kind of hot. I felt his body press up against my back, and had to force myself not to lean into him.

"Maci." Bryce spoke as though Connor never had and wasn't currently standing behind me. "Do you know how ridiculous you're making yourself look right now? Let's go."

"I've never understood what you see in this tool," Connor mumbled under his breath. Stepping around me, he walked up to Bryce.

Even though Connor was a few inches shorter, it wasn't hard to see why Bryce backed up. Connor and his intensity. I wanted to smile.

"I can't stop Maci from seeing you, because she's an adult. But I can make you leave my apartment, and I strongly suggest you do it voluntarily, before I force you to." He didn't stop walking toward him, and he didn't stop talking. "I don't like you, never have. You don't take care of Maci, and even after all this time with her, you don't have the balls to step up and be the man she needs and deserves."

Whoa, whoa, whoa. Hold up. Who the hell is this, and what did he do with Connor Green? My eyes were probably bulging out of my head as I watched Bryce step toward the open doorway.

Bryce's head shot up, his eyes piercing mine. "Maci, get over here. We're leaving."

"I don't know who the fuck you think you are, but if I ever hear you talking to Maci like she's a child again, this is your only warning that I won't even bother waiting for her brothers. I'll make it so you'll never want to look in her direction again, do you understand what I'm saying?"

"Mac—"

"Leave."

I watched in disbelief as Bryce backed out and Connor shut the door on him. I grew up with four older brothers. Brothers who wouldn't let other guys get near me, but also didn't cut me slack when it came to . . . well . . . anything. I'd always had to fight for everything, growing up. So I didn't need Connor coming to my rescue, but, hell, that was the hottest thing I'd witnessed in a long time.

And now I was confused all over again. I thought I was *Mini* to him not even twenty-four hours ago. I thought he'd been making it obnoxiously clear that I didn't mean anything to him. *He's so damn confusing. And why the hell does this baby powder itch so freaking bad?*

Connor turned and walked quickly back to me, but I'd just remembered why I'd come into his apartment in the first place. He opened his mouth, but before he could say anything, I punched him in the stomach as hard as my little muscles would allow.

"Fuck, Mace!" he wheezed.

"This shit burns, and it itches really bad! I keep scratching my head and skin like I have lice, or a rash or something, and it got in my mouth! Since when does baby powder itch like this?"

He laughed as he straightened up, his hand rubbing at his stomach. Pussy. "It's not baby powder."

I stopped mid-scratch before starting up furiously again. "You have five seconds to tell me what I'm covered in."

"Itching powder. Good to know it actually works."

No words came out of my mouth as I stood there gaping at him. After floundering for something to say and coming up empty, I did a very girly and unattractive screech before stomping around him and back to my apartment. Bryce was pacing inside, and as soon as I entered, he leveled me with a glare and pointed in the direction of Connor's place.

"Who the hell was that?"

"My neighbor. He's one of my brothers' best friends, so he's kind of protective."

"I don't like you living next to someone like him, and I don't appreciate you letting him order me around."

I slammed my hand down on the counter after grabbing my phone to research how to de-itchify myself, and turned to look at him. "Are you serious right now? I didn't *let* him do anything. You were being a douche and he didn't like that you were ordering me around. Neither did I. You know what? I don't even know why you're still here! You should go, Bryce. I'll see you tomorrow or Sunday when you're not being such an ass."

"Maci, this is dumb. We've got to stop this game we've been playing. It's stupid, and your neighbor kinda had a point, even though he didn't seem to have all the facts. It's not just me keeping us a secret, but I'm done with it. I'm almost twenty-four, Maci. My parents expect me to be married by the time I'm twenty-five."

"Oh Jesus," I whispered when he started walking toward me.

"I become a partner in Dad's firm on my twenty-fifth birthday, I can't go into the firm single. You know this."

No, I *so* did not know that.

He grabbed my hips and pulled me close, his eyes roaming over my whited-out hair. "We'll get your hair back to blond, and we'll take this out," he murmured, tapping the small hoop on my left nostril. "As for the tattoos . . . we'll cover them when we make appearances."

"Appearances? Wh—"

"Babe, you know I think you're hot . . . God you're so sexy, but I need the tame-looking Maci in public. You can be *this* when it's just us. Okay? As soon as you look normal again, we'll announce our engagement."

I'd known Bryce had always thought we'd end up together. Just like I'd known he'd expected me to go back to the old me. I just hadn't realized that when the conversation would finally happen, it would hurt so much. When we were with friends, he didn't care who saw us together. But saying that if we were to continue with an actual relationship, I could only be me in private? That I needed to get back to "normal?" This was my normal.

My eyes welled up with tears and my throat tightened as the crashing realization hit me that not only was I not good enough Connor Green. I wasn't even good enough for someone like Bryce anymore. It'd been my idea to keep us in the friends-with-benefits zone. But he'd still been the only guy to ever show any type of affection toward me. The only guy to show he cared about me as something other than a sister.

"Babe, don't cry. It's just, like this, you look like the mistress . . . not the wife. I need you to be my wife."

A sob burst from my chest and I slapped my hand over my mouth as I tried to pull away from his arms.

"You and I both know it's time. It's time for us to move forward, and it's time for you and me to grow up. We need to stop acting like we're still in college, and we need to look ready for the world. No one is going to take you seriously when you look like this and dress the way you do. It was one thing in school, but now—"

"Get. The fuck. Out."

My eyes shot up past Bryce's shoulder to see Connor standing there. His face was slowly turning red in anger.

"I swear to Christ I will break your neck if you say one more word to her."

Bryce breathed heavily through his nose before turning his head to look over his shoulder. "Now *you're* in an apartment that isn't yours. It's your turn to leave, we're talking about something important."

"Yeah, no, I heard. You can talk about it again another time when you're not making her cry. And I'll give you a clue if you haven't caught on yet, she's not crying because she's happy."

"You're really starting to piss me off."

"Go," I choked out. "Please, go."

One of Bryce's arms left my waist to gesture toward the door. "You heard her."

"You, Bryce."

He turned back to me, his eyebrows pinched together. "What?"

"Go. Just . . . please. We'll talk later."

"Fine," he huffed softly and released me. "I'll call you tomorrow, babe. I know you have a lot to think about."

I did. I had so much to think about, but not about what he was insinuating.

He left after a long glare directed in Connor's direction, and once the door was shut, Connor looked at me like I'd betrayed him. He closed the distance between us and stood there watching me for a few moments before setting an Aveeno box down on the counter.

"It's an oatmeal bath to help with the itching," he answered my unspoken question, and looked at me sadly. Grabbing my left hand, he glanced at it for a brief second before dropping it and stepping away, his head shaking slowly back and forth. "I hope like hell you didn't say 'yes' to him."

I JOLTED AWAKE and grabbed at my phone, ringing loudly, and almost dropped it in the process of answering it.

"'lo?"

"Wake up, bitch! It's the first of December, Christmas decorating day!"

I groaned and rolled over onto my back. "What time is it, Amber?"

"Who cares, and did you just groan? You don't groan when there's anything in your immediate future that has to do with Christmas. Get your ass out of bed. I'm coming to pick you up."

After Connor had quickly left my apartment last night, leaving me stunned and sobbing; I'd texted Amber letting her know I wasn't going out, and got in the tub with the Aveeno. I'd spent hours repeating everything Bryce had said, and poring over all that had happened between Connor and me in the previous forty-eight hours. None of it made sense with Connor, and half of what he did left me wanting him more, and thinking that in some insane alternate universe, I could have a chance with him. The other half had me feeling like a child, and added to Bryce's words . . . a joke.

When my tears had stopped, an embarrassing amount of time later, I'd called Bryce and more or less told him to screw himself. That I wouldn't marry him, and I wouldn't change for anyone, including him. Funny thing about that is, I couldn't help but stare at myself in the mirror for an hour after, trying to convince myself that I was happy with who I was and that I didn't want to go back to the old Maci.

Bryce had told me to sleep on it.

"Maci!" Amber sang my name, drawing it out.

"You are not a morning person, go back to sleep!"

"Too late, I'm already on my way."

I started to groan again, but stopped myself. "Okay, I'm up. Pick up coffee and a muffin, and I'll blast Christmas music while I get ready, that will get me in the mood."

"Consider it done! See you in twenty-ish."

I hopped out of bed and ran over to my radio to turn on the Christmas station. Once it was on and the music was loud, I practically bounced around my apartment as I sang along with the songs and rushed to get ready. I checked the weather app on my phone and sighed. It was finally December, and it was still in the mid-sixties. Stupid California weather.

Once I was dressed and ready, I grabbed the box of remaining oatmeal bath packets and walked over to Connor's door. Just before my hand grabbed the door handle, I heard a feminine laugh followed by Connor's, and froze. Letting the box slip from my fingers, I left it in front of his door and went back to my apartment, waiting for Amber to call me. There was no way he could stand up for me the way he did, and say the things he said all day yesterday . . . especially last night . . . and me not be affected by them. Or not be upset that he had another girl, or Sadie again, in his apartment.

"You ready to get decorations, and Christmas-out our apartments?" Amber said with an excited look on her face as I got into her car.

Taking the pastry bag from her, I pulled a piece off the muffin and popped it in my mouth. "Mmm-hmm!"

"This weather sucks though, huh? It needs to be gloomy or something at least. But, no, it's bright and sunny, barely cold enough for a hoodie. Whatever."

I smiled to myself. That is why Amber and I were friends. "Oh well, not too much longer and we'll be in Mammoth."

"So excited! I can't wait to see the snow! Well, and stay with your brothers in a cozy cabin."

I started choking on the muffin and grabbed for my coffee to help it go down. "Seriously, Amber, gross! I'm going to tell my mom you suddenly have the bubonic plague or something, and can't come with us."

"Now that's just not nice."

"Admit it, you only love me because of my brothers."

She shrugged and made a face at me. "It's true."

I laughed and cautiously put another piece of the muffin in my mouth, speaking around it. "Bitch."

"Your favorite bitch. And don't be all lame just because you won't make a move with the neighbor dude."

I paused from grabbing my coffee, and laughed sadly. "Yeah, well, like I said . . . that won't be happening."

Pulling out my phone, I sent Connor a text and vowed to get it through my head that he was just my older brothers' friend, and my neighbor. Nothing more. I also told myself that the girl in his apartment this morning wouldn't bother me, nor would any other girl after her. Nothing was about to bring down my mood today.

Connor

I ARMY-CRAWLED AFTER my nephew and scrambled away when he stopped, and obviously started making good use of his diaper.

"Ugh! Oh my God, that is—" I gagged and brought my shirt up over my mouth and nose. "How do you deal with that?"

My sister laughed loudly and waited until my nephew started crawling again before going to pick him up. "When it's your kid, it's different. You do it because it needs to be done."

"No, no! God, Amy! Wait until I'm out of the room before you start changing him. You trying to kill me or something?"

"Chill, jeez. I still have to get the diaper bag and get him ready." She walked toward me with little Ben and I practically ran to the kitchen. "It is good to see you though, Connor."

I raised an eyebrow at her, still keeping my shirt over the bottom half of my face. "I see you every Saturday morning unless I'm working."

"I know, but ever since that girl who—"

"Amy," I said her name in warning.

"Ever since that girl who went back to Texas, you

haven't been the same. I don't know what's happened to you since you came over last week, but you're a completely different person. You're back to my little brother . . . well, almost."

I shrugged, and let the hand that wasn't holding my shirt go out before dropping back to my side. "I'm always me."

"No, and you know what I'm talking about. Just because you think you hide it from me, doesn't mean I don't see it. There's still something today, you're not completely back yet, but it's a huge difference."

I nodded, not knowing what to say. I didn't know what to think or say about there being that much of a difference when I'd thought I'd been hiding everything from her. She'd spent so much time protecting me from our bastard father when we were little that I'd been trying to protect her from any and everything ever since we'd been adopted from him. Including my own struggles. Amy had known about Cassidy, but she hadn't known how hard it had been for me after—or apparently she had.

And I didn't know what to do about the fact that everything she was seeing had everything to do with the girl next door.

The girl I couldn't feel this way about.

The girl whose god-awful singing, as she blasted the Christmas music she loved so much, had Amy and me cracking up just half an hour ago.

The same girl who, just last night, might have

gotten engaged to that fucking creep who did nothing but degrade her.

My phone went off in my pocket, pulling me out of the memories that were sure to piss me off all over again. Grabbing it, my eyes widened when I saw her name, and I hurried to open the text.

Maci Price: All things considered, it's not your place to tell me who I should and shouldn't be with . . . or to give an opinion on my life at all. Watch yourself, Detective. We wouldn't want people thinking you're jealous or give a shit.

I gripped my phone in my hand and started storming out of my apartment, grabbing my keys on the way.

"Where are you going?"

"I'll be right back," I answered, and avoided looking where she was changing Ben.

As soon as my door was open, I kicked the box of oatmeal bath packets sitting there out of my way and went next door. When Maci's door didn't immediately open, I unlocked it and let myself in to walk through the apartment as I called her name. Nothing. Pulling up her contact in my phone, I pressed on her name and ground my jaw when it went straight to voice mail.

"It's Connor. We're talking about this when you get home."

I locked her door behind me and walked back into my apartment. Amy was standing there holding her son, a confused look on her face that slowly started changing.

"I'm sorry, I just had to—"

"What is going on between you and Maci Price?"

My eyebrows shot up. "Nothing, she's just driving me insane right now."

She hitched Ben higher up on her hip and pursed her lips at me. Ah fuck. She was in mom mode. "I know you're lying to me, and why do I have a feeling she has something to do with the difference I'm seeing in you?"

I sucked at lying to my sister. Especially when she went into mom mode. Throwing my hands out to the side, I let my keys fall to the floor before bringing my hands back to grip my hair. "She's a *Price*, Amy. They would fu"—I glanced at Ben and tried to filter myself—"freaking murder me."

Amy gasped and a massive smile crossed her face as she dropped to the couch. "How long has this been going on?"

"That's just it," I laughed humorlessly. "It hasn't been. Nothing's happened between us."

"Connor."

"I'm being honest. Nothing has happened, and nothing will. She's my best friends' sister, I can't touch her."

And apparently I'd done something to fuck up anything that could have happened between us . . . and I had no idea what exactly that was.

Maci

AFTER HOURS OF shopping, then decorating Amber's apartment and my own, we were finally done. I had a smile on my face that only this time of year could put there, but there was still something missing. Christmas was my favorite holiday, and I loved decorating day more than anything, but I still hadn't gotten Connor or his words out of my mind.

Amber flopped down next to me on the couch and admired our work. "We did good."

"That we did."

"Hey"—she elbowed me—"what's going on? You're usually bouncing off the walls and I can't get you to stop playing *Elf* or singing Christmas music. You're just kind of . . . blah today. Is it still what Bryce said?"

"Kind of." I shrugged. *Barely.* I couldn't forget his words if I tried. But it was Connor who was ruining my day, and I hated that I let him have that much power over me.

"Fuck him, Maci. He's a douche, and I think he did you a favor by finally showing his true self. Now you can move on and find someone else."

Was it sad that I couldn't figure out if she was talking about Connor or Bryce, even though I knew she didn't have a clue about Connor?

"I don't want to find someone else . . . I just want to forget about him." Forget the words he'd said. Forget that I'd let myself think he might feel something. Forget the other girls in his apartment. Forget it all.

"Then let's do it! Let's forget the bastard!" Amber shouted and jumped off the couch, jolting me from my thoughts. I hadn't realized I'd said any of that out loud and was glad I hadn't said Connor's name.

"Should I be worried?" I asked when Amber held a hand out for me. I let her pull me up and push me toward my room.

"Hell no. You want to forget about the dick, that's what we're gonna do. So slut it up, get yourself looking hot, and let's go shout from the rooftop that your vagina is finally free!"

I laughed and shook my head. "You're disgusting, you know that?"

"You love my kind of disgusting though. Hurry up, I want to run home and change too."

Turning around, I pointed at her. "I just want to go have fun, I don't want to find another guy."

"Yeah, yeah. Whatever. Let's get a few shots in you and see if you feel the same."

Note to self: Buy a chastity belt and wear it whenever going out with Amber.

Chapter Five

Connor

I SHOOK MY head and drained my beer as Dakota leaned over far enough that he was about to—oh, never mind. There he went. Dumbass fell out of the damn chair leaning over to watch the girl leave with her friend.

"Shit, Kota, you already got her number, you don't need to look like a fucking loser wishing he'd had the balls to talk to her." I signaled the waitress for another beer and held out my hand. "Keys. You're not . . . driving." *Shit.*

My eyes landed on long, vibrant red hair. Messy in a way that only a girl like Maci could pull off.

". . . not drunk, man," Dakota's voice filtered in as I shamelessly stared at his sister. "I just couldn't stop looking. Did you see her ass?"

"Yeah," I answered automatically. "Definitely saw it." And I was still staring at it.

Maybe I shouldn't be driving tonight; because other than having a death wish, a guy would have to be drunk to continue checking out his friend's little sister right in front of him.

"Maci!" Dylan called out her name when he caught sight of her from where he was working on a table of girls I was positive had used fake IDs to get in here.

Maci's body stilled before turning to the sound of her brother's voice, followed by Dakota's once he finally spotted her. She caught sight of me, and her eyes widened before narrowing. Her gray eyes didn't leave me the entire time as Dylan walked her and that girl that was always at her apartment over to our table.

"I said where the fuck is he? Which one, Mini?" Dylan growled toward her ear, but loud enough that Dakota and I could still hear him.

Maci tried to shrug Dylan's arm off her shoulders, and when he didn't give, started pushing at his side. "I've already told you—"

"Is her boyfriend here?" Dakota asked and stood up quickly, his eyes scanning the area where she'd just been standing.

"There's no boyfriend! For fuck's sake, can't you leave me alone for one day?"

"Hi, which one are you?" Maci's friend asked Dylan as she pressed against him.

"Amber, no, gross! Seriously, back off my brother.

We're leaving, you boys have fun getting wasted and hitting on girls too young for you. I've told you a dozen times there's no boyfriend, and there isn't," Maci said, and her eyes met mine again. This time they were stone cold, and all expression had left her face. "There's no man in my life, because not only do you all make it impossible, but every guy I've come across has proved to be nothing but an asshole."

There was no way to take that as anything other than a direct attack. I still had no idea what I'd done this time though.

"Amber, get off my brother, we're leaving." She finally succeeded at getting out of Dylan's grasp, and pulled on Amber's hand.

"Maci, should you be driving? Do you want me to call you a cab?" She didn't look intoxicated, but she looked pissed . . . and if I was being honest with myself, I wasn't ready for her to leave where I could keep an eye on her. But just as soon as she turned to look at me, eyes bigger than I'd ever seen, I realized exactly what I'd done.

"And since when do you give a shit about me, Connor Green?"

I could feel Dakota and Dylan's eyes on me, and had to force myself not to react to her question. Instead, I shrugged and sipped at the new beer that had been placed in front of me. "I'm a cop, Mini . . . it's ingrained in me to make sure everyone is okay to drive."

With a slow shake of her head, she stared me down for a few tense moments before walking backward, with Amber in tow. "I'm fine. The last thing I need is you looking after me. I already have four brothers, I don't need another."

I'd deserved that. I'd called her the name she hated the most coming from me, judging by her reaction yesterday in her office. But I couldn't think of anything else to do without her brothers thinking something was up. When had I ever stopped her from leaving when it turned out we were all at the same bar together? Never. But, fuck, having her call me her brother hurt. Not nearly as bad as the way those gray eyes went from challenging to hurt in a split second, though.

What was happening between us? Had I been missing these small signs from Maci for months . . . years, even? Or was I just imagining things because for the first time in my life, I couldn't get this frustrating girl out of my mind?

Dakota pounded on my back and I had to throw my arm out over the table when the beer in my hand sloshed over on me. "Scared me for a second there, bro. You've never offered to call a cab for Maci."

Think, Connor, think. "It's just usually when I see her coming back to her apartment with that girl, they're pretty trashed. Guess I was just automatically thinking ahead for the night."

"They're fine. Mini knows not to drive drunk, but, shit, Amber gets hotter every time I see her." Dylan said, and looked over his shoulder at the door. I didn't

need to look with him, I'd watched out of the corner
of my eye until Maci had left.

Dakota held out a fist over the table and Dylan
smacked his own on it. "Hell yeah she does, and she's
going to Mammoth with us this year. You're still
coming, right, Connor?"

"Yeah, of course I am. When have I missed a
winter with you guys up there?"

"Fifty says I get with Amber first," Dylan said,
challenging his brother.

Dakota snorted and chugged his beer. "You're on."

*Fifty says I don't last until Mammoth before I lose my
fucking mind trying to stay away from their sister.*

MY EYES FLASHED open and I automatically, and quietly, reached for my Springfield XDm on my nightstand. Slipping out of bed, I took slow and calculated
steps, with my arms raised in front of me. More noises
came from the front of my apartment, and I stopped
just at the turning point in my hallway, trying to listen
to figure out how many people were in my apartment.
It sounded like one, and whoever it was wasn't trying
to be quiet. Just before I rounded the corner, I heard
it. That damn raspy voice I'd been dreaming of the
last two nights.

"Shit. Fuck. Sorry, lamp! Shh! Stay quiet," Maci
whisper-yelled in the front of my apartment.

I dropped my arms and let out a huff as I rounded

the corner and found her fumbling with a lamp on the table at the end of my couch. I scratched at my forehead and dropped my hand to cover my mouth when I started to laugh as I waited for her to get it stable again.

"Good boy, lamp. Now, stay!"

"Maci."

She whirled around so fast that her purse hit the lamp and knocked it off the table and onto the floor. "Fuck! I'm sorry! I told you to stay," she hissed down at the lamp, and fell half onto the couch, half onto the floor, bending over to see where it had fallen.

"Damn it," I mumbled, and ran over to put my gun on the bar countertop before going to Maci. "You okay there?" I asked as I pulled her fully onto the couch and brushed her wild hair back from her face.

"Connor! Hi," she was still whisper-yelling, and her face looked like she hadn't known I was there. God, she was so fucking wasted.

"Hey, Mace. Little bit drunk tonight?"

"What? No, I just wanted to—hi."

I couldn't help it. I cracked a smile and had to drop my head when I started laughing. "Hi, Maci. Baby, do you know what apartment you're in?"

"Where'd you come from?" she asked her massive purse as she took it off her shoulder, stared at it, and let it fall to the floor.

I just shook my head and repeated my question. "Maci, do you know what apartment you're in?"

She looked back over at me, and her eyes widened

when she saw me. "Connor! Hi! I wanted to come home and then, here am I! I am? Sam I am!" she giggled as she kicked off her shoes and grabbed at the bottom of her shirt and started to pull it up.

"Maci, stop! Stop, undressing." I grabbed her hands and kept them from going higher. "Maci. Do you know that you're in my apartment?"

Maci looked around confused for a second, and then nodded slowly before leaning all the way to the right to whisper to a pillow. "Did you bring me here?"

"Did you drive home?"

"Ooo, I love him. He's soft, and my face is in love with him."

"Oh, Jesus Christ. Maci, it's a pillow." I sat her up and gripped her chin with my hand. "Did. You. Drive. Home. Tell me now."

She started giggling until she was laughing loudly and leaning into my bare chest. "Of course not, *Detective Green*."

"Thank God. Who drove you home? Was it Amber?"

Maci sat up so fast I was afraid she was about to throw up, but she just looked around and pointed at random things in my apartment. "No, Amber . . . where'd Amber . . . oh, Amber's boyfriend came."

"He drove you home?"

"No, no. This guy I met at the bar we went to, he was so sweet! I think his name was John, or Josh . . . or . . . . where'd my pillow go?"

I had to let go of her so my hands wouldn't hurt

her as they clenched into fists. I wanted to yell at her
for letting some random guy drive her home. I wanted
to tell her about how many times I'd had calls where
girl's bodies Maci's age and younger were found
dumped on the side of the road. But she was so gone
right now, it wouldn't even matter. Then something
else occurred to me.

"Maci, Maci wake up!" I pulled her up from the
pillow and made her look at me again. "Did he walk
you upstairs? Did you tell him which apartment was
yours?"

"No, no . . . he just dropped me off."

I let go of her and ran my hands over my face.
Thank God Maci had some kind of sense when she
was wasted. But I sure as shit wasn't letting her go
back to her apartment tonight. I still didn't trust the
guy who brought her home, or what she might have
told him.

"I love you."

My hands froze and I dropped them slowly as I
turned to look at her, but she was cuddling the damn
pillow again—*oh dear God she just kissed it.*

"All right, I think you've had enough time with
this pillow. Come on, let's get you to bed." I pulled
her up and she struggled against me as I tried to take
the pillow away from her.

"No, he's so soft! My face loves him!"

"I know, you've professed your love for my pillow
a few times now, but I'm gonna get you taken care of
and in bed now. Okay?"

"No"—she whined—"pillow!"

I stood with her in my arms and laughed when she reached toward the couch. "I have softer pillows on my bed," I whispered into her ear.

She froze for all of two seconds before throwing her arm out and pointing in the direction of my bedroom. "Pillows!"

"Christ, you are so fucking drunk," I mumbled to myself. "How about this: you help me take care of you, and I'll give you all the pillows you want. Deal?"

When she turned to look up at me, our faces were so close that everything in me halted for a few seconds as I fought with the dreams and fantasies I'd been having.

Maci's face scrunched in concentration before nodding. "Deal."

I swallowed hard and nodded to get my mind working again. "Right. Okay, kitchen first."

I walked her in there and placed her on the countertop, making sure she was stable enough to keep herself sitting straight up without falling off. Grabbing a few aspirin and a Gatorade out of the fridge, I walked back to where she was sitting and handed her the pills.

"Do you feel like you're going to throw up?"

"Nope, nope, nope!"

Smiling, I handed her the bottle and made sure she had a firm grip on it. "Take the pills and drink that entire bottle."

She frowned after she took the pills. "But I'm not thirsty."

"Take as long as you need, but drink the whole bottle, or no pillows."

Her bloodshot eyes narrowed at me as she brought the bottle back to her mouth and continued drinking. Once the bottle was empty, I helped her off the counter and walked her into my bathroom before turning on the shower.

"I don't wanna," she whined, and stamped her feet like a child.

"You smell like a bar. You're not getting in my bed smelling like this. Would it make you feel better if I went to your apartment and got your shampoo?"

Maci swatted at me and moved toward the shower as her hands went to her shirt again. I grabbed at them and kept them down. "Wait until I'm out of the bathroom please." *For the love of God, please wait until I'm out of here.* "Are you going to be okay alone in here?"

She pushed at me and waited until I released her. "I'm fine," she drew out the word. "Go . . . go, wherever you go."

My eyes roamed over her face as I judged just how drunk she was. "Okay," I said softly. "I'm going to bring you clothes to wear when you get out, okay?" When she just nodded and turned back toward the shower, I grabbed under her chin again and made her look at me again. "Please don't fall asleep or pass out in there. Yell for me if you need anything, okay?"

"Yeah, 'kay."

With a sigh, I walked out and shut the door behind me, letting my head fall back against it as I fought with myself. If it was any other girl, I wouldn't let her take a shower without me making sure she was okay the entire time. Hell, if it was any other girl, I'd usually just be leaving her place, or I'd make her leave mine. She wouldn't be about to go sleep in my bed after this. But this was Maci, and I wanted her too much and didn't trust myself enough to let myself stay in there. Groaning, I pushed off the door and went to my bedroom to grab a shirt and pair of gym shorts for her, and went back to the bathroom.

I cautiously stepped in, and sighed in relief that she was in the shower, and it sounded like she was still conscious and actually making use of it.

"You doing okay, Mace?" She just grunted and I shook my head. "Clothes are on the counter, okay?"

"Pillows?"

"They're coming right after this, promise. Just finish up and get dressed. I'll be waiting outside the bathroom."

"Mmm, pillows."

Less than ten minutes later, Maci was walking out of my bathroom door, red hair wet, and hanging down over her shoulders . . . and in my fucking clothes. Shit. I hadn't thought that one through. My arms automatically moved up to grab for her, and I forced myself not to pull her closer.

"Feel any better?" I finally asked, trying to concentrate on something else other than the way she looked. Anything else.

"Yeah, I'm tired. I just want to sleep."

"All right, let's go," I said and walked her into my bedroom.

After I got her situated in my bed, I stood and froze when she grabbed my hand.

"Connor? I'm sorry for coming over like this," she said huskily and pulled me back so I was sitting next to her. "I wanted to come talk to you . . . just, not like this."

Whatever she was about to say, I didn't know if I wanted her to say it when she was drunk. Because all I could think about right now was how much she'd consumed my mind in the last couple days, and how perfect she looked in my bed. "We'll talk in the morning, Maci. I need to talk to you too."

Her heavy-lidded eyes fluttered back open and her brow scrunched. "You do?"

I smirked at her and pushed back some of her wet hair. "Didn't you get my message from this morning? I don't know what I did to piss you off, but we need to talk about it."

Her confused face softened into something that instantly made me want to hold her. "Oh, right. The girl in your apartment this morning, I'd been able to forget about her until you brought up this morning again. Thanks for that, hope she was worth it." Maci rolled away from me and grabbed at the comforter. "Good night, Connor."

"Whoa, what? Maci . . . worth it? What are you talking about? My sister was here with my nephew this morning when I got your text. She'd been here for a couple hours."

She stopped stroking one of the pillows, reminding me that she was still completely trashed, and turned back to me. "Amy was here? It wasn't just some girl . . . ?"

"No," I drew out the word. "Why?"

"I—I thought that . . . that maybe after what you did last night that you had . . . that there was . . ."

I draped my arm over her, caging her to the bed, and leaned closer. "After what I did last night? Maci, what are you talking about?"

"You . . . you stood up for me. You cared about me," she whispered and turned her head to the side to look away from me. "For once."

Using my fingers to turn her face back to mine, I shook my head slowly and tried to find the words for a few moments before finally whispering, "What do you mean for once?" My breathing deepened as I waited for her to respond, but her eyes just bounced back and forth between mine. "Maci, what do you mean for—"

She sat up and crushed her mouth to mine, and for the life of me, I don't know why I didn't push her right back down onto the bed. The fingers that had been pressed to her cheek slid through her wet hair, holding her face to mine as I deepened the kiss, eliciting a moan from her that shot straight through my body. Her hands slid down my bare chest, to my stomach, causing the muscles to contract; and, Jesus Christ, I wanted her to continue. But the second she whispered my name, and the alcohol barely masked by the Gatorade registered in my mind, I remembered why she was even here in the first place, and what I was doing.

I grabbed at her hands and pinned them to the bed as I sat up. "No, Maci. Shit . . . no, this can't happen. Not like this, not when you're drunk." Not at all . . . her brothers would kill me.

"I'm not dru—"

"Yes, you are. Maci, you're trashed; you were falling in love with my pillows not even half an hour ago. This can't happen . . ." *Leave it at that. Leave it at that.* ". . . like this. Let's talk in the morning, okay?"

She looked hurt, but I didn't even know if she'd remember this in the morning, or if she'd hate herself for doing it.

"Just go to sleep, we'll talk tomorrow, I swear. Okay?"

"Yeah, okay."

It took everything in me to force myself away from that girl, but I stood and walked to the door, turning just in time to see her start stroking the pillows again. *Yeah, she isn't going to remember any of this.* "Good night, Maci Price," I whispered as I shut the door.

I walked around my apartment shutting off lights, bringing my gun to the end table, picking up her purse and the lamp—that, thank God, hadn't broken—and locking the door before settling on the couch and shutting my eyes. But sleep didn't come easy after that. All I could see was the way she looked as she'd come out of the bathroom, and in my bed, and my body was still very vividly remembering every second of that kiss.

It was going to be a long night.

Maci

MY EYES OPENED slowly, and I looked around confused at the strange room that still somehow reminded me of my own. I let go of the pillow I was holding to my body, sat up, and grabbed at my head when I felt like I was going to fall back over; but after a few seconds, the feeling passed. It was then I noticed the clothes I was wearing that definitely weren't mine, and smelled . . . oh, holy mother of God . . . smelled just like Connor fucking Green. I looked wildly around the room for any sign of him, and stood up, only to sit back down on the bed when I felt like I was going to faint.

Shit, how much had I had to drink last night? And what on earth did I do to end up in Connor's clothes and bed?

I stood, slower this time, and cracked open the door to tiptoe down the hall. I almost thanked God out loud when I found Connor passed out on the couch. Going quickly back to the hallway, I paused outside his bathroom and looked in at the pile of my clothes on the floor. *Oh, God, they smell like alcohol and smoke.* No wonder I was wearing his clothes.

Trying to remain quiet, I went back around his apartment until I found my purse near the couch, and stuffed all my clothes in there before looking for paper, a pen, and tape. Once my note was attached to his door, I slipped out of his apartment and quickly made my way over to my own.

After searching for my phone, I pulled up Amber's name and shot off a text before changing into some of my own clothes and pulling up my messy hair. It was obvious I'd taken a shower and slept on wet hair, I just hoped like hell he hadn't had to help me, or that I'd thrown up in his apartment. My phone dinged and I picked it back up.

Amber: Dude. So. Hung-over.

I'm not as bad as I should be, but I still need a greasy breakfast. I don't know how I got back last night, when I checked out the window, my car wasn't in the lot.

Amber: I'll come get you. Greasy breakfast so needed. Then we'll go look for your car. Give me . . . like . . . a million hours to come get you

I woke up in Connor's apartment. In his bed. In his clothes.

Amber: SUPER HOT NEIGHBOR?! Holy shit I'll be there in ten!

I smiled to myself. I knew that would hurry her up. Too bad the only thing I had to tell her was that I'd dreamed I kissed him and woken up snuggling a pillow. Definitely not the most exciting experience of my life, and when it came to Connor Green, my dreams usually left me more satisfied than I felt right now.

Right now I was just confused and praying that I hadn't made an ass out of myself last night.

Connor

I GRUNTED AS I sat up on the couch, and ran my hands through my hair before standing up. Trying to stay quiet, I walked back to my bedroom and cocked my head to the side when I noticed the door was open. I stepped in and walked quickly back out. The bed was empty. Looking in the bathroom, I cursed when I saw her clothes were gone, and jogged over to the couch to look for her purse. But on my way there, I saw something attached to my door, and knew that I wouldn't find her purse where I had left it last night. Stepping up to the note hanging there, I clenched my fists as I read her words.

Hey . . . so I don't know how I ended up in your apartment last night, but I'm so sorry. I hope I didn't make an ass out of myself, and if I puked anywhere, uh . . . can we just pretend like that didn't happen?

Regardless if I did or didn't throw up anywhere, thanks for taking care of me. I know you didn't have to do that.

See you around.
Maci

She didn't remember a goddamn thing from last night, including the kiss. I'd known she wouldn't, but that bothered me more than I'd thought it would. From the words on her note, the cryptic words she'd said to me in my bed last night were something she hadn't meant for me to ever hear.

But it was too late. I'd heard them. She'd kissed me. I'd had the smallest taste of what having Maci would be like.

Grabbing my keys, I walked over to her door, and unlocked it when it didn't automatically open.

"Maci?" I called as I walked around her empty place. "Fuck!"

I locked up and ran back to my place to grab my phone.

When are you coming home? We need to talk.

I sat there staring at the screen, waiting for her response.

Maci Price: Like I said, I'm really sorry if I threw up or did something stupid.

It's not about that. When are you coming home?

Maci Price: I don't know . . . later? I'm having a late breakfast with Amber right now, and then I'm supposed to go meet up with Bryce.

That fucker from the other night? She was still seeing him? God, I'd never even found out what had happened with his fucked-up proposal. Not bothering to respond, I let my phone fall to the couch and fought the urge to punch something as I went to take a shower.

Last night, I'd stayed up for hours, finally deciding that when Maci woke up this morning, she and I were going to talk, and I was going to find out what was happening between us. But if she thought so little of herself that she would stay with that asshole, then what was the point? I'd tried to get her away from him without being as bad as her brothers, and a little over a day later, she was going back to him.

Fuck it. This was a good thing, wasn't it? I needed to stay away from her. So if her staying with Bryce was what kept me from her . . . then I needed to stay out of it and be happy she was making this easier on me.

Who was I kidding? I'd just realized that I wanted the girl next door more than I'd wanted anything since Cassidy; nothing was about to make this easier.

Chapter Six

Maci

I'D SUCCESSFULLY AVOIDED actually speaking to Connor for two days. Two days that felt like years. Okay, *successfully avoiding* might not be the right words to use here. He wasn't exactly talking to me, and I couldn't figure out what to say whenever I saw him. When I'd gotten home from having breakfast with Amber the other morning, and then going to see my mom for a few hours—since I'd told Connor I was hanging out with Bryce—he was locking up his apartment and turning to leave just as I reached my door.

He stopped abruptly and just stared at me, his intensity filling the space between us. With two large steps, he closed the distance between us and looked down at me. Those bright blue eyes held mine, the question in them one I still didn't know. Just as I'd opened my mouth to apologize again for whatever I might have done the night before, he grabbed my left hand, looked at it, and then dropped it before walking past me as he shook his head.

I'd all but fallen against my door and blown out a large breath I'd been holding when he walked out of sight, and had to sit there trying to catch my breath from one of the more intense interactions I'd ever had with him. And there hadn't even been any words.

Since then, we'd crossed paths a few more times as we came and left the apartments; each time the looks got longer, and the air got thicker. But I was still being a pussy. I was afraid of what I'd done while I was drunk that he'd want to talk to me about. At least yesterday I'd gone back to work, so I was able to have a legitimate excuse for not being able to talk to him.

My alarm went off again, and I groaned as I tapped the screen on my phone to shut it off. I'd already snoozed it twice to try to stay in the dream I'd been having of the intense blue-eyed man next door . . . but I needed to get to work before my brothers came busting down my door looking for my "boyfriend."

With a heavy exhale, I practically fell out of bed and stumbled to the bathroom. I wanted to go back to sleep so I could be in a place where I could stare at those blue eyes whenever I wanted. Where I could imagine the way his lips would feel against my neck as he pressed me against a wall. *I wonder if I can get away with saying I have cramps today so I don't have to go to—oh wait, shit, I did that last—*

"Oh my God! Holy shit, what the fuck?" I screamed and jumped back off my toilet when it popped like gunfire underneath me. Thank God I hadn't started peeing yet. But, seriously, what . . . the hell . . . had just happened?

My hand cautiously reached for the toilet seat, like the inanimate object might jump out and bite me. And with a determined huff, I grabbed it and threw it up.

"Connor!" I screeched and ripped the bubble wrap off the toilet bowl. "You son of a bitch, I know you can hear me!"

Pulling up my underwear and sweats, I stormed through my apartment, unlocked my door, and flung it open. A scream tore through my chest, and I jumped away as a trash can filled with water fell into my apartment as my door swung open. Mouth and eyes wide open, I just stared at the water-covered entrance and living room for long seconds before my mind started working, and I took off running for my bathroom again. Almost going into the splits on the way there from running on the wet hardwood.

"I will kill you for this! You flooded my apartment!" I yelled, knowing full well he could hear me.

Grabbing all the towels in the bathroom and linen closet, I ran back to my living room and started throwing towels everywhere as I continued to scream and curse Connor Green. Not five minutes into trying to dry everything so there wouldn't be permanent damage, two different neighbors stopped by because of my screaming, and graciously lent me piles of their towels too.

"What happened?" an older guy who lived across the hall from Connor asked. "And what's with the trash can?"

I gritted my teeth as I gathered soaked towels to take them to my laundry room. "All I'm saying is this, if you hear my neighbor yelling tonight . . . just know that he's getting what he deserves."

The guy jerked his head back before continuing to pat dry my throw rug. "The guy I'm across from?"

"The very one," I hissed.

He shook his head and huffed. "You're saying this is because of him? I don't buy it. That guy is the quietest neighbor I've ever had, and isn't he law enforcement?"

My face drained of expression as I stared at him. "And what exactly is that supposed to mean for me right now? I grew up with him. Pranks are kind of a phase we go through every now and then."

He just continued with shaking his head. "Just doesn't seem like that kind of guy."

I wanted the guy to leave, but he was helping me dry my apartment. So instead of responding again and being snotty, I just walked back to the laundry room and threw the towels into the washer.

Once we were done, I went to Connor's apartment, but wasn't surprised to find him gone. I figured he was at work, with how long he'd been off. Part of me was

happy that there had been a prank at all. A very. Very.
Small part, mind you. Because that meant that whatever weirdness had been going on between us was,
hopefully, ending. But I was absolutely livid that he
almost gave me a heart attack as I'd sat on my toilet,
and then flooded my apartment.

*Shit just got real, Connor Green. I'm going to enjoy piss-
ing you off.*

Connor

PICKING UP MY phone off the desk, I glanced at the
screen and didn't give it a second thought when I
saw PRIVATE NUMBER. I always had informants calling
from blocked numbers, and since my partner, Detective Sanders, and I were getting nowhere fast with a
homicide that wasn't adding up from two nights ago,
they were expected and wanted.

"This is Detective Green."

"I'm interested," the deep voice said.

"Excuse me?" I grabbed for a pen and pad of paper,
and waited for the voice to start up again.

"I'll call you 'Daddy.' "

The hell? "I'm sorry, you have the wrong number."
I pressed END and stared at the screen for a few seconds before shaking my head and putting the phone
back on my desk.

"Who was that?"

I looked over at Sanders and shrugged. "No clue.

Okay, every lead we've gotten has been a dead end. Let's review the footage from the store again, look at all the people who entered after him and left before or right after he did. Let's get all the cars we can see from the outer cameras, and make sure they all match people who were accounted for in the store." I loosened my tie and ran a hand through my hair. "I need more coffee first, want some?"

Sanders looked over at me like I was stupid. "We've been at this for almost thirty hours. What do you think?"

"That you need to get your own damn coffee if you're going to be a bastard, gramps. I got called in same time you did, I'm just as tired as you are, and I'm just as lost about this case as you are. Don't be a dick to me because we're not getting anywhere," I snapped and walked over to the coffee station.

Sanders and I were complete opposites, but when we worked together, we were damn good. To have a case that left us completely clueless was frustrating for both of us. We needed to go home and get some fucking sleep before we tore into each other.

The victim had been shot three times as he'd exited a store in a nice part of the city. He lived alone, and nothing had been stolen or happened to his house before or after the shooting; he still had his wallet with all his money and credit cards on him, and he had no ties to gangs or drug trafficking. No witnesses saw him get shot, but the way it was done was like someone was getting revenge, or sending a sign. And where he'd been standing was out of range of the outside cameras. All his immediate and extended family lived in the Midwest and couldn't believe what had happened when we'd called. According to them, and everyone he worked with, he was the nicest guy and kept to himself. I'd been sure we'd find something when we tore apart his apartment, but there'd been nothing. We'd just finished going over his phone records when my phone rang. Other than work and family . . . there was nothing. Murder was what I faced with my job; more often that not, it was gang or drug related. But these cases where the victims were completely innocent were something that just tore you apart. The need to solve them intensified, so you could give the family some kind of peace.

After getting both Sanders's coffee and mine, I walked back over to our desks and handed him his. "Come on, let's go review the footage again."

Two and a half hours later, Sanders and I were more frustrated than we'd been before. There was nothing, and in the large gap between outdoor cameras, there were multiple lanes the shooter's car could have gone down, but none had gone through both cameras at the right timing. We were getting ready to do a press briefing with news outlets about what had happened, asking for help and any information, before we called it a night, when my phone rang again.

I practically lunged for my desk, hoping for some kind of information. But it was a call much like the one I'd received after we'd finished going over the phone records. Different voice—this one actually had a number—and, unfortunately, he tried to keep the conversation going as he kept calling me Daddy. When I ran the number through the system, it came back as a pay phone, and I was left even more confused . . . and seriously fucking disturbed. But I was so drained, discouraged from the case, and pissed off for the victim and his family that I couldn't muster the energy to want to figure out what was going on with the phone calls.

When I got home, taped to my door was an envelope with the words "Bro, have you seen this? They're everywhere!" scrawled across it. I pulled out the brightly colored paper as I looked up and down the hall for anyone who might have left the note, unfolded it, and did a double take when I saw my picture blown up on it. Across the top in large, bold writing was SWM LOOKING FOR SBM WHO WILL CALL ME DADDY. IF INTERESTED, CALL ME! SMOOCHES.

Honest to God, below my picture was my cell number.

Too far. Too far. Too fucking far. I wasn't breathing, and the hall was spinning around me. My hand shot out in front of me to grip the frame of my door as I took deep breaths in and out until I felt like I could stay standing again.

When I hadn't been at work, or when I'd taken breaks to clear my head from the case, I'd been miserable thinking about how Maci and I still hadn't talked. I hated thinking about her marrying that self-entitled douche, and yet, I still couldn't make myself do anything about it, because I knew I should leave her alone. Cassidy had ruined me for half a year, and even she hadn't consumed me like Maci was.

I don't know why everything suddenly changed between us, and I don't know why I'd never noticed her. It'd been a week since she'd brought me out of the Cassidy-haze. And it didn't matter that it'd only been a week, or that half that time had been us pissed at each other. Those seven days had somehow felt like years of torture as I kept myself from her. But then she goes and pulls this shit? I flipped through my keys until I found hers and stormed into her apartment, already yelling before I even found her back in her bedroom.

"You're messing with my career! Maci, don't you get that? I'm a detective, people on the streets know me, there are a lot of law enforcement who will see that picture and know it's me!"

She sat up and a soft smile crossed her face briefly before she could hide it and give me a puzzled look. "I don't know what you're talking about."

"I don't have time for your bullshit!" I slapped the flyer down on her bed near her feet and alternated pointing between it and her. "Where did you put all of these? You need to go take them down! You really think this is funny?"

That coy smile was back and she crossed her arms under her chest as she shrugged. "Actually, yeah, I did kind of think it was funny."

"You went too goddamn far today! I'm done dealing with your shit."

"Really . . . you're done? Then why do you keep playing this game with me, huh?"

I grabbed at the flyer and threw it toward her. "This isn't a game, this is my life!"

She threw her hands up before folding them under her chest again. "What the hell is with you tonight? The whole thing is a joke, I didn't actually make a bunch of flyers! I just made the one; the two guys who called you are my friends. It was all just a joke! They're the ones that helped me make it and put it on your door. You need to calm down, do you really think I would do something like that to you?"

My chest moved up and down rapidly as I took quick, hard breaths through my nose. "Yeah, I do! Why the hell wouldn't you do that? You've been a fucking pain in my ass for the last week . . . for most my life." I closed my eyes, cracked my neck and shook my head before turning to leave. "All of this, we're done. Both of us," I called over my shoulder.

"So when a prank sucks for you, we're done. But you can do them with no consequences?" she asked, and I heard her feet hit the hardwood floor behind me. "You flooded my fucking apartment yesterday!"

"I'm just done, Maci. Done with this, done with you." The more we did this . . . the more I interacted with her . . . the more I would want her. She was marrying someone else. I couldn't keep doing this.

"I've known you most of my life, we're neighbors
. . . you're just going to act like I don't exist now?"

Scrubbing my hands over my face after I unlocked
my door, I pushed it opened and started taking all my
gear off my belt and slamming it down on the kitchen
table. "I don't know, maybe. Look, I got called in a
day early on a case that is killing me, it's been a long
thirty-six hours, I'm fucking exhausted, just give me
some time alone without dealing with one of your
pranks. And swear to God if there's something in my
apartment, you better tell me now."

"There's nothing, and seriously, sue me. All I
wanted was for you to come back to life. Like I told
you, you were a zombie a week ago, is it wrong for me
to want to change that? What even happened to you?"

"That's really none of your business."

"Why won't you just talk to me? Tell me what happened half a year ago, and tell me about the case. This
isn't like you, maybe it'll help to get it off your—"

Turning quickly, I put a hand to her chest and took
two long steps until I had her pinned to the wall. "I
said it's none of your goddamn business! Stop pushing
for something you have no right to know! If you want
to talk so fucking bad, why don't you tell me why the
hell you're going to marry that douche even though
I know you don't want to. You don't even want to be
with him, Maci, I know he doesn't do anything for
you."

Her chest rose and fell rapidly, and her eyes narrowed. "Who the hell are you to say that I don't want

him or that he doesn't do anything for me? Why the fuck do you even care?"

"Because I've had to listen to you moaning his name! I've had to listen to you pretending that what he's doing is working for you."

"And it is!"

"Do you moan louder to piss me off? Does he know that show you've been putting on is more for me than him? I swear to Christ if I have to hear you say his name one more time, I am going to lose my ever-loving mind."

"Why? I have to listen to your whor—"

"Because the name you're moaning should be mine!"

Her gray eyes blinked rapidly and she licked her lips. "W-what?"

"I guarantee you, if it were me inside you . . . the noises you'd be making wouldn't be faked or forced . . . fuck, Maci, you wouldn't be able to stop them from happening even if you tried."

I closed the distance between us and brought my mouth down onto hers. A high-pitched moan sounded from her chest, and her arms came up around my shoulders, bringing me closer. Cupping her face in my hands, I traced her bottom lip with my tongue and bit down when they parted on a gasp.

"Don't marry him, Maci," I whispered into her mouth.

"I'm not."

Pulling back, I looked at her and watched as her eyes fluttered open. "You're not?"

"Of course not."

I searched her eyes and breathed a "Thank God" before claiming her mouth again.

Maci's hands slid down my chest and stomach, resting on my belt for just a second before she grabbed at my shirt and began pulling it out of my pants. Her fingers quickly worked through each button as I pulled off my tie just before she was pushing the shirt off my shoulders and down my arms. I grabbed the back of the undershirt I was wearing, and pulled it over my head, letting it fall to the floor

I groaned, and the muscles in my stomach contracted when she lightly ran her nails down my torso.

"Maci, tell me to stop," I pleaded with her as I grabbed the waistband of her pajama pants and started pushing them down.

How we'd gone from yelling at each other about pranks, pasts that needed to stay there, and current partners, to where we were now . . . I had no idea. But with the way her body was reacting to mine, I knew I wouldn't stop. She had to be the one to stop this, or I was going to take what I'd been keeping myself from.

She responded by curling her hands over mine, and pushing her pants the rest of the way down before stepping out of them, and I stepped back to look at her body as she pulled off the thin shirt she'd been wearing. Fucking beautiful.

I captured her mouth with mine again as I ran my hands over her bare skin, and when they hit her thighs, I grabbed them and pulled her up to press her against the wall. A raspy giggle left her that quickly turned into a moan as I bent forward to pull one of her nipples into my mouth. Her hands went into my hair and pulled my head closer to her body. I didn't know how I could move from where we were right now, but that moan had to be the most amazing sound I'd ever heard from her. And I wanted to hear it over and over again. Remembering the fake sounds I'd always heard her make, I knew I needed to make this about her, no matter how much I wanted to take her up against this wall. For once, Maci needed someone who took care of her; and a quick fuck against the wall wouldn't do that, and wasn't what I wanted for my first time with her.

Pushing away from the wall, I released her breast and stared into her gray eyes as I walked us into my bedroom. Laying her down on the center of my bed, I was hit with every fantasy I'd been having of her over the last week. Part of me couldn't believe she was actually lying on my bed; hair splayed everywhere as her hooded eyes followed my every movement. The other part of me couldn't believe I was about to be stupid enough to take what I wanted.

My hands went to my belt, and I kept my eyes trained on hers as I slowly unbuckled it and slid it through the loops before letting it fall to the carpet Popping the button on my pants, I crawled onto the bed and over her, and about died when her face lit up with a come-get-me smile. I kept my hands planted on either side of her head, and lowered myself until

I could tease her lips, and pulled back each time she tried to deepen the kiss.

A soft growl left her, and her eyes leveled a glare at me before I pressed my mouth firmly to hers and prompted her to open with my tongue. Her growl turned to a needy groan, and her hands went back to my pants. I pressed into her hand when she palmed me where I was straining against the material, but the second her hand went to the zipper; I sat back and moved her hands away.

Quickly leaning forward to kiss her confused face, I kissed a trail down her jaw to her ear as I moved off her body and whispered, "Let me take care of you."

Running the back of my hand down her flat stomach, I gently prodded her legs open as my lips explored her neck and collarbone. My fingers trailed over her, and she whimpered when I groaned. She was so wet, so ready, and I'd never been more turned on in my life. Slipping two fingers into her, I pressed my thumb against her clit and made teasing circles as she pressed harder against my hand.

"Oh God," she breathed when I quickened the pace. "Connor, please."

"Please what?" I asked against her throat, and placed an openmouthed kiss there.

Her breathing was getting ragged as she rocked her hips against my hand, and I knew she was close. "Please—just don't stop. God, don't."

"Don't do this?" I pulled my hand away from her, and slammed my mouth down onto hers just before she could voice her frustration. "Trust me, Maci, I'm not done with you yet," I said against her lips and moved down the bed and in between her legs.

Her eyes widened, and she looked like she was about to stop me, but the second my tongue swiped against her, her hips thrust off the bed, and a loud moan left her. I laughed against her swollen lips and gave another slow lick before sucking on her clit and bringing my hand back up to tease her entrance. Maci whimpered before begging me to continue as her hands threaded into my hair to hold me where I was.

"Holy shi—oh my God!" she cried out as her body shattered around me, and I continued through her orgasm.

Once her body went limp on the bed, I pulled away and stood from the bed.

"Commando?" she asked, her tone somewhat teasing as I shed my pants and searched for a condom.

I turned to look at her and winked. "Does that bother you?"

"No, but I was wrong."

I paused when I began crawling back on the bed. "Wrong?"

"I've wondered for a long time, I'd finally decided boxer briefs," she said with a coy smile.

Laughing loudly, I grabbed her hips and pulled her closer to me; loving that her legs automatically wrapped around me. "So you've thought about this before, huh?"

She shrugged and feigned indifference. "A time or two."

"Uh-huh, a time or two." I bit down on her collarbone and pressed against her entrance. Maci rocked her hips against me, and I spoke against her flawless skin. "I don't know if I can be easy with you right now, Maci. I'm trying to hold off until I feel like I have more control, but you're driving me crazy."

Cupping my neck, she brought my face to hers and pressed her thumbs under my jaw until I was looking into her eyes. "Then don't be easy," she said so softly, I almost didn't hear her.

"Maci—"

She rocked against me again, and with a growl, I slammed into her. Her nails dug into my shoulders, and a whimper mixed with pain left her.

"Shit, are you okay?"

"Move, Connor, oh God, please move," she urged, and rocked her hips.

I cautiously began moving inside her. Terrified of causing her any more pain, I focused on her movements, and smiled when she glowered at me.

"If this is you not being in control," she said breathlessly, "I'm worried what you're like when you're in control."

Leaning back, I pulled almost all the way out before slamming back in over and over again. Using one hand to raise myself off her, I watched as her eyes rolled to the back of her head and she urged me to go harder as I continued pounding into her.

"Oh God, I'm—" she cut off when I shifted up onto my knees so I could quicken the pace.

Grabbing her legs, I brought them around my waist and leaned back over her, resting one hand on the bed, and letting the other trail to her sensitive bud. The second I rolled my fingers around it, her back arched and my name tore through her throat as she began shuddering around me, almost causing me to fall over the edge with her. Gritting my teeth, I rode her through her second orgasm and grabbed the hand that was trailing up my chest and slammed it down on the bed as I came harder than I ever have before.

Maci unlocked her legs from around my back, and I rocked onto the side that wasn't holding her hand, bringing her with me. Her body was shaking subtly, but when I looked down at her face, there was nothing but the brightest smile there. Releasing her hand, I wrapped my arm around her body and held her close as we both calmed down. With a soft kiss to the corner of her mouth, I uncurled my body from hers and walked to the bathroom to dispose of the condom and wash up. When I walked back into my room, I stopped short, and the high I'd been riding ever since I'd kissed her in my living room suddenly left me.

She wasn't in the room, and when I walked down the hall, she was putting her clothes on from where she'd taken them off earlier.

"What the hell are you doing?"

Her gray eyes widened, and she quickly pulled her

pants up as she faced me. "Isn't this what you want? Don't you want me to leave?"

"Why the fuck would I want you to leave? What was that just now for you?" *No, this isn't fucking happening. She's said too much for me to think that she doesn't care about me.*

"You always make your girls leave," she whispered, and looked around the room, avoiding eye contact with me. "I thought when you got up, that's what you wanted me to do."

I'd never seen Maci so unsure of herself and timid-looking. I quickly closed the distance between us and pulled her close, cupping her face in my hands. "If all you wanted was for me to fuck you, then go. But, Maci, you're not like those girls. I don't want you to leave."

Those eyes shot back up to mine, and a soft smile crossed her face. "Really?"

Letting go of her, I shook my head and shrugged helplessly. "Jesus Christ, Maci. I haven't gone more than a few minutes without thinking about you this entire week. I've been going crazy keeping myself from you because I know this is going to turn out so bad for us. Your brothers will kill me. But after that . . . fuck. You can't walk away from me . . . not after that. I can't go back to avoiding whatever's happening between—"

She launched herself at me, wrapping her body around mine, and kissed me until our breathing was ragged.

"Does this mean you'll get your ass back in my bed?"

"I'm kind of wondering why you aren't already walking us back there, Detective."

I bit down on her bottom lip and was suddenly ready for round two when another sexy moan sounded in her throat. "I hate it when you call me that."

"I know."

"Watch it, Maci," I said in a teasing warning.

"Or what?" she whispered against my lips. "You'll lose control with me again?"

I smiled and began walking to the bedroom. "You haven't seen me lose control yet, baby."

Chapter Seven

Maci

I woke to Connor's lips kissing a soft trail down the back of my neck, and turned in his arms to face him.

"Morning," his deep voice rumbled as he pushed my hair away from my face.

"Morning." I dropped my head against his chest when I started to yawn. "What time is it?"

"Early. I have to go back to the office, we only left last night because we needed to sleep before Sanders and I tried to kill each other."

Looking back up at his face, I noticed the dark circles under his eyes and reached up to trace them. "You look like you still didn't get any sleep."

"I didn't."

"Why?"

Connor took a deep breath in and held it for a few

moments as his eyes glazed over. "Just had a lot on my mind."

"Like?" I asked cautiously.

"This case I'm working . . . you . . . your brothers," he gritted the last two words out.

"They won't find out," I said, hoping to assure him and trying not to panic that he was already regretting last night.

He smiled sadly and kissed me before getting off the bed and heading to his closet. I frowned when I saw he was already mostly dressed to leave for work. Sitting up in his bed, I pulled the comforter up to cover myself, and watched as he walked back out, buttoning up a gray shirt, with a blue tie the same color as his eyes draped over his arm.

Not willing to let him see my inner freak-out, I squared my shoulders and stated with blatant indifference: "You regret last night."

"What—no." His head snapped up, his eyes wide. "Maci, shit, why do you do this?" He dropped the tie on the bed and walked over to lean close to me.

"What?"

"This," he said softly, his eyes boring into mine. "You act like you don't care, and I know you do. You put on this brave face and say shit like this, and you get ready to push me away rather than find out what's happening between us. Its like you're prepared for me to upset you, and are trying to act like you couldn't care less."

"Have you met my brothers?" I tried to laugh. "I

have to be tough around them, or they'd give me so much shit."

"Bullshit, Maci." I opened my mouth, but he stopped me by talking over me. "I know you have to act tough around them. I know you have to act like you don't give a shit about anything around them. But I'm not them, so why do you do this with me?"

I stayed quiet for so long that he started to ask why again before I said anything. "Because you've never cared about me, and all of a sudden you do? It doesn't make sense. Nothing you ever say to me makes sense. There are the rare days when you defend me against Bryce and take care of me when I'm wasted. But then you call me Mini, you always call me a child or tell me to grow up; last night you came into my apartment yelling at me that you were done with me. Why wouldn't I be ready for you to hurt me? You're—" Something in Connor's blue eyes shut me up. It wasn't his intensity, which I was so used to, and loved. It was the smallest flash of fear, before his hands were cupping my cheeks.

"I've been an asshole to you, I know that, and I'm sorry. Last night . . . Maci, I was going off no sleep, and this case is really getting to me. I was already beyond frustrated, and feeling defeated when I got home, and then when I saw that flyer . . . I just flipped. It doesn't excuse it; it's just what pushed me over the edge yesterday, and I took it out on you. I'm sorry, you have no idea how much I hate the times I've yelled at you; but, Maci, I will never hurt you, I need you to know that."

"You say that now, but you can't know—"

"No. Maci. I swear to you I will never hurt you."

We'd gone from a six-month hiatus of even speaking to each other, to pranking each other and pissing each other off, to a night of the most mind-blowing sex I've ever had. He couldn't be that sure of something because of one night. But with the way his blue eyes were pleading with me to understand what he was saying, and believe him . . . I just nodded my head and forced a smile.

"And I know you act like a badass around your brothers, but I've seen you cry, Maci. I know you're not heartless, and I know, from drunken ramblings and what happened last night, that you're in this just as bad as I am. So stop waiting for me to show you to the door, and stop acting like you don't care."

I'd stopped breathing at *drunken ramblings.* "What did I say to you when I was drunk?" I asked, horrified.

A massive smile crossed his face seconds before he kissed me hard. "Enough for me to know that you want me, and more than enough for me to be pissed off that you were gone the next morning."

"Connor. What. Did. I—"

We both looked over at his phone on the nightstand, and with a huff, he pushed away from me to grab and answer it.

"Green. . . . When's she coming in? . . . All right, I'm leaving now."

Shoving his phone into his pocket, he finished buttoning his shirt and tucked it into his pants before grabbing the tie off the bed.

"Work?"

"Yeah, I need to get down there to interview some-one who may have information."

I waited until he was done with his tie before I started climbing out of his bed; but he just put a hand on my bare shoulder and pushed me back down.

"You can sleep a couple more hours before you have to get up for work. You don't have to leave."

"Are you su—"

"Maci," he said my name low, and hard. "I'm sure. Stay, and stop questioning this, okay?"

" 'Kay."

After a slow and firm kiss, he straightened up and smiled widely. "I'll see you later, sweetheart."

I lay there with the biggest smile on my face, trying to convince myself that I wasn't dreaming until I heard his front door shut. There was no way I could go back to sleep now. I needed to call Amber, and my phone was still in my apartment. After jumping out of Connor's bed and getting dressed, I ran into my apartment and grabbed my phone.

Less than one minute and five sentences later, I was rushing to put on normal clothes to meet her at our favorite coffee shop before I had to go into work.

I DIDN'T SEE Connor that night or this morning before work due to whatever case he was working on. But he'd texted me two hours after I'd gotten to work this morning letting me know he was on his way home, and was going to crash as soon as he got there.

I was eager to see him; I was still in such a state of disbelief with this that I wanted to be near him to make sure I hadn't dreamt the entire thing. Even telling Amber yesterday morning, I kept questioning my sanity as I gave her most of the dirty details from the night before with Connor. She'd seemed more excited about it than I was, but, then again, she'd been afraid I would get back with Bryce. So to say she was hoping this night with Connor had snapped me out of my "obviously liquor–induced Bryce phase," was an understatement.

A loud clap directly next to my ear mixed with Dakota yelling my name caused me to jump and throw my wireless mouse across my office. I noticed my computer had come back to life when I'd moved the mouse, and wondered how long I'd been sitting there daydreaming when I saw a half-finished game of solitaire on the screen.

"Jesus, what the fuck are you trying to do? Give me a heart attack?"

He just smirked as he picked my mouse up off the floor and tossed it back at me. "Not my fault you were somewhere else and didn't see me walk in here."

I started clicking on the old game and rolled my eyes. "Can I help you?"

"I'm just making sure you got all your shit done."

"And what shit would that be exactly? Playing

games on the computer, or the hour I actually spend on my job?"

His face fell into an expressionless mask seconds before he kicked my rolling desk chair away from the desk until it hit the wall.

"What is it with you and Dylan kicking me away from my desk?"

"We wouldn't do it if you weren't such a bitch. Did you get all the reports done today and get everything ready for the weekend?"

"Fuck you too, big brother. And, yes, I got everything done forever ago. Reports and pictures are uploaded to the site. Stuff's ready for the guys working this weekend."

"Funny how you seem to do everything, but I only ever see you playing games."

"I've been doing this job for Dad and Craig since I was thirteen because I was mad I was the only one who didn't ever get to go in the office. I could do this shit in my sleep. Now if you're done being an asshole, I obviously have a game that I need to get back to."

My dad owned a private security company, and later on, Craig bought in to own it with him. The rest of my brothers all worked for them somehow, and did security work for them when they were old enough, and I basically sat here. Uploading reports and pictures for our clients to read used to take me all day . . . and when I say "used to" I mean ten years ago; now it takes about an hour. Making sure the security officers had whatever they needed for working that night or weekend took me fifteen minutes, tops. Which led to me being bored most of the day. I couldn't complain though. I worked for my dad, for crying out loud. I had a cushy job, especially since I was his only daughter.

Dakota grabbed the mouse from my hand and flipped me off as he walked back down the hall that led to the rest of the office. Asshole.

Just when I stood to go fight him for it, my phone vibrated in my pocket, and I sat right back down in a rush with a smile on my face when I saw the name.

Connor G: Good morning sweetheart

Don't you mean afternoon? ;) How'd you sleep?

Connor G: Like I hadn't slept for 72 hours.
When will you be home?

I glanced at the clock, and frowned when I saw it wasn't even four. I was so anxious to see him. And I was still smiling like a freaking giddy-ass girl.

About an hour and a half.

Connor G: Do you think you can leave early? I need to see you.

Heat quickly flooded my veins, and my stomach curled in the most delicious way possible.

I'll see what I can do.

Not waiting to see his response, I shoved my phone back in my pocket as I stood to go talk to my dad; and thank God I did. I hadn't even taken two steps when Dylan and Dakota both walked into my office.

"Why are you smiling?"

"Can't I smile? I smile all the time."

"Considering you looked bored as shit about five minutes ago when I was in here, and now you look like you're ready to go to a Justin Bieber concert, it doesn't really make sense," Dakota answered for Dylan. "Here's this back." He threw the mouse at me, and I barely caught it before it hit my face.

"Bieber? Seriously? Do you not know me at all?"

"Whatever. You look like a freak, why are you so happy all of a sudden?"

Dylan's expression suddenly fell. "Oh, hell no. Who is he?"

Well shit. "For fucking real! There's no one! Will you all get off this whole thinking I have a boyfriend? Jesus, it's really getting old. I just made some plans with Amber, and I was on my way back to ask Dad if I could leave early."

"You can't," they said at the same time.

"It's barely over an hour, and it's a Friday!"

"No," Dylan said at the same time Dakota looked over at him and said with a competitive grin. "Amber can wait."

"You can leave," Craig said as he walked down the hall, and smacked both twins' heads. "We're all leaving early, that's what they were supposed to come out and tell you."

"You're both so annoying, and whatever that look was for, Dakota, forget it. Stay away from my friends."

He raised his hands in surrender, and Dylan smirked. "Who said we were the ones who had to stay away? She's the one coming on to us."

I leveled a glare at Dylan and pointed at him. "You stay away too!"

"Stay away from whom?" Sam asked as he walked down the hall with Dad.

"My friend, Amber." I turned and grabbed my purse out of my lowest desk drawer, and stood to face them. "Good-bye. I hate all of you. Except you, Dad, I love you!" Kissing his cheek, I didn't wait for my brothers to say anything as I practically sprinted out of the office and to my car.

Not bothering with my apartment, I let myself into Connor's and walked around confused when I didn't find him. Pulling out my phone, I called him as I locked his door and then unlocked my own.

"Yes?"

"Um, I'm home. But you're not . . . ?"

He laughed low, causing a shiver to run up my spine. "I'm where I need to be."

"And that would be?"

"Walk toward your room."

Dropping my purse on the little table near the door, I quickened my steps, a smile threatening to break out on my face. Just as I hit the hallway, he rounded the corner from my bedroom, and I paused . . . phone still to my ear, smile now on my face as I just stared at him. Blue Henley shirt on, and jeans riding low on his narrow hips. His lips tilted up on one side into a smirk, and he took slow steps as he continued speaking softly into the phone.

"Are you just going to stand there?"

"Maybe." My voice came out soft and breathy.

When he reached me, he took my phone from my hand and hung both ours up before putting them in his pocket.

"That was a lot faster than an hour and a half," he said as he stepped even closer to me, cupping my right cheek in his hand.

"I wanted to see you."

"Good answer," he whispered just before his mouth came down onto mine. "You look beautiful, by the way, and you took way too fucking long to get back here."

Goose bumps covered my skin, and I smiled against his lips. "Did I?"

Turning us to the side, he pushed me a step back until my back was pressed against the hallway wall, and his lips went to my neck as his fingers went to the zipper on my hoodie. My body heated when I felt him harden against my stomach, and my hands went for the button on his pants. I loved knowing that as soon as I had them undone, there would be nothing there covering him from me.

He groaned when my hand covered his length, and pushed against it. "Do I need to answer that?"

"No."

Connor pulled my hoodie down my arms, and I only released him long enough for him to toss it to the floor and pull my shirt over my head before I was gripping him and running my hands up and down his length.

"Fuck, Maci . . ." he growled, and his hands went to my pants to shed me of them, and my underwear.

When my bra was all I was left in, and his shirt had joined the rest of our clothes on the hardwood floor, he bent to suck on my hardened nipple through the lace, and my head fell back against the wall.

"Open your legs," he said after a teasing bite.

I did, and almost came the second his fingers touched me.

"God, I love that you're so ready for me."

I couldn't even be embarrassed about that; his fingers pressing against me and pushing into me had my mind blurring. His words were only turning me on more.

My stomach tightened, and blood rushed through my veins as I gripped at his hair to pull his face back to mine.

"Please, Connor," I pleaded against his mouth.

"Please what?"

"Don't make me wait any longer."

Before the words had finished leaving my mouth, Connor was gripping the backs of my thighs and lifting me up against the wall, his cock already pressing against my entrance. I tried to move, but the way he was holding me left little room, and an agitated groan left me.

When he didn't move, I practically whimpered, "Please."

He smiled and nibbled softly on my bottom lip. "I just wanted to hear that word out of your mouth again."

I cried out when he roughly pushed into me, and all I could do was hold on to his shoulders as he slammed into me over and over again. His thrusts got harder and faster, and the moans that I was trying to quiet continued to get louder as the muscles in his back and shoulders tightened under my fingertips from holding me up. A growl built up in his throat, and he bit down on my shoulder as he pushed into me a few more times, his whole body shaking as he came.

"Jesus Christ," he breathed.

I still couldn't speak, so I just nodded and moaned when he pulled out and set my feet gently down. His fingers went back to touch me, and suddenly his body stilled.

"Condom."

Still in my daze, I blinked slowly and pressed down against his fingers. "What?"

"Condom, Maci, fucking condom; I wasn't wearing one."

"Ok—"

"No, I've never *not* worn one."

"Okay, Connor. It's fine."

He shook his head and backed away from me. "Maci, I'm so damn sorry."

"It's all righ—"

"It's not," he cut me off. "I don't . . . fuck . . . I don't do this! I even had them in my jeans. I'm sorry."

Pushing him back, I bent down to grab my clothes and had taken a few steps toward my bathroom before he grabbed my arm to stop me. "I swear to God, Connor, if you apologize one more goddamn time I will punch you in the face."

"Maci, I just don't—"

"You don't do that. I get it. I've never done it without a condom either, but I've also never had that," I gritted out, pointing at the wall, "and now all you're doing is pissing me off. I'm on the pill . . . and looking at your face, that still doesn't mean shit to you."

With a huff, I turned and walked into my bathroom to start the shower. I angrily yanked my bra off, and put my hair up in a high bun before stepping under the hot stream of water. Almost immediately after, Connor was pushing back the curtain and stepping in behind me.

"You have your own shower right next—"

He turned me around, and grabbed the back of my head to bring me closer to him and kiss me thoroughly.

I pushed against his now-wet chest, but he didn't go

far. "No, you don't get to pull that shit, and then just come in here and act like you didn't just completely fuck everything up."

"Just listen to me. I'm sorry for reacting like that. I've *never* had sex without a condom on, and I hadn't even known until I looked down. Yes, it scared the living hell out of me when I realized that I hadn't worn one, but I also couldn't get over the fact that for the first time, that hadn't been my first thought, and main thought during. But, Maci, I told you that you're not those other girls I've been with. It's different with you, and I'm not going to lie to you, part of me is terrified by that. But the rest hated watching yo

u walk away from me just then, and hated knowing I'd pissed you off after that."

I wanted to punch him. I also kind of felt like I was about to cry, and wanted to throw my arms around him. I hated that he could mess with my emotions like this, but I loved the way I felt when he touched me, looked at me . . . talked to me. I was still scared that this was all just going to be gone.

He'd said he'd been thinking of me for a week the other night . . . I'd been craving him for years, and finally had him. I was in too deep way too fast; I knew I was beyond what he could be feeling for me. So he'd freaked over not wearing a condom, understandable. It was the fact that he'd still looked at me with such a horrified expression even after he'd known I was protecting myself that had killed me. But I couldn't let that be a reason for me to push him away, and gaging from our conversation the other morning, he probably wouldn't let me anyway.

"Maci, please say something."

I focused on his bright blue eyes, and came up empty on how to respond to all he'd said; so, instead, I slowly closed the distance between us and brought his face down to mine.

"I'm sorry," he whispered and kissed me firmly.

"Stop apologizing."

Wrapping my arms around his neck, I deepened the kiss and leaned my body into him when his hands slid down my waist to grip my hips. The kiss escalated quickly, and soon our hands were searching, and I couldn't get enough of him.

"Turn around."

I looked up at him, confused; but turned when he prompted me again, and looked over my shoulder to see his blue eyes. The air in the bathroom had thickened, and not just from the steam of the shower. Connor's intensity was quickly filling the enclosed room, I could literally feel it radiating around me; but I had no idea what had changed so suddenly.

Reaching above me, he grabbed at my showerhead, and pulled off the detachable part. "I didn't know you had one of these."

"Uh . . ."

"Do you trust me?"

My eyes widened as the spray of the warm water got lower and lower, and I jerked back into his chest when the spray went to the jet setting.

"Do you?"

"Yes."

"Put one foot on the edge of the tub," he said in a demanding tone, and I quickly followed his instruction. "Hold on to me, sweetheart."

I brought my hands over my head, and let them run over his hair and down his neck when the spray hit me. My back arched, and I moaned as the continuous spray put pressure against my clit, and Connor's other hand ran over me.

"Holy shit." My breathing quickly turned ragged as I got closer to coming faster than I ever had before. "Oh God, don't stop."

The heat in my stomach intensified, and I grabbed at his wet shoulders as I prepared for what I knew was going to be the most intense orgasm I'd ever had.

"Still trust me?"

"Yes, just don't stop!"

His deep laugh sounded in my ear. "Put one hand against the wall, and grab the showerhead from me."

"What?"

"Do it, Maci."

I didn't want to move. I was so close. But the way his voice had dropped even deeper, and the room got even thicker with his intensity; I would have done anything he'd told me to.

Leaning forward, I put one hand against the wall, and grabbed onto the showerhead. His hand let go, and both went back to my hips, his hardened cock pressing against me. I wanted to feel him inside me again, but I didn't want what'd happened earlier to make a repeat appearance.

"No, you're not wearing a condom. Don't do this to prove something to me."

"I'm not." He bent over me and his lips moved to my ear, and the deep tone of his voice had my knees growing even weaker. "I'm doing this because I want to. I've never had sex in a shower, and I don't want anything between us when I do it with you."

Without warning, he was inside me, and I was screaming as I came. My entire body shook with the force of how hard it hit me, and as soon as I came crashing down from the high of it, I dropped the showerhead and my legs gave out under me. Connor caught me easily and told me to put both hands against the wall.

"Are you okay?"

I was more than okay. I felt like I was dying in the best way possible, and I wasn't ready for the feeling to end. "Keep going," I managed to choke out, and had to remind myself to breathe when my second orgasm started as soon as the first ended. "Oh God!"

Connor's fingers dug hard into me as he thrust two more times before stilling as he came inside me.

Helping me stand, he made sure I was able to stay upright on my own before grabbing the showerhead and returning it to the top portion.

"You okay, baby?"

I sagged against his body and nodded my head. "I feel like I'm going to faint."

"What?" his voice had gone from deep and powerful to terrified in no time.

"No, no. I'm fine . . . I just stopped breathing there for a while."

His chest rumbled against my back when he laughed, and he bent to kiss my neck. "Okay, I'll get you in your bed soon."

He quickly cleaned us both up before turning the shower off and helping me out of the tub. Wrapping a towel around his hips, he grabbed another and wrapped it around my body before dipping down and lifting me into his arms.

"Oh my God! Put me down," I laughed. "I can walk, I said I was fine."

"I know you are, but I'm having more fun this way."

He dropped me down onto my bed and crawled on after me. Pulling me close, he kissed me softly and settled down beside me.

"Where have I been, Maci?"

My suddenly heavy eyelids slowly blinked back open. "What do you mean?"

"Why did it take me so long to finally notice you . . . notice this?"

I studied his eyes for a few moments before finally lifting one shoulder in a shrug. "I don't know; I'm just glad you did."

With a soft smile and another lingering kiss, he pulled me into his chest and held me there as I drifted to sleep from the exhaustion of the last hour.

Three hours later, my stomach woke me up.

Connor cracked one eye open, and his lips tilted up into a smile. "Jesus, woman, was that you?"

"Mmm, don't judge me. I didn't have lunch today, I'm starving."

"Well then, let's feed you." He jumped off the bed, and tried pulling me with him, but I forced my way back down.

"No, the bed is so comfy right now. I don't wanna."

One dark brow rose. "Are you about to fall in love with *your* pillows this time?"

I sat straight up, and didn't even bother with the towel when it fell to my waist. "Fall in love with *my* pillows? As opposed to . . . ?"

Grabbing my hands, he pulled again, and this time I let him take me off the bed. "Let's just say you're a very affectionate drunk."

My face fell into a look of what I'm sure was horror. "Oh no. What did I do? You still haven't told me."

"I'm not sure I remember. Do you want Chinese food?"

"Connor . . ."

"Pizza?"

My stomach rumbled again, but I was still glaring at him and wondering what I had done almost a week ago.

"Pizza it is. Come on."

"You're not going to tell me, are you?"

"Ha. Fuck no. I need to have something to hold over your head."

"I'm going to punch you."

He kissed my cheek quickly and pulled me into the hall. "I'm sure you will."

Pulling on his jeans, he leaned back down to grab his shirt, and I stole it from his hands. When he looked up at me, his blue eyes were dark, and he began biting on his bottom lip as he watched me put it on. He reached for me, and I twisted away from his grasp.

"Hey, you were the one who wanted to get out of bed. This is what you have to deal with now."

After another few seconds of shameless staring, he shook his head and grabbed my hand and dragged me into the kitchen. "You're going to kill me, Maci. I have no doubt of that."

Depositing me on my kitchen counter, he felt around in his pockets until he found his phone and pulled it out. After dialing the number and ordering a medium pepperoni, half with black olives on it, he positioned himself between my legs, and I just sat there shocked.

"How'd you know I wanted olives?"

"I may not have noticed you, sweetheart, but that doesn't mean I don't know you."

I smiled and leaned into his next kiss, slowly putting my arms around his shoulders when his tongue began teasing mine.

"Holy fucking hell, you weren't shitting!"

I jumped, and Connor gripped my body harder, pulling it closer into his chest like he was getting ready to protect me.

Turning my head, I huffed loudly and eyed Amber standing in the doorway. "Jesus, don't you knock?"

She snorted and rolled her eyes. "Don't you lock your door?"

"When I leave . . . but, fuck, you scared the hell out of me! What are you even doing here?"

"Considering I just ran into your brothers, and they asked where you were . . . I'm saving your lying ass."

Both Connor's and my body locked up. "Oh my God, I forgot to call you on my way home." Looking back over to Connor, I explained, "That's how I got away from them so fast. I said I had plans with Amber."

Connor was still tense when he looked over my shoulder at Amber. "What did you tell them?"

"That you'd gotten a beer thrown on you and went home to change, because that's kind of what I felt like doing to you when I realized you were using me as a cop out, and I didn't even know about it." She sat down on my couch, and I looked at her like she was insane.

"Um . . . I love you for saving me, but you're kind of interrupting."

She looked at her phone and then looked up at the ceiling as she counted on her fingers. "We've *supposedly* been together for four hours. I'm sure you've had more than enough time for me to interrupt, and I'm still saving you by not leaving your side in case they come to check on you."

I looked up at Connor, and laughed lamely as I let my forehead fall onto his chest. "Christ. She's really not going to leave, you might want to go get another shirt, because I'm not taking this one off."

"Oh no," Amber said loudly, "he doesn't need to put on a shirt. I'm enjoying the view."

"Amber," I groaned. "Seriously, go put on a shirt; I'm going to put on pants."

Connor smiled softly and kissed me quick and hard before helping me off the counter. "I'll be right back."

As soon as he was gone, I crossed my arms over my chest and glared at her. "Pizza is on its way, but, really? Could you not see I was busy?"

Amber was practically bouncing off the couch. "OhmiGod! He adores you! Did you see the way he was looking at you?"

My scowl turned into a smile, and I felt my cheeks heat. "We'll see." I shrugged and failed at sounding like I didn't care.

"Oh, whatever. Go put some clothes on. It's fun to look at him half naked. You . . . . not so much."

I flipped her off as I turned and began walking toward the hall. "Love you too."

Grabbing all my clothes off the floor, I took them into my room and found a pair of sweats to put on. I wasn't exactly thrilled I was spending my night with Connor with Amber as well . . . but I loved the shit out of her for having my back with my brothers. And as soon as I was back in the living room, I let her know by tackle-hugging her on the couch.

Chapter Eight

Maci

"Tell me more," Amber prompted, and I smiled against the lid of my cup of coffee.

"There's not a lot more to tell."

"Come on! I just got done with the worst shift other than the time I had some drunk bitch vomit all over her birthday shoes, and that's all you're going to tell me?"

Raising an eyebrow, I pointed a finger at her and whispered so the people near us couldn't hear. "That's not fair. You can't keep holding that night over my head!"

"Just saying! I want to hear more about your crazy hot sex with cop man."

The old man at the table next to us turned and eyed us for a second before going back to his paper.

"Detective. And you do realize not everyone is as lucky as you and Aaron are. His schedule is all over the place, there are some times he goes in and is home not long after I am, there are some nights where he doesn't come home from work at all. So, excuse me for not having enough stories for you because I don't practically live—and work—with my boyfriend."

"Boyfriend? You just said 'boyfriend'! That was a detail I missed!"

I sighed and slumped down in my seat. It had been a week since Amber had shown up at my apartment and interrupted Connor and me, and she was enjoying dragging out every piece of information from this past week about as much as I had, experiencing it with him. "No. No you didn't. Connor and I aren't . . . anything really. I was talking about you and Aaron."

She gave me a lazy eye roll, and pushed her empty cup at me. "You aren't going to do the same thing with Connor that you did with Bryce. You and your whole can-only-stay-friends thing is bullshit." Amber looked over at the old man looking at us again and held up a hand. "Sorry, excuse my language."

"I'm not. I'm not making us stay anything. We just *aren't* anything. There's a big difference here."

"Yeah, I could tell last week. The way he kept looking at you and always touching you like he was making sure you were still there. I was getting turned on and nothing was even happening."

I checked my phone for the time, and grabbed my

purse as I stood up. "That's one of the more awkward things you've said this morning."

"It's the truth!"

"Ha. Go home and get some sleep, I need to get to work before my brothers start hunting down random guys."

"I'll see you tonight for a repeat of last week!"

I turned and hushed her as I looked around the coffee shop. "Please don't interrupt us again tonight, I haven't seen him since Wednesday."

"I kid. I kid," she said with a wry smile. "But I want details of your monkey sex tomorrow!"

My face had to be as red as my hair by now. I widened my eyes at her and laughed lamely when she blew me a kiss. "Sometimes I just want to punch you."

"You love me!"

"I do. Seriously, go get some sleep. You look like the crypt keeper."

Amber threw her head back when she laughed. "Ah, bitch. I love you too."

I laughed and ran out the door and to my car. My phone went off right after I'd pulled into my parking spot at work, and I frowned when I saw Connor's text. He hadn't been able to come home last night, and didn't think he would beat me back today.

Which also meant I couldn't make my day go by faster by talking to him since he would be busy with work.

Seven hours, thirty-six games of Minesweeper,

and twenty games of solitaire later . . . and I was now all cozy in my desk chair as I read from my Kindle. But I was distracted. Other than one more text from Connor saying he was hoping to be able to leave soon, I hadn't talked to him today, and I had a feeling that once he got home he was going to crash. I hated and loved that I was this anxious and worried about not seeing him, when I'd seen him two nights before.

Bryce and I would go a week without talking, and I wouldn't give it a second thought. A week and a half with Connor, and I felt like I was falling deeper every day. I craved him. Craved his touch, his kisses . . . just craved being *near* him. Part of me was worried he'd see how much I cared, and I'd scare him away . . . the rest of me loved the rush of feelings and emotions I had, just thinking about him, that I'd never experienced with Bryce.

"What's this?"

I almost tipped my chair backward when I flung my legs off the desk and reached wildly for the Kindle that had just been ripped out of my hands. "Give it back, Kota!"

"And his throbbing member—"

"Ew! You know it doesn't say that. Give it back, asshole."

He tossed my Kindle on my desk and sat down next to it. "What's up, brat?"

I reached forward for my e-reader, but he slapped my hands away. "Ugh, what do you want?"

"What? I can't check on my favorite sister?" he said with a charming grin.

"I'm your only sister, fucker. And, no, you can't. You only ever come up here to piss me off somehow."

"Not true, and I'm offended," he grabbed at his chest dramatically. "I'm being nice and you're just wanting to hurt me."

"What do you want, Dakota?" I repeated as I crossed my arms over my chest.

"I need to know if you took care of the setup for the new clients we got this week."

"Yes, I finished it as soon as Craig gave me the information, and the security officers have been informed of the new places."

"See? Favorite sister."

"Why are you *really* in here?"

He leaned forward, his hands gripping the edge of the desk as his expression got serious. "I want Amber's number."

"Um, no. Definitely not. She has a boyfriend, and I told you both no already!"

"I just want her number, I didn't say I was going to try anything with her."

My eyebrows rose up, and I laughed humorlessly. "You honestly think I believe you right now?"

"Hell no, but you can't blame me for trying."

Jumping off the desk, he grabbed my Kindle and began walking away. "Put. The Kindle. Down." When he didn't stop walking, I spoke louder. "Don't make me use the 'daddy' card."

Dakota froze and hung his head before he turned around. "Bitch," he hissed under his breath as he roughly tossed it back on my desk.

"Aww, and here I thought I was your favorite."

"Doesn't change the fact that you're a bitch."

"I learned from you."

He huffed and turned back around. "Tell Amber I'm looking forward to Mammoth with her in a little over a week."

"I'll be sure to tell her you have syphilis."

Dakota shuddered and looked back at me. "That's just cruel."

"It's up to you, try something with her and I'll make up a massive list of STDs that you miraculously and suddenly got overnight."

"You don't play nice."

I shrugged and inspected my Kindle to make sure he hadn't damaged it. "Neither do you."

Sam came up behind him and shoved him into the wall, pinning him there. "We're closing up, Mace. You can go home if you're done with everything."

"I am. I'll see you Monday." I grabbed my purse, yelled an "I love you" to my dad so I wouldn't have to pass Dakota, and made my way outside.

Once I was home, I tried reading again, but I couldn't even remember the main character's name, so I did something else to pass the time.

I cleaned.

I know, I was *that* desperate for time to speed up.

A couple hours in, I'd thoroughly deep cleaned my

apartment and was rearranging Christmas decorations when my phone chimed.

"Freaking hell. Finally!" I yelled at my phone as I raced to get it off the counter.

> Connor G: I'm about to leave. I want you in my bed and waiting for me when I get home.

My face broke out into a ridiculous smile, and I hurried to hop in the shower so I could clean up before going to his place.

Connor

GRIPPING MACI'S HIPS, I gritted my teeth and tried to hold off until she was ready. Judging by the sounds she was making, she was close, but watching her ride me was making it almost impossible to keep myself from coming first.

I forced my right hand to release her hip, and brought it in between us to tease her clit.

"Oh, shit!" she cried out and threw her head back.

Her movements became frantic until she started shuddering, and her body bowed over mine as she tried to continue moving at the same pace. But the force of her orgasm had sent me into my own, and my hands gripped her soft skin to stop her movements as I finished pumping into her.

Maci's forehead was resting on my chest, her

shoulders and back rising and falling from her erratic breathing. Placing a soft kiss on my chest, she turned her head so her cheek was resting against me, and I ran one hand through her vibrant red hair as I wrapped my other arm around her.

"Come here," I commanded gently and pulled her up to me so I could kiss her lips, which were still swollen from the rough sex we'd had earlier.

There was still a line from where I'd bitten down a little too rough on her bottom lip, and I ran my thumb over it. She quickly bit down on the tip of my thumb and grinned.

"I didn't mean to hurt you," I tried to assure her.

"You didn't," she said with a smile. "I didn't even feel it. I wouldn't have known if you hadn't noticed the blood." Her face fell and she brought a hand up to cup my face. "Connor, I swear, it didn't hurt. To be honest, it was really hot."

But I'd made her bleed. I fucking hated that. All I'd been able to think about in those first few seconds of seeing the blood on her lip was what if next time, it wasn't during rough sex? I opened my mouth to respond, when loud banging came from my door.

Maci and I both froze, and her eyes got massive when we heard the voices.

"Get out here, you pussy! Let's go get a beer!"

She was off me and scrambling to find her clothes so fast that she stumbled into my dresser, and hissed a string of curses as she started to dress. I'd just grabbed a pair of jeans and was stepping into them when the banging got louder and they started up again.

"We're busting down your door if you're not out here in ten seconds! Ten, nine . . ."

I grabbed Maci's face, and kissed her hard. If they found out tonight, so be it. But I would really rather it not happen this way. Not when their little sister looked like we'd just had a night like we had. The lamp was broken on my bedroom floor; her shirt—that she'd given up trying to put on before grabbing one of my own—would never be able to be worn again; the handle of my bedroom door had put a dent in the wall; the comforter and sheets were on the floor; and the headboard to my bed wasn't even up against the wall anymore.

". . . six, five . . ."

"Don't let them back here," she pleaded and walked toward my closet.

". . . four, three . . ."

I finished buttoning up my pants, shut my bedroom door, and tried to stay silent as I ran to the door.

". . . two, one! You asked for it, Green! We're coming in!"

I swung open the door and saw Dylan, backed up, his leg raised in the air like he'd been getting ready to kick down my door.

"What the hell is wrong with you two?" I hissed, and stood in the doorway.

"What took you so long?" Dakota asked and

pushed past me, quickly followed by Dylan. "It's Friday, let's go out."

"Uh . . ."

"Man, you look like shit," Dylan said on a laugh and dropped onto my couch.

The same couch that just earlier, I'd started literally tearing Maci's clothes off her.

"What's wrong with you? Not going to say anything?"

I tore my eyes from the couch and looked at Dakota. "I'm exhausted. I went in Thursday morning and didn't get back until a few minutes ago." *Or a couple hours.* "I had just started falling asleep when you came beating on my door."

"Ah, shit man, I'm sorry," Dakota said with a sympathetic look before throwing his arms out. "Sorry you turned into such a bitch. Get ready, we're going out."

"Why are you breathing so hard?" Dylan asked suddenly, and I had to force my body not to stiffen.

"I woke up to you bastards yelling and hitting my door. I thought someone was breaking in and I was going to have to shoot someone. So I have a shit ton of adrenaline coursing through my body right now."

"Boo-fucking-hoo. Are you coming out with us or not?"

"Not. Dakota, I told you, I'm fucking exhausted." At least that was true. "I'll go out with you tomorrow night."

"Fine, fine. But get some damn sleep, because I'm

holding you to that." He stood and Dylan followed. "Maybe Maci wants to go out with us, I'd bet she brings Amber with her."

Oh shit.

"Oh fuck yeah, let's go talk to her."

"She's not there," I said suddenly and tried to school my expression when they turned back around.

"What do you mean? Her car's in her spot," Dylan walked toward the front door, and I thought of anything that would make sense right now without me looking suspicious.

"Yeah, she was getting in Amber's car when I got home. From the way they were dressed, they're probably not hitting the bars around here tonight."

"Fuck, if she comes back with a guy, you better fucking call us."

I just nodded and walked toward my door.

"I'm serious."

"I hear you, Dylan. If I hear a guy in her apartment, I'll let you know."

"All right, see you tomorrow. Seven sound good?"

I nodded and pounded my fist against Dakota's. "Yeah, see you both then."

Dylan punched my arm as he walked out my door. "Get some sleep so you're not such a pussy tomorrow."

"Well, if you'd leave, I would!"

As soon as the door was shut, I locked it and went over to the window to watch Dakota's truck. Once they took off out of the parking lot, I practically ran back to my bedroom and flung open the closet door.

Maci launched herself at me, and crushed her mouth to mine.

"Please tell me Amber won't be at the bar tonight," I begged against her lips.

"No, no. She got called into the hospital before you even got home."

"Thank God," I breathed and kissed her again, stopping when I finally noticed her body. "Why are you shaking, sweetheart?"

"I just—I thought—I . . . fuck," she cried, and her head hit my bare chest as a sob tore from her throat.

"Maci, no . . . don't cry. Please don't cry." Holding her close, I walked us over to my askew bed, and sat down with her in my lap.

"I thought they were going to find out. They can't find out," she said between strained sobs. "They'll make us stop seeing each other."

"No they won't." I didn't even believe what I was saying.

"Yes they will, you know they will. You heard them just then, they wanted you to tell them if I brought someone home tonight. You've seen how they always act."

"It's not their decision if I see you or not. Just because that prick you were seeing would have listened to them doesn't mean I will."

"They'll *make* you stop, Connor!"

I shook my head and grabbed her chin, waiting for her to look up at me. "There's always a choice, Maci.

They can tell me to stop, but like I said, that doesn't mean I will."

Her gray eyes stared at me as more tears fell down her face, and I brushed my thumb against her cheeks with the hand that wasn't holding her to me. I hated seeing her cry, but something deep inside me was happy that she would get this upset over us not being together.

I turned and laid her down in my bed, and brushed my lips across her cheek as a lone tear slipped down. Bringing my hands to the pants she was wearing, I pulled them off her, and let them fall to the floor. Sliding my hands up her waist, and underneath my shirt, I unclasped her bra, and worked at getting it off through the shirt before leaving it on the floor as well. I kissed her gently and took my time looking at her like this in my bed. Nothing but my shirt and her underwear. Fucking perfect.

Walking over to my dresser, I took off my jeans and pulled on a pair of loose sweats before grabbing my comforter and crawling onto the bed. Once we were both covered, I turned her body so she was facing me, and pulled her close.

"I'm sorry," she whispered. "I didn't mean to start crying."

"Don't be." Pressing my lips to her forehead, I held her body tight as the last of her shaking stopped. "Go to sleep, sweetheart."

I was exhausted from being up for so long, and from a case Sanders and I had just finished—and was physically exhausted from the hours with Maci before her brothers had shown up. Sleep came quick, but the last thought on my mind was how I understood her completely. I was terrified of losing Maci, but I knew that regardless of her brothers, I someday would.

Chapter Nine

Connor

WAKING UP TO Maci in my arms was rapidly becoming one of my favorite things. The hard exterior she always wore from being raised in a house with only brothers was gone. Other than the few times I'd seen her cry, this was the only time when her guard was completely down, and I loved seeing her like this. But every morning I woke with her was a blaring reminder that I was one more morning closer to losing her.

My body was sticky from having been covered in a thin sheen of sweat when I'd woken thirty minutes ago, and like I was every morning, I was thankful I didn't act out my nightmares. Maci would always still be asleep in my arms when I jolted awake, and only tried to move closer to me when my frantic breathing changed the quiet and calm air between us. But after making sure she hadn't been hurt, I always crawled out of the bed and away from her to try to calm myself from the too-real scenarios my dreams played out.

Pushing her wild hair from her face, I grimaced and my heart rate sped up as I was assaulted with images from the latest nightmare. My hands around Maci's throat. Her hands clawing at my arm as she struggled to breathe. Her face bruised, and blood dripping rapidly from her hairline. Her arms covered in varying stages of bruising.

I squeezed my eyes tightly shut and moved my hand away from her to cover my face as I pushed away the dream. I kept reminding myself over and over that she was fine, that I hadn't touched her . . . but it didn't take away the fear that one day it could be real.

I can't do this to her. I can't do this.

But I'm not ready to let her go.

Opening my eyes, I stared at her unmarked skin and took deep breaths in—letting her sweet scent wash over me as I looked over every exposed part of her body and reminded myself that she was fine. That I hadn't hurt her.

When my breathing had returned to normal, I glanced at the clock behind Maci and stifled a sigh. Brushing my knuckles against her cheek, I leaned in and kissed the corner of her lips gently. A soft whimper sounded in the back of her throat, and she curled her body closer to mine as she dug her head into my shoulder.

"Wake up, sweetheart," I whispered into her ear.

"Mmm, nu uh."

Laughing softly, I kissed a trail down her jaw, and then up to her mouth. "I have to leave."

She'd been leaning into my kiss, but jerked back when I spoke. "Where are you going? I thought you were off."

"I am, but it's Saturday. I need to go see my sister."

Maci nodded in acknowledgment and studied me for a few moments before asking, "How is Amy?"

"She's fine," I said automatically.

"You don't talk about her much."

"There isn't much to say."

Another minute went by before Maci pulled from my arms and started to get off the bed.

"Where are you going?"

She looked over her shoulder at me as she grabbed her pants from the floor and pulled them on. "You said you have to leave, so I'm going."

"I don't need to go yet, I planned on spending some time with you first."

"It's not a big deal, really. Have fun with my brothers tonight."

I sat up and pushed the comforter off me. "What the hell, Maci, what's wrong? What changed from last night to this morning?" Last night she'd cried because she was afraid her brothers would make us stop seeing each other, and now she wouldn't even stay with me? My stomach churned when I realized I *might* have done something to her in my sleep, and that's why she was rushing to get away. "Maci," I said again when she reached my bedroom door, my voice ragged as lifelong fears clawed at my chest.

She stopped and held the handle of my door, like she was going to shut it behind her, for a few seconds before finally looking back at me. "I don't believe you."

My brows pinched together in confusion. "Wait, what? About what?"

"Your sister. That there's nothing to say . . . I don't believe it."

I let my face go into the expression I wore during interviews and interrogations, and hoped like hell she hadn't noticed how I'd just gone still.

"You're extremely protective of her. So much that I think I've only seen her twice in my life? And you pushed her into another room one time, the second toward her car. Have my brothers even met her?"

"What difference does it make?"

"You wouldn't be that protective of her if there was nothing to say. You told me this week you see her every Saturday unless you're at work. So all that says to me right now, is you're lying. You're keeping something from me."

"Maci, don't start this—"

She shook her head and crossed her arms over her chest. But it wasn't a defensive stance, it looked like she was curling in on herself. "No, Connor, don't tell me what to do or not to do. You didn't like that I kept waiting for you to hurt me, that I acted like I didn't care about you. Why is it okay for you to get frustrated when I lie because I'm shielding myself from being hurt by you, but it's not okay for me to get upset when you lie to me?"

"I won't hurt you." My body felt hot and cold at once as I remembered making her bleed last night, and the nightmare I'd just repressed came flooding back.

"You keep saying that. I know. But you're keeping something from me."

Shaking the disturbing images from my head, I flung my arms out to the side, and tried to remember what we were talking about. "I don't understand why you're getting this worked up over my sister."

"Don't say it like that. You know why I'm upset. You freeze up whenever anyone mentions her, and you did it with me just now. If you want me to keep being open and honest with you, you need to be honest with me. I *know* you're hiding something, Connor."

"No, you *think*—"

"Save it. Have a good day."

"Maci!"

She didn't respond, and I didn't go after her. Because she was right . . . I just couldn't tell her. Sharing my past with Cassidy—and people who could benefit from my story—was one thing. Telling Maci was another. She'd had no idea that Amy and I were even adopted. And if I told her about my past, I'd have to tell her about my fears of the future. I wasn't ready for that. I wasn't ready to lose her.

Once I heard both our doors open and shut, I

slowly got out of the bed and went about straightening it up before picking up the broken pieces of my lamp. I tried to stop the thought that by keeping Maci in the dark . . . and keeping *her* . . . I'd actually just lost her.

Letting our night together flood my mind instead, I took a shower, dressed, and headed over to Amy's to spend time with her and my nephew.

AMY HAD SPENT most of the last two hours watching me carefully, and I'd hated that she was doing it. I knew what she was doing. She was about to go all mom mode on me, and she'd see right through my bullshit.

With a sigh, I sat up with Ben in my arms and focused on her. "Just say it. Let's get it over with."

Her lips pulled up on one side in a sympathetic smile. "What happened between you and Maci? You were so happy when I saw you last week."

Knowing it was pointless to lie, I told her about this morning, and waited for five agonizing minutes as she studied me.

"You still haven't told her about us?"

"Still?" I asked, a little confused. "I don't know what you mean by 'still.' We've only been seeing each other for a week and a half."

"You told Cassidy and you weren't even seeing her," she said, accusation coating her voice.

"Cassidy was different and you know that. She had a past worse than ours, she understood."

"But you weren't in love with her."

I sat there, waiting for her to correct herself . . . or maybe for myself to realize I'd heard her wrong. But the way her eyes speared me, I knew I'd heard her correctly. "I'm sorry . . . but I'm not in love with Maci either."

"Maybe not yet, but she's different for you. You can't deny that."

Ben started squirming in my arms, so I let him go to crawl around the floor between us. "It doesn't matter if she is or not, nothing can come of it and you know it."

"Why not, Connor? What is so wrong with marrying Maci Price? You're fearless, her brothers can't scare you that bad."

I looked at her, horrified. "I can't marry her."

"You would have married Cassidy."

"She would have understood, Amy! She would have understood *everything*!" I tried to calm down as I waited for her to respond. But she just sat there shaking her head at me. "What?"

"Kevin didn't have our past: was it wrong for me to marry him? Was it wrong for *me* to have Ben?"

"Amy"—I sighed and ran my hands through my hair—"you don't have problems with your anger like I do."

"You don't have a problem with your anger. You're afraid of getting angry, period. There's a difference. You can't always be afraid to turn into him, Connor. We don't have his genes, who knows what either of our biological fathers were like? Mom sold herself so she could get coke. What you should have been afraid of all this time was developing a drug problem, because our fathers probably had one too. The man you're afraid of turning into just took his anger with our mother out on us. You need to get that through your mind."

I sat there staring at the floor and chewing on the inside of my cheek, trying to stop myself from saying what I so badly wanted to. But, in the end, it still came out. "When we were adopted, you were terrified of new men. Anytime you saw a man that was older, you would start shaking. It took you years of being asked out by guys at school before you finally said yes, and then you came home crying because you were afraid he would turn out just. Like. Him. Until Kevin came along, the only man you ever trusted was Dad. I have nightmares of me being the one to beat *my* future family. I never once judged you or said a word; I was just there for you. So don't start judging me because of this."

"I just want you to be happy. Cassidy may have understood better than most, but you have to know that you wouldn't have done anything to her or your future family with her if it had ever even gone that route. But all you can see, or think about, with her is that she would understand. You're not letting yourself realize that even *you* understood that you wouldn't hurt her. You won't hurt *anyone*, Connor."

I looked up and instantly felt like shit when I saw

her crying. "Fuck, Amy, I'm sorry. I shouldn't have said that. I just—I don't know. I shouldn't have said that, though."

"I've seen how much Maci has changed you, and I saw how happy you were last week. I know you won't turn into him. But if you won't let yourself have that, then don't lead Maci on with the pretense that something will happen between you two. I can see it, you may not realize it yet—maybe because you just don't want to—but you love her. She's going to see it too, so don't do this to her. Don't break her heart when you know that you can't give her what she's going to want."

I knew what she was saying, and knew I needed to listen to her. My head started to nod, but shook instead. "I can't stay away from her. I tried, but Cassidy didn't even consume me the way Maci does. It's like, now that I've finally pulled my head out of my ass, I'm trying to make up for all the time I've already lost with her. I can't get enough of her, and I hate when I'm not near her. I hate that she's mad at me right now, and it's killing me because I know I still won't tell her when I go home."

"You have to tell her."

"Amy, I just told you—"

"Tell her, or stop wasting her time. I know you've tried to protect me since Mom and Dad adopted us, and I appreciate what you did. But, I love you too much to let you ruin yourself and Maci like this."

I just sat there, not knowing what to say after that. If only it was as simple as she made it seem.

Maci

TURNING AROUND TO face Amber, I blew out a deep breath and asked, "Okay, I look hot, right?"

"For the tenth time, yes, you do! I still don't know why you're trying to make him drool over you when you left his bed just this morning, but whatever."

Amber wouldn't understand what had happened between Connor and me this morning. It would seem stupid on my part, but she hadn't seen the way Connor had hidden and protected his sister for as long as I'd known him. She was a huge part of his life, and I didn't know what it was, but whatever it was he was keeping from everyone had everything to do with her.

Turning back toward the bar that I knew my brothers were at with Connor, I squared my shoulders and said, "Just want to make sure I drive him crazy tonight."

"Mission accomplished. I'm betting he won't last the entire time we're here before he makes a move toward you."

I smiled to myself. I was betting the same damn thing. I was wearing my dark skinny jeans with ridiculously high heels I'd borrowed from Amber, but the shirt . . . well, we'd gone on a hunt for it today. What little fabric there was, was a bright green color that connected in a knot low on the small of my back, and with a gold chain around my neck. The front was cut so low that I couldn't wear a bra—not like I needed one anyway. It'd cost a stupid amount of money since all it covered was my boobs and stomach, but I was hoping it'd be worth it.

I'd spotted them sitting at a table with a pitcher of beer among them as soon as we walked in, and like he could sense I was there, he turned and his eyes went wide when he saw me. I watched as he took me in, and loved when his blue eyes met mine again. They were dark with want. Good.

Walking past their table, I paused when Dakota called my name, and tried not to smile. "Amber, please remember to stay away from my brothers tonight."

"But they're so—"

"You're dating Aaron!" I hissed before turning around to walk toward their table. "Can I help you?" I asked lazily and eyed Dakota before punching Dylan's arm when I caught him checking out Amber.

"The fuck are you wearing?" Dakota asked.

"Um . . . clothes?"

"You need to put more on," Dylan added, and grabbed his jacket off the back of his chair.

"I'm not putting your jacket on, I look fine. Was there something else you needed?"

Dakota pinched my arm, and I smacked his hand as I jumped away from him. "We'll be watching you, Maci."

"That's nice." Grabbing Amber's hand, I turned without looking at Connor. Everything in me wanted to rebel against the action, but I had this planned out.

Twenty minutes after we'd walked away from the

table, I walked toward the restrooms and waited in the hall, hoping like hell I would be right about this. And not two minutes later, Connor was storming down the hall toward me, a determined look on his handsome face.

Grabbing me around my waist, he hauled my body against his and pressed his lips down onto mine as he forced me back up against the wall. "You trying to kill me, sweetheart? Wearing something like this when you know I have to sit next to your brothers?"

Looking around the hall, he grabbed my hand and walked us into the women's restroom and locked the door behind us. His hands were all over my bare back, gripping and pulling me closer, and he moved the front of my top aside to suck on one of my breasts.

I pulled on his hair, until he released my breast, and brought my mouth to his for a few seconds. "We have to get out of here. My brothers are going to realize I'm not with Amber and go looking for me."

"I know, I know. Just . . . fuck. I can't sit there next to them while you're walking around looking like this."

Looking at him from under my eyelashes, I rubbed my hand over his hard-on and bit down on my lip, loving when his eyes rolled back. "Then what are you going to do?"

"Give me a few minutes, I'll check my phone and tell them I'm going to meet up with a girl. Ten minutes after I leave . . . no, fuck that. Five. Five minutes after I leave, you and Amber leave. If they ask where you're going, tell them to another bar—and apologize to Amber for me for cutting your night short."

"Her boyfriend is waiting for her at his place, she'll be fine."

With another hard kiss, Connor pushed away from me and moved my shirt back into place. "Five minutes after I leave, sweetheart. I'll be waiting in your apartment."

"See you soon."

His eyes raked down my body one last time, and he harshly whispered, "Fuck!" before unlocking the door and walking out.

When I didn't hear yelling from my brothers immediately after, I followed him out into the hall and smiled when he turned to wink at me before leaving the hall. I was so focused on him, I didn't even notice the girl walking down the hall toward me until she was talking to me.

"Don't fall for it, honey."

I jerked back and looked up at the busty brunette. "Excuse me?"

She pursed her lips and looked back over her shoulder. "Connor Green." She said his name like he was a legend or something. "I get it, I swear I do . . . but don't fall for it."

"Fall for what, exactly?"

"You think I don't know you two were just in the bathroom together? This is just the start for him. He'll call you 'sweetheart' and say all the right things to get in your pants."

I stopped breathing at "sweetheart."

"He'll make you feel special for a little while, but then he'll leave you . . . and he'll do it without a second thought. Then he'll move on to the next one. It's what he does; I'm just warning you so you don't get hurt."

Tears burned the backs of my eyes, and I forced myself to smile at the bitch. "Thank you. So, so much. I'm glad you warned me before anything else happened."

She gave me a sympathetic smile that was as fake as her breasts, and patted me on the shoulder. Walking quickly back into the bar, I found Amber, grabbed her hand, and began towing her toward the front door.

"Mini, where are you going in such a hurry?"

When I looked up, I noticed Connor was still there with my brothers, and he looked confused. "Go to hell."

"Hey!" Dylan and Dakota said at the same time, but I didn't stop.

"Oh my God, what's going on? Are you okay?" Amber asked when we were finally outside and making our way to my car.

"Fine."

"Maci!"

I choked back a sob and walked faster.

Once we were in my car and I was reversing out of my spot, Amber spoke again. "Okay, I saw him follow you, what happened? What did that fucker say? I'll go shank him!"

"He didn't . . . didn't. Son of a bitch!" I yelled and

blinked back the tears. I couldn't figure out if I was more upset or angry. "Gah, he didn't say anything bad. He . . . we made out, it was actually really hot. This girl approached me after; obviously it was someone he's been with, because she knows that he calls me 'sweetheart.' She was warning me, she said how he'd treat me and then how he'd leave me."

"Well, Maci, you knew he'd fucked random girls before. This isn't news, and he said you weren't one of them, didn't he?"

"That's what he said, but he called them *all* sweetheart. That's what he calls me."

Amber was silent, but kept watching me, until we made it to Aaron's apartment complex. When I pulled to a stop in front of his building, her voice was careful. "Maybe he just—"

"Amber, I know for a fact that he called his random hookups that, because he didn't want to bother remembering their names. I just don't know why I'd forgotten that until tonight."

"But he knows your name."

"He's also known me for years. Those girls he'd just picked up at bars."

After a few silent minutes, she squeezed my hand and opened the door. "Call me tomorrow. Love you."

"Love you too."

Almost immediately after I'd gotten home and started undressing, my front door flew open, and I could hear Connor charging through my apartment.

"Maci!"

I'd only taken my shoes off, and I really wanted to throw them at him.

"What the hell was that?"

I turned on him and threw my arms out. " 'Sweetheart'? Really?"

Connor's head jerked back. "Wait, what?"

"You call *me* 'sweetheart.' "

"Yeah . . . and? Maci, you're really fucking confusing me right now."

"I was stopped in the hall by one of your random fucks, and she was so kind as to remind me that you call all your one-night stands 'sweetheart,' and that you'd say all the right things and make me feel special for a little while before leaving me, like you've done all the rest."

"Maci—"

"I can't believe I was fucking stupid enough to forget that you called them all 'sweetheart.' I was so happy that you and I were finally together, that I didn't even realize it when you called me that. In fact, I loved it." Connor opened his mouth, but I kept talking. "I'm not going to be one of your random hookups!"

"You're not! When have I ever treated you like one? I've told you from the beginning that you weren't like them. Did I ever let *one* of them stay over? No! And you know that. I'm sorry calling you that made you think that, but you have to know by now that I would never do to you what I did to them. I was an asshole to them, and, granted, I've been an ass to you so many times. But, Maci . . . can you really not see that you're everything to me? I can barely make it through a shift because all I want to do is get home to see you. I've been going out of my mind all day knowing you were mad at me, and I just—you know what? Fuck it. You're never going to believe me. This is what you've been waiting for. You've been waiting for something to give you a reason to get pissed at me again. So now you have it."

Laughing loudly, I ran one hand roughly through my long hair and tried not to start crying again. "You found me out. Congratulations! Obviously you know your way out. So, have an awesome fucking life, *sweetheart*."

Connor had started walking out of my room, but stopped, and turned back toward me. Quickly closing the distance between us, he grabbed me and crushed his mouth to mine. I pushed against his chest, but he didn't move away.

His lips only left mine long enough to say, "I'm not letting you do this to us."

"Connor—"

"Maci, I know I took a long time to finally realize what you mean to me, and I know it's only been a week and a half. But I know you're in this deep . . . just as deep as I am. Do you think I'd risk my friendship with my two best friends for some random fuck? No. You know I want you, and, Maci, I want you so goddamn bad, it's all I think about. And don't say it's just about sex with you, because you know it's not. I don't know what I'll do if I can't wake up with you in my arms tomorrow morning. I hate watching you walk away from me, I hate getting out of bed when you're in it with me, and I know you feel the same."

"I don't."

"Then why are you crying?"

"Because I seriously fucking hate you right now," I choked out.

Connor's thumbs brushed back my tears and he shook his head. "No you don't."

His mouth fell onto mine again, and it was all I could do to hold onto him. He moved us until my back was pressed to my bedroom wall, and his tongue teased my lips until I opened them for him. A whimper rose up my throat when our tongues met, and I moved my hands over his broad shoulders and up his neck so I could run my fingers through his hair.

Slowly, his hands ran over my waist and dropped to my hips. Usually we were ripping each other's clothes off, but the controlled way he rid me of my jeans—his mouth leaving mine to make a trail down my bare chest as he took them all the way off—had my breath accelerating. Lazy, openmouthed kisses made a trail back up my body, and his hands went to the scrap of fabric covering my torso. With movements just as slow and calculated as before, he pushed the fabric up over my shoulders and down my arms, pushing the rest of the shirt past my hips so it fell to the ground.

Gripping the backs of my thighs, he pulled me up against the wall, pinning me there so I had no option but to wrap my legs around his still-clothed body. But the moment my legs locked around his hips, he was turning us and walking us toward my bed. My hands went between us to grab at the bottom of his shirt once he'd laid me down and stayed hovering inches above me. With help from him, his shirt was thrown over the edge of the bed, and my hands eagerly went to the belt on his jeans. I barely had the belt and jeans undone, and down to his thighs, before he was already pushing against my entrance. The second they hit the floor, Connor was slowly sliding into me, and I couldn't stop the erotic moan from leaving me.

Every movement against each other was slow, and in sync. Every movement had my blood rushing through my veins, and my stomach tightening in a delicious way. Every movement had the tears falling faster down my face and into my hair as I finally accepted that I'd fallen in love with him.

He hooked a hand behind one of my knees and brought my leg to rest on his back as he gently made love to me for the first time; and his lips met mine briefly before going to my wet cheeks to kiss away the tears. When our movements quickened, nothing about the passion that was flooding my room changed. Everything still felt like it was going in slow motion, and every time his body moved against mine, I struggled with not telling him the three words that were repeating themselves over and over in my mind.

I gasped, and my body felt like it burst into a million pieces seconds before Connor stilled above me.

He'd been rough, he'd been intense, he'd finally lost control with me, and he'd exuded raw power every time we'd been together. I'd craved more, and loved every second of us together the last week and a half. But he'd never been like this. He'd never been gentle; he'd never been this loving; it had never felt like this; and I wanted it again and again.

My eyes opened when his thumbs rubbed lightly against my cheeks, and I found bright blue eyes directly above me. In them, I found everything I was feeling being reflected back at me. I wanted to tell him that I was done pretending. That I was in love with him, but I ached to hear him say those words and knew I would wait until he did.

"Never doubt what you mean to me," he murmured, and watched me until I nodded before kissing me slowly and thoroughly.

Pulling back the comforter, he helped me slip under before sliding in next to me and pulling my back up against his chest. Curling around my body, he grabbed my hands and held them tight as he pressed his lips to my shoulder.

"You're everything," he said against my skin before I felt his body relax as he fell asleep.

Everything.

That word continued playing in my mind, and I decided right then that I was done hiding. I was done protecting myself from a heartache that may or may not happen with Connor, because all I'd been doing was pushing him away. I was done pretending that he didn't matter, and that I didn't care. And I was ready for anything and everything with him.

Chapter Ten

Connor

I TOOK THREE deep breaths in, and tried to tell myself that this would go in my favor. Because it would. They knew me. They trusted me. They would trust me with their sister.

Right?

Opening the door, I walked into the sports bar and looked around for Dakota and Dylan. Looking to the right, I faltered and almost walked right back out of the bar. One of their other brothers, Sam, was at the table too. It was one thing to tell my best friends first, to get a feel for how the rest of the family would react; but to have Sam there too?

But I knew I had to do this now; we were all going to Mammoth tomorrow, and there was no way I could stay away from Maci while we were there. And in case it went bad, I really didn't want Maci present for whatever went down.

I'd thought I was in deep when Amy had tried to give me an ultimatum last week, but after making love to Maci that night . . . I knew that what I'd felt for her had been nothing compared to now. I craved her constantly. When she wasn't near me, it felt like I'd go crazy waiting until I could be near her again. A week of not being able to look at her or touch her would drive me insane.

With another deep breath in, I straightened my shoulders and walked over to where they were already drinking.

"Connor!" Dylan yelled, and Dakota sent off a girl I had no doubt he'd be going home with later. "Aw, come on now. You couldn't even take off the detective getup to have a beer with us?"

I just smirked. Honestly, I couldn't have gone back to my place. Because if I had, I would've seen Maci and then I would've never made it out again.

Sam grabbed my arm and pulled me in to clap my shoulder, and I flinched out of his grasp. *Jesus, when did I become such a bitch?*

"Good to see you, Sam," I forced out, trying to make up for how awkward I'd just acted. "How's the family?"

"They're really good. Caden is almost two, and Jessica just found out she's pregnant again . . . which is why I am here," he joked, but held up his empty beer glass, looking around for a waitress.

"Congrats, man. I'm excited for you."

His smile showed how happy he really was when he turned to look at me again. "Me too, so what about you? I know these two aren't settling down anytime soon, but I always thought you were an old soul. Figured you'd find a girl and settle down early."

I had to be careful how I answered, because what I said in that moment could determine how they reacted later. Before Cassidy, I would've sworn up and down I would've never gotten married because I was terrified of having children and what I might do to my future family. Then she'd come back into my life, and Cassidy had been like an antidote to my fears, or at least had blinded me from them . . . making me want to have it all. Even though I wasn't ready to think of marriage with Maci yet, since it hadn't even been three weeks since we'd actually gotten together. I knew with my life that was exactly where Maci and I would eventually lead.

There was still one problem, though. She wasn't Cassidy. Don't get me wrong . . . I was glad she wasn't. I knew now that Cassidy hadn't been the girl for me; she had just been someone who would understand me, with absolutely no judgment. Finally finding that in someone had been the one thing that triggered my want to keep her in my life forever. Of course she had been sweet, brave, and strong. But sweet, brave, and strong weren't what I needed or wanted.

I wanted feisty. I wanted obnoxious. I wanted stubborn. I wanted Maci . . . *needed* her. But a part of me felt like I needed that piece of Cassidy that understood everything I had gone through as a child. And I still hadn't brought myself to tell Maci about my past and my fears of the future because I couldn't know what her reaction would be.

There had never been a need for the Price family to know what had happened to Amy and me, but I knew I needed to tell Maci in order for our relationship to continue. I was just terrified that after finally opening my eyes to her, and having her in my life even for a short time, I would tell her and she wouldn't be able to understand . . . and then she would be gone too.

I looked Sam right in the eye and told him the truth. "I hope to soon."

He cocked an eyebrow and took a sip of the new beer that had just been placed in front of him. "Really?"

Dakota snorted. "We obviously need to get you a beer if you're starting to talk about settling down. Everyone knows that's not about to happen." He caught the waitress's eye and pointed toward me.

"I don't want a drink."

"What?" all three said at once.

"You feelin' okay?" Dylan asked.

"I'm fine, but uh . . . I." *Shit.* "I need to talk to you three about something."

None of them said anything; they all just sat there staring at me. When the waitress walked over, Dakota waved her away without taking his eyes off me.

Sitting down, I tried to figure out the best way to say it, but in the end, it still came out all kinds of fucked up. "I want your . . . I'm . . . I plan to marry Maci one day."

They were still sitting there staring, but now none of them were blinking or moving. It was fucking terrifying. I rushed to get the rest out.

"I'm not going to ask your permission to date her, because we're already together. And I'm not asking her to marry me anytime soon because our relationship is still raw; but I needed you to know how serious I am about us. She's not just some girl; I know she's it for me. I'm not going to hide us."

Dylan burst out laughing, cutting off when he realized no one else had joined in with him.

"This better be a fucking joke," Dakota sneered, his face slowly turning red.

"What? No," Dylan said, shaking his head. "No way. Not Connor and Mini. Of course he's joking."

I quickly glanced in Sam's direction; he was scowling at me but didn't look like he was ready to kill me, like Kota did.

"How long has this been going on?" Sam asked.

"A few weeks."

"A few"—Dakota slammed his hand down on the table—"a few fucking weeks? Are you shitting me?"

"No, listen—"

"No *you* listen. How many times have we seen or talked to you since this started happening, and you didn't say anything?"

"I'm sorry, you have every right to be pissed about that. I should have told you right away."

Sam still wasn't talking; he was now studying me. And now I was wondering if he was figuring out the most painful way to kill me. Dylan was sitting there, blinking rapidly, as if he was trying to come out of a daze.

"Krista!" Dakota barked at the waitress, and lifted his empty glass before looking back at me. "Did you tell Maci you were going to talk to us?" When I shook my head, he nodded, scratched at his jaw roughly, and then dropped his head to look at the table. "You're not going to tell her you talked to us. You're gonna break up with her, and we're gonna forget this shit ever happened."

"No. I'm not leaving her."

Dakota's head shot up, and he stared in Sam's direction for a few seconds before turning to look at me. His gray eyes narrowed. "If it were anyone else, I wouldn't have asked, Connor. I would have just made sure they never wanted to even think about her again. You're my best friend, but you have five seconds to change your mind before we change it for you."

I shrugged sadly and ran my hand through my hair roughly. "I'm sorry you feel that way, but I'm not changing my mind."

Dakota was out of his chair and lunging across the table so fast, I didn't have time to register his fist coming at me until I was already falling out of my chair.

"Stay the fuck away from Maci!"

I stood and worked my jaw a few times before spitting blood on the ground. A few of the bigger workers had surrounded us by then, so I held up a hand.

"We're fine. Just a misunderstanding. It's over."

We knew them all well; we'd been coming to this bar since we could legally drink. So after a few warnings, they walked away and we all sat back down.

"Connor, you *will*—"

"No, Dakota. I won't. You got your hit in, hopefully that's enough for the three of you for now. But I'm not going to leave Maci. I told you, I didn't come to ask your permission, I just wanted you to know. You can't keep doing this to her, you've been scaring her from having relationships, and you've been keeping guys away from her. She's twenty-three, she's an adult, you need to let her have her life."

"Fuck you, Green!"

"I agree with Connor," Sam said, surprising the hell out of us. "At least it's someone we all know and can trust her with."

Dakota leaned over the table toward Sam, but pointed at me. "He's not good enough for her!"

I threw my arms out to the side before letting the drop. "I'm your best friend! If I'm not, then who is? No one will ever be good enough for your sister. That's how I felt with Amy, but I couldn't stop her from getting married!"

"Kota's right," Dylan said softly. He wasn't looking at any of us, he just sat there with his arms crossed over his chest, but he looked sad. "I'm sorry, Connor, but I can't let you date my sister . . . let alone marry her."

"I hope this shows you how much she means to me. I'm willing to risk eighteen years of friendship because I don't give a fuck what either of you are saying. I'm not leaving her." I stood, and everything in my body froze when Dylan spoke again.

"Connor, we know about you. We know what happened when you were a kid."

"Excuse me?"

"After Cassidy left—"

"How the fuck do you know about Cassidy?"

"You got trashed and told us about her when you came back from Texas, you told us everything that night. What happened to you sucks, and we would've never brought it up again because it was obvious you didn't mean to tell us all that shit," Dakota said. His voice was dark. When he spoke again, the warning was clear. "I'm not about to let my sister be with a man who is constantly fighting that kind of demon."

"What the hell are you talking about?" Sam asked. He looked back and forth between his brothers before looking at me. But I couldn't answer. It felt like I couldn't breathe.

"Short story of his past," Dylan began, and my hands clenched into fists on top of the table. "He had a druggie, absentee mom, and his old man beat him and Amy. Almost killed them. The Greens adopted them after that. *That* would never sway my decision on this situation. But now? Connor is always living in fear that he's going to turn into the guy who raised him. His anger scares him, and he told us that he was afraid if he had kids, he'd do the same thing to them."

"Holy shit," Sam said under his breath and scrubbed his hands down his face. "Connor, man, I'm—"

"So you can see our reasoning," Dakota said, cutting him off. "I love you, Connor, really, man, I do. But I can't let you be with my sister. I have to protect her, and letting her be with a man like you would be the exact opposite of protecting her. You would ruin her."

"Dakota," Sam snapped.

"He said it himself! He said he would ruin his future family, *destroy* it. Those were his words. I don't care if he was wasted, don't we always say drunks are the only honest people?" Dakota stood, and leaned over me, his voice low. "Break up with Maci . . . tonight. If you still want to go to the cabin with us tomorrow, then come. We want you there. None of us will say a thing about tonight, like I said, we'll act like none of this shit happened."

My eyes flashed up to his, then down to Dylan's. He looked away and cleared his throat. "I'm sorry, man, I didn't want to bring that up. But you had to know why we can't let you be with her."

With a hard nod, I ignored Sam calling my name, and walked out of the bar.

I knew what I had to do.

I just didn't know how to do it in a way that would convince her.

"CONNOR, WHAT ARE you already doing home? I thought you were going out after work."

I stood there staring in my fridge, trying to ready myself for this. After I'd figured out how to do it, I'd been telling myself over and over that this was for her own good. That it might upset her at first, but in the long run, it was what she needed.

"I didn't know I had to give you a play-by-play of what I was doing."

"Whoa, what's wrong? Did something happen at work?"

I grabbed a beer and shut the door with more force than necessary. "Jesus, Maci. Nothing is wrong. Is it so wrong that I wanted to have a night away from you?"

Her head jerked back, and her eyes widened. "What?"

"I'm tired of constantly babying you. Did you ever think that maybe I need time to see other women? That that's the way this usually works?"

"*What* works?"

"Sleeping around with people." I turned away from her, and took long pulls from my beer. Trying not to choke at the thought of being with anyone else, or her with another guy. "I wanted to prove something to you, Mini. I wanted to show you what you were missing by just being with that preppy guy. I think I more than proved that, and I'm done catering to you."

"What. The hell. Did you. Just call me?"

I was going to throw up. I tried to blank my expression when I turned toward her again, the way I did when I questioned people. But this was fucking Maci, and I could hardly look at her without wanting to pull her to me.

"God, Maci, grow up. It's just a damn name."

"Why are you doing this? What happened today?"

"Nothing happened." She reached out for me and I grabbed her wrist, walking her out my door and toward hers. "You can't be in my apartment, I have someone coming over."

"You—what? Connor!" she cried out my name and clutched at her chest when I released her. "Why are you being like this? This isn't you."

"Shit, enough! Stop making this out to be so dramatic when it really doesn't have to be. I'm just tired of pretending with you."

"Pretending?" she whispered to herself, her eyes looking everywhere but at me.

"I'm sorry if I let it go on too long, but you need to find someone else. Get a boyfriend or something, one that you're not afraid to introduce to your brothers."

Her head snapped up, her gray eyes pleading. "Is that what this is? Because I haven't told them yet? I'll tell them right now, I swear!"

"No, fuck, that's not what I meant. You need to find the guy you're meant to be with, and I'm not him. Obviously you've gotten too deep in this, but *this* should have never happened."

"How can you say that? I belong with you . . . *to* you. I'm yours, Connor! Completely. Yours. Why can't you see that you own me?"

I watched as her gray eyes filled with tears, and I wanted to die.

I'd been looking for any kind of emotion since Cassidy had left. I'd searched for it in so many women. This girl . . . for so many reasons she shouldn't have been the one to start evoking all these feelings again—and yet, she had been. My best friends' little sister. My neighbor. The girl next door. Everything cliché and everything I had overlooked for years. I wondered for the hundredth time tonight why I couldn't have actually *seen* Maci years before.

Another sob tore from her chest, and I wanted to take her in my arms and brush away the tears that had just started falling down her face. I wanted to tell her that she had all of this backwards. She owned me. But I couldn't do this to her. Not only would her brothers never allow it, especially after tonight, but they were right . . . I would ruin her.

I had fears she couldn't understand, a life that she'd had no idea about, and too many secrets I wasn't willing to taint her world with. I would ruin her and our future family, and I wouldn't be able to live with myself when that happened.

My body was shaking, and I tried to focus on anything other than the way her expression was breaking my heart. *I'll destroy her. I'll ruin her.* I continued to chant those words and focused on the fact that I could never be the type of man that she needed.

Swallowing past the tightness in my throat, I scoffed. Scoffing was good. It made me sound like that much more of an asshole. "You can't start crying every time you aren't getting your way, Maci. You're an adult, start acting like one."

"Connor!" she cried when I turned to leave. "Why are you doing this to us? I know you, I know you want to be with me too. Is it Dakota and Dylan, did they find out? Are they making you do this?"

I stopped walking when I reached her door, but couldn't look back at her when I said, "You don't know anything about me. The fact that you somehow made yourself believe there was an *us* is proof of that. There is no *us*."

"How can you sa—"

"Because we fucked, Maci, that's all we did!" I turned to look at her beautiful face, filled with pain. "It's not my fault you let yourself believe we could be something. It's not my goddamn fault you don't know how to keep your feelings and your needs separate."

Her head shook slowly back and forth, and her hand came up to cover her mouth as a strangled sob left her. "You're lying," she choked out. "Please don't do this!"

"Goodbye, Maci."

"Connor!" she sobbed when I shut her door behind me.

I hurried into my apartment and threw the can of beer at the wall, suppressing an agonized roar as I stormed into my bedroom. For the rest of the night, I stood with my forehead and palms pressed against the wall that connected our bedrooms, and listened to her sobs. And for the first time since I was last beaten at seven years old, I cried.

Chapter Eleven

Maci

"UP! COME ON, get up!" Amber yelled as she charged into the room we were sharing.

Glancing over at her when she jumped on my bed, I looked back up at the ceiling and suppressed a sigh. "I think I'm going to call it an early night. I'm exhausted from traveling up here."

"Bullshit you are! You're moping and being all stupid depressed because Connor turned out to be a dick!"

My chest ached, hearing his name. "Amber . . . please, just let me be upset about this for a while."

"Nope, no. Not going to happen. As your best friend, it is my duty to make sure you get back to being all happy happy because it's almost Christmas, have an awesome fucking vacation, and get laid by some random hot ski instructor."

I actually cracked a smile. "Ski instructor? Really now . . ."

"Yes, and it will be perfect. It will take your mind off the asshole, you won't have to see the guy again until next year—*if* you even see him again."

"Ahh . . . no thanks. But, really, have at it."

Standing up, she grabbed my ankles and started dragging me down the bed.

"Holy shit! You're such a fucking bitch. Oh God!" I wheezed when my back hit the floor with a hard thud.

"I'm *your* bitch, and it's why you love me. So let's slut it up, hit a few bars and—"

We both looked toward the hallway when one of my brothers yelled my name.

"Why do I feel like I'm about to be in trouble?" I whispered to Amber when she helped me up off the floor.

"Maci, get the fuck up here!" one of the boys yelled seconds before I heard him pounding down the stairs.

We stood there frozen as we waited, and I jumped when my door was thrown open so hard, I was sure it left a dent in the wall.

"Jesus, Dyl—"

"Shut the fuck up and get your ass upstairs. Now."

"Excuse me? Don't be fucking rude! Get out of my damn room, you son of a bitch!"

"Maci!" Came another voice from upstairs. Seconds later, Craig was standing behind Dylan. "You might want to come upstairs." It wasn't a suggestion.

It was a command, and he sounded just as pissed as Dylan.

I looked up at my ceiling when I heard my dad yell, "Calm down, Dakota! Let the man talk."

Connor. My heart raced and ached at the same time. My stomach started churning, and I was afraid I was about to lose what little of dinner I'd actually eaten. I didn't want to see him, but why would he be here and upsetting my brothers if it weren't for me?

Grabbing Amber's hand, I pushed past my brothers and tried to ignore the way their glares made my skin crawl. Running up the stairs, my shoulders slumped and I had the ridiculous urge to start crying when I saw him standing there.

Connor hadn't come for me. Bryce had.

The loss I'd been dealing with over the last twenty-four hours since Connor had thrown me out of his life seemed to double. That little glimmer of hope that he'd changed his mind had been crushed when I saw Bryce instead of the man I loved standing there next to my dad.

"What are you doing here?" I asked Bryce. His family vacationed here every winter, just another reason why we'd been close for so long. But when he'd texted me to see if we could talk while we were here, I'd thought my 'Fuck off' response had said it all.

"You lying bitch," Dylan said under his breath as he and Craig shoved past me, pushing me into Amber.

"Hey, baby," Bryce said, a smile lighting up his too-perfect face.

"Baby?" Amber and I said at the same time.

"Oh, hell no. I thought we were finally done with you," Amber sneered.

Bryce sent a glare her way before looking at me again. "As always, Amber, what a pleasant surprise to see you."

"Somehow I doubt that."

I held my hand up to keep them from going into one of their fights, and stepped forward. "Bryce . . . why are you here? I told—"

"I was just telling your father about our plans."

Plans?

"Maci,"—my Dad began—"this young man has just informed me that you're going to be getting married within the year . . . ?"

"What? No!"

"You don't have to keep lying just because your brothers are here," Bryce said as he stepped up to me. One arm went around my waist, the other cupped my cheek. His eyes roamed my face before zeroing in on my nose. When he spoke again, it was soft enough that only Amber and I could hear him. "I thought we agreed you were going to take that thing out? And please tell me your hair will be blonde again soon, I was planning on announcing our engagement at the beginning of the year."

"You are such a little piece of shit."

Bryce kept talking like Amber had never spoken. "I told you, Maci, no one will take you seriously when you look like this. You're the mistress . . . remember? I need a wife. It's time to grow up, baby."

The air in my lungs left in one hard rush. It had hurt the first time Bryce had said that, but now, after Connor? It was killing me. He was right . . . all I was, like this, was a fuck buddy. I wasn't relationship material, and, according to Bryce, I wasn't marriage material either.

"I know," I said as I nodded my head in his direction. Suddenly, I felt a large presence behind me.

"I suggest you leave," Dylan said.

"Now. And if you don't stop touching my sister, I swear to God you will spend Christmas in the hospital," Dakota added.

Okay, make that two large presences.

Bryce actually had the balls to look up over me and say, "I'd like to speak to my future wife, if you don't mind."

"Nah, man. That's not about to happen. You'll leave; we have to talk to her. Seeing as you just dropped this on our whole family when none of us even had a clue about you, I'd say this is the wrong time for you to be here." Dylan grabbed my arm hanging limply at my side, and pulled me back toward him, and away from Bryce.

"Maci?" Bryce looked at me.

"Let me walk you out," I choked out, and wrangled my way out of Dylan's grasp.

Not looking back to see if he was following me, I turned and headed toward the front door. Once I got there, I waited until Bryce was near me before jerking the door open and stepping outside with him.

"Mac—"

"Leave, I don't want to see you again. I thought I'd made that clear to you before, apparently I was wrong."

"Don't you realize how well I'll be able to take care of you? After how much history we have, Maci, you can't tell me you don't want this. If it's because I'm telling you to change your appearance, I'm only helping you. I've told you no one takes you seriously looking like this, you aren't going to find a man that wants to make you his wife when—"

"Stop," I cried out and slapped a hand over my mouth as I tried to collect myself a little bit. "You need. To leave. Don't call me, don't come back here . . . and don't come to my apartment when we're back in Mission Viejo. You need to find someone who would be happy in your life, but I'm not her. God when did you even turn into this person?" I asked and waved my hand at him. "You're turning into your dad!"

"Maci," he said as he reached toward me, but I stepped back.

"No. Go. We're done. Good-bye, Bryce."

Walking back inside, I shut and locked the door behind me before turning to face my family. My mom and sisters-in-law looked confused, Amber looked annoyed, Dad looked disappointed, and my brothers all looked pissed beyond reason.

All at once, my brothers started yelling at me about keeping something like that from them, how much they couldn't stand him, and how I wasn't supposed to see him again.

I looked to my mom and dad for help as Amber came and stood by my side. She grabbed my hand, and waited out the screaming with me as my parents tried to get my brothers to stop talking. Tears were steadily falling down my face from having heard those words from Bryce again, having my heart broken and wishing Connor had been the one to come for me— and realizing he wouldn't—and having to listen to my brothers trying to run my life again.

I was so used to turning off these kinds of emotions around them, but I couldn't anymore. I was too close to breaking from everything. My tough exterior I showed my family was cracking, and I knew I only needed one of them to poke me before I shattered into a million pieces. The moment they saw the tears, each one of my big brothers froze and looked like they were going to lock me away somewhere safe before going on a killing spree for whomever had made me cry.

Sam and Dakota were the first ones to start toward me, but I held my hand up at the same time a sob burst from my chest, and they both stopped their advance. Their gray eyes wildly searched my face, and it looked like Dakota was struggling to find something to say to me, but I didn't wait to find out what. I turned and headed toward the stairs with Amber.

Once we were in our room with the door locked, Amber grabbed me in a hug and let me cry against her shoulder. She didn't say anything, she just stood there and slowly ran a hand through my long hair, trying to soothe me as we listened to my family flipping out upstairs.

Four different times, people came to the door and spoke through it. Sometimes it was my brothers and the last was my parents. My brothers were freaking out over seeing me cry, but were still pissed off over Bryce; and my parents just told me they loved me and would talk to me about Bryce tomorrow.

"Did you think it would be Connor?" she asked when my parents had left, my body had stopped shaking, and the tears had dried out.

I nodded against her shoulder and released my death grip on her. Turning around, I headed toward our bathroom and wasn't even shocked when I saw how horrible I looked. I felt even worse; the streaked makeup was just the cherry on top. Grabbing my makeup remover and face wash, I turned on the water and went about cleaning up.

Looking at myself in the mirror when I was done, I let everything Bryce and Connor had said to me in the last day race through my mind.

"I do look like the mistress," I whispered to my reflection.

Amber did a double take from where she'd been standing at the entrance of the bathroom. "I'm sorry, what did you just say?"

I took out the hoop in my nose and set it on the counter as I continued staring at myself in the mirror. "Bryce is right, I need to stop being like this." A short, pained laugh burst from my chest. "Both he and Connor were right. I need to grow up. At my hair appointment in two weeks, I'm going to start going back to blonde."

"No, Maci . . . don't do that because of what that douche said."

"The only two guys I've been with have both told me to grow up within a short time. There has to be truth to that, and if this is part of the process of growing up . . . then it's what I'm going to do. I know it won't bring Connor back to me; I never meant anything to him." I winced saying those words out loud. "But I can mean something to someone. I just—it's just what I need to do," I said resolutely before walking out of the bathroom and crawling back in bed.

Amber slid onto my bed instead of going to her own and wrapped an arm around me, holding me tight. "They're both assholes if they couldn't see how amazing you are. You're going to make some guy ridiculously happy just the way you are, Maci. Don't change because of two guys."

But I'd already made up my mind. I knew what had to be done. I was just hoping that my physical makeover could somehow help with the heartache I wasn't sure I could get over.

Connor

MY PHONE RANG somewhere beside me, and I slapped my hand around on the bed until I found it. I didn't know the number, but that didn't mean much, I just hoped like hell it wasn't work. I'd just gotten back from my parents' house and had endured hours from them, Amy, and Kevin over what I'd done to Maci two nights ago. Like I didn't already hate myself enough as it was. After that, it was safe to say I really didn't want to deal with work when I was supposed to be on vacation.

"This is Detective Green."

"I had high hopes for you. What the hell did you do to her?"

I sat up and glanced at the screen again. "Excuse me, who is this?"

"Maci's been walking around this cabin like she belongs on *The Walking Dead*. Of course, I'm the only one that knew about you, so I know this has to do with you. What did you do to my best friend?"

"Amber, look there's a lot about Maci and me that you don't know."

She snorted. "I know that you're a dick, and you broke her heart! I know that she's taking out her piercings and saying she's going back to blonde. I know that Bryce is in Mammoth too and telling Maci's dad that he's going to marry her, and I'm pretty sure after the shit you pulled, she's considering it!"

I was already off the bed and running through my apartment, looking for my keys and wallet. "Why the fuck is Bryce there?"

"Surprised you never noticed that his family has a cabin up here too."

"She can't marry him, he doesn't fucking care about her! He wants to change her; he wants to make her into what he thinks a wife should be. Not who Maci is."

"You know, for a guy who said all he did was *fuck* her," she sneered, "you sound more pissed off than you have a right to be."

"Amber, I told you, there's a lot that you don't know. I . . . shit."

I slammed my fist on the frame of the door and tried to talk myself out of driving up there. She needed to find someone else. I was hearing those words repeating themselves in my mind, but I wasn't understanding them. Because at the moment, all I could think about was the sick feeling spreading through my stomach at the thought of her with Bryce. With anyone. She was mine. Fuck her brothers.

"I'm on my way."

"It's about damn time! Freaking hell."

I shook my head as I locked my door and ran down the hallway. "I thought you were mad at me."

"I saw you and Maci together, there's no way you can tell me you didn't care about her. I also know you're Dylan and Dakota's best friend, and I saw the way they flipped out over Bryce talking to their dad last night. For Maci, I wanted to hate you and castrate you. But I knew there was something about this whole situation that just didn't make sense. After seeing the twins' reaction, I started piecing it together. This phone call just confirmed my suspicions."

"It was ugly when I told them about us. I can't imagine it's going to go over well when I get there—just be there for her now. I'll be there as soon as I can."

Chapter Twelve

Maci

MY HAIR WAS naturally straight, I usually just messed with it enough that it had that just-fucked look. But even so, I used Amber's flat iron to make sure it was perfect, before pulling it back in a low bun and stepping back to look at myself in the full-length mirror. Even with still having red hair, I hardly recognized the person staring back at me. My makeup was a little lighter, the nose ring was still out, my hair was smooth, and I looked like I probably belonged on Bryce's arm with the black peacoat I had on over my cream long-sleeved shirt. But it wasn't those changes that made me unrecognizable.

I usually smiled. I usually looked happy. Right now there was nothing, no emotion, no life in my eyes. I looked like I should be going to a funeral instead of a late Christmas Eve dinner with my family.

Forcing a smile, I immediately let it fall when it came across looking pained.

I shouldn't be this upset about Connor, but I was. I shouldn't have let myself fall in love with him, but I had. And at the moment, I didn't know how I was going to make it through another family meal acting like everything was fine when it wasn't.

Amber walked into our room and stopped quickly, a fake smile immediately pulling at her lips. "Don't you look . . . different."

"Why thank you, why don't you just tell me I look like shit?"

Rolling her eyes, she crossed over to my bed and sat down. "Because you don't. You're really pretty, Maci. Like, you have no idea how much it pisses me off how gorgeous you are. You just don't look a thing like my friend."

"I don't say anything when you endlessly go back and forth from blonde to brunette other than the fact that you're killing your hair. You change the way you look, I'm changing—"

"You. You're changing *you*, not the way you look."

I blinked slowly at her and turned toward the door. "We talked about this—it's time for me to grow up. Come on, let's go upstairs."

"It's Bryce's version of you growing up. You don't need to change anything about the way you look, and it's killing me to watch you do this to yourself. You're trying to kill off my best friend. You're shutting her up. You're hiding her, however you want to see it, but you and I both know you won't be happy like this."

I stopped at the door and turned on her, whispering in case anyone was in the hall. "You only think that because I'm not happy right now. I'm going to be fine, I'm growing up, and I'm moving on. If you have a problem with it, then get the fuck over it. I don't need my best friend telling me that I shouldn't be a certain way!"

Amber's head jerked back, and her eyes got massive.

"Look, I know I'm being mean right now, but you have no idea how tired I am of everyone constantly telling me what I should or shouldn't do. You always told me not to see Bryce, and now you're telling me not to change the way I look. My brothers won't let me date anyone and are incessantly bugging me about that. Bryce always told me to stop cussing and told me I had to change the way I look because I looked like a mistress instead of a wife. And for some goddamn reason, every man in my life except for my dad is telling me to grow up. Obviously, whatever I've been doing is wrong, so I'm changing that. The only person who is just telling me to be who I want to be is my mom, and I can't even tell her about being in love with someone because it will get back to my brothers. Do you understand how fucking tired I am?"

She blinked quickly and looked away for a second. "Yeah, I'm sor—"

"I'm always hiding a part of me, there is only one

person who has ever gotten all of me. My family gets a certain Maci, my friends get a certain Maci, and Bryce had a certain Maci. Connor had all of me . . . the good and the bad. For the first time I didn't have to hide a part of my life or my personality, and it was so freeing. But he didn't want me; I didn't mean anything to him. And like everyone else, he told me to grow up. So I am. Can you please just be okay with that?" I wiped at my eyes and blinked back the wetness in them.

"Maci, I called—"

The door swung open and my mom popped her head in. "Dinner is about done, you ready? You both look beautiful."

"Thanks, Mom, we're coming up."

She focused on my eyes for a few seconds, but smiled and shut the door behind her as she left.

"What were you going to say?"

Amber chewed on her bottom lip and shifted her weight. "I'm sorry for what I've said to you. I just didn't want you to change because of what Bryce said, and—and I'm just sorry," she said as she walked past me and opened the door again. "Be whoever you want, and date whomever you want; I'll love you the same."

My shoulders sagged when she walked out of my room, and I felt like such a bitch. Again. I really shouldn't have said that to her, I was just so tired of everyone telling me how to live. Turning around, I walked into the hall and up the stairs. Everyone was already at the table when I got up there, and I was positive that if their wives hadn't been there, Craig and Sam would be glaring at me just the same as Dakota and Dylan were.

Good to know we're still not past the whole Bryce thing.

Dakota kept pulling my chair away from me every time I went to sit in it, and after a smack on the back of the head from my dad, he finally shoved it toward me hard enough that I fell into my sister-in-law Sarah's lap.

"Dakota, that's enough," Dad chastised him, and I had the urge to put Dad between Kota and me.

No one said anything about Bryce, or my hidden relationship, throughout the rest of dinner. But just as I started to stand to help my mom and sisters-in-law clear the table, Dakota grabbed my arm and yanked me back down.

"Is there anyone else? Because you went a damn long time not telling us about Bryce; and that got serious enough that he's still thinking he's marrying you."

"I'm not going to marry Bry—"

"I know you're not. You think we would let you?" he hissed in my ear. "I know you think we've been keeping you from having a relationship to be mean, but I promise you we're just looking out for you. All we want to do is protect you from assholes like us, okay? We can't do that if you're keeping them from us."

I yanked my arm from him and grabbed my plate, but lowered my head toward him before I stood.

"Well you really haven't given me another option, have you?"

"Maci, who else." It wasn't a question. It was a demand. But there was no point in telling them about Connor.

After grabbing his plate as well, I took a few steps past him, turned back around, and shook my head sadly. "You know the funny thing about what you just said, Dakota? You say that you all want is to protect me, and that you're looking out for me; but I don't feel like I can even come to you guys if I need protecting. You're my brothers, I'm supposed to feel safe because of all of you; instead I just feel like I need to hide everything about myself from you because you won't approve or won't allow it. You four are the last people I would think to call if I was in trouble."

I ignored the shocked looks everyone was giving me and rushed into the kitchen to put the dishes on the counter. I turned to leave, but my mom grabbed me in a hug from where she was standing at the sink.

"I'm sorry, my sweet girl. I'm so sorry you're hurting." Cupping my cheeks, she pulled back to look in my eyes, and smiled sadly. "There's something else, Maci, I can see it. Maybe someday you'll talk to me about what's going on with you? It hurts me that you feel like you can't."

My chest started burning and my throat closed up as tears pricked the backs of my eyes. Tonight was definitely not one of my finest. Yelling at my best friend, telling my brothers that they pretty much suck at being brothers. My heart breaking for my mom because I'd kept myself so closed off and had kept everything from her. I needed to get out of there. I just needed to go.

I squeezed my mom's hands and removed them from my face before running out of the kitchen and through the house toward the front door. Just as my hand reached it, I was turned around, and my body sagged in defeat against the door when I saw Sam.

"Where are you going?"

"I just need to go, I need to get out of here and get away from everything for a minute and just think."

"We're your family, don't run away from us. Dakota and Dylan are being dicks. What's new? They'll get over it."

I shook my head quickly and grabbed the knob behind me. "You don't understand, Sam. There's so much going on right now that you just don't understand. I need to be alone for a while, okay?"

His mouth pulled up on one side as he thought, and then turned to look behind him where the sounds of our family could be heard. "If you're going outside, then I'm going with you." He grabbed the first jacket he touched on the coat rack and shrugged it on as he stepped up right next to me. Not giving me the option to go alone.

"Despite everything we've said and done, you can't let us stop you from having relationships," he said after we'd been walking for a handful of minutes. "And I don't mean hiding them, I mean actually having them. Bringing the guy around to meet the family, that sort of thing."

"You're not," I said automatically.

He laughed humorlessly and shoved his hands in his pockets. "I need to tell you something," he mumbled and stared off at the dark sky as we continued to walk.

"Are you going to tell me, or are you just going to make me wonder what it is?"

"I know about Connor," he said suddenly, and stopped walking, turning his body so he was facing me.

My heart skipped painful beats hearing someone else say his name, and it took a couple seconds for me to understand what he was saying. My eyes widened as I slowly turned to look up at him.

"We . . . shit. He came and talked to us the day before we left for Mammoth, he wanted us to know that you were together. Dylan and Dakota forced him to leave you. I'd sided with Connor, but when I saw you the next day, I knew he'd listened to them."

The way Connor had been acting that night played through my mind, and I felt sick. Sick over losing him, and over the fact that he *had* tried to stand up to my family, and my brothers had convinced him to leave me. I would expect that from Bryce, but not Connor.

"Wait! You sided with Connor? Why?"

Sam shrugged and a huff left him. "Because he's a good guy, and he . . . well, after all he said. I knew he wanted to be with you forever, not just to screw around with."

"We fucked, Maci, that's all we did." I sniffed and rubbed at my frozen nose before crossing my arms under my chest. "Well you were wrong about that, and it doesn't matter. If he's going to let them keep us apart, then he's not worth it."

"I'm not buying that, and I can tell you don't even believe the shit you're saying."

"I will one day," I countered, and his face morphed into a sympathetic smile.

"Maci, I had no clue you were with him; but from what he said, and what I'm seeing these last couple of days from you, I don't think you will. He is worth it: What guy has ever had the balls to talk to you after we've told them to back off for just *looking* at you, let alone actually confront three of us at once and *tell* us he's with you and not leaving you? Dakota and Dylan . . . they said some pretty fucked-up shit. They hit him low, and they hit him hard. I'm still pissed off at them for what they did, but they really left Connor with no choice."

Little puffs of clouds filled the space between us from our breath for silent minutes as tears filled my eyes, and eventually spilled over.

"There's always a choice, Sam," I choked out as I remembered Connor's words the night my brothers had shown up at his apartment, and turned to head back to the cabin. "I just wasn't enough for him, apparently."

Sam grabbed me and pulled me back. "Don't let anyone make you feel like you're not enough. And if that's what this is"—he gestured toward me—"Maci, you look beautiful, but this isn't you. This isn't my little sister."

"God, not you too. It's just time for a change," I repeated mechanically. "Why is that so difficult for everyone to comprehend?"

"If you wanna change, then change. But do it because it's what you want for you and your life, not because other people have made you feel like you need to. After what I heard from the prick that's high on his daddy's money last night, you're not doing this for you."

"I'm not doing it for Bryce either."

"And thank Christ for that. Deep down though, I think you're letting everything he's said to you—and what happened to you and Connor—get to you, and you think this is what you have to do. You don't: all you have to do is be the Maci everyone loves, and let the rest fall into place, okay?"

Tears continued to fall down my face, but I didn't try to brush them away anymore. The corners of my mouth lifted in a shaky smile and I cocked my head to the side as I looked at my brother.

"Who are you and what did you do with Sam?"

He laughed loudly and pulled me in for a hug. "Come on, let's go back in. It's freezing, and whichever twin's jacket this is, it smells like he had prostitutes hanging all over him. Jessica is going to freak when she smells me."

I didn't have to ask what he was talking about. You

could smell the jacket from a mile away. "I'll back you up that it isn't your jacket as long as you do me a favor. Don't hold me back when I go ape-shit on Dakota and Dylan's asses when we get back."

"Deal."

But when we got back, Sam didn't have to worry about holding me back. Craig and Dad were trying to moderate a yelling match that was getting closer and closer to a brawl between Dakota, Dylan, and Connor.

Connor

PARKING BEHIND THE multiple cars at the cabin, I started cursing at the icy walkway as I tried to run up to the door. Without knocking, I walked in and walked toward the living room, where I could hear voices.

"Connor!" Dakota said loudly, his voice deceivingly happy. His eyes looked dark when he noticed my mood.

"Where is she?" I huffed as I looked around the room. I heard a bunch of women talking in the kitchen and turned that way.

"We told you," he began as he stood in front of me, stopping me from getting closer to the girls.

"I said where the fuck is she?"

"Hold on here," Mr. Price said, standing up from one of the couches. "What the hell is going on?"

"Connor," Dylan said in warning as he shook his head.

"Maci!" I yelled toward the kitchen, and Dakota pushed me back with a hard shove.

"We told you to stay away!"

"The fuck?" Craig said as he came to stand behind Dakota.

"And I should have never listened to you! Maci!"

The women began pouring into the living room, and I looked wildly for her.

"She's not here," Amber said, her face breaking out in a smile when she saw me. "She left, but Sam followed her."

"Left? Left for where?"

"It doesn't fucking matter, because we told you to stay the hell away from her!" Dakota yelled, and started coming toward me, but Craig stopped him.

"Now everyone just shut the hell up!" Mr. Price yelled and walked into the triangle Dakota, Dylan, and I were making. "This has been the most dramatic Christmas vacation I think we've ever had. Now someone better explain to me what's going on, and I mean right now."

Dylan opened his mouth, but I spoke over him. "I'm in love with your daughter."

"Oh, Jesus Christ, not again," Craig groaned.

"He can't—"

"No," I cut Dylan off, and kept talking. "Whatever that asshole told you last night, don't listen to him. Maci doesn't want to be with him, I've seen the way

he treats her, all he does is order her around and be-
little her."

"Like that's much better than what you would do
to her?" Dakota sneered.

"I won't hurt Maci!" I yelled at him, and turned
back to his dad. "I've been seeing your daughter all
month. I know that's not a long time, but I also know
that there isn't another girl for me out there."

"Connor, I swear to God you better stop talking."

"Dakota Price! Shut your mouth and let him talk!"

I looked over to Mrs. Price, and sent her a grateful
smile.

"If you're so in love with Maci, tell me why my
little sister looks like she wants to die?" Craig asked
before I could say anything else.

Mr. Price raised a graying eyebrow at me, and I
shrugged lamely. "Because I listened to Dakota and
Dylan when I shouldn't have."

"Wait." Craig released Dakota and pointed at his
brothers. "You both already knew about this and
didn't say anything?"

"He came to talk to us about their relationship the
night before we came," Dylan started, and his dad cut
him off.

"What I'm not understanding is what I'm seeing
right now. You three have been inseparable since you
were kids, and now this?"

"They forced me to break up with Maci! Do you
understand how much it killed me to do that, how
much it killed me to have to lie to her so she would

believe me, and then listen to her cry for the rest of the night? I feel like I've been suffocating ever since I left the goddamn bar after talking to you three!"

"Wait, three?"

"Sam was there," I answered Craig.

"Why the fuck did everyone know except for me?"

"I hadn't planned on Sam being there, I wanted to talk to Dakota and Dylan first."

"Yeah," Dylan started, "and we already told you our answer. You can't date or marry Maci!"

"That's not your fucking decision! You're my best friend, but I never should have listened to you in the first place!"

"You know why we can't let you be with her!" Dakota yelled back.

"Why can't he be with her?" Mr. Price asked, the only calm male left in the room.

"Dakota, I swear to God I will die before I hurt your sister."

"You don't fucking know that!" He started toward me again, and Craig grabbed him to stop him.

"You told us—"

"I know what I said, Dylan. But I will do everything to make sure I never hurt her!"

"You already have."

All of the men froze, and some of the women gasped from where they'd been whispering to each other. Forcing myself to turn to the left, it took all my willpower not to run up to her and grab her in my arms.

"Maci," I breathed. And when I saw her face covered in tears, I automatically started toward her, stopping when she held up a hand.

"Sam told me they made you do it, and for the record, I will not forgive either of you for that," she looked at her brothers, and wiped at her face when she turned back to me. "But, Connor, you told me there was always a choice. You made yours."

"Maci, no, you don't understand. You have to let me explain."

Sam bent down to whisper something in her ear, but she shook her head at him and spoke loud enough for us to hear. "I already told you, he let them tell him what to do." Looking back up at me, my heart broke when she choked out, "That told me all I need to know. Just go home, Connor."

My mind flashed back to Cassidy for the first time in a month. Having her tell me to leave the way Maci just had . . . but at the time, I'd listened to her and had left. Maci was different, I couldn't leave her . . . not again. "I can't."

She turned toward the door, before looking back at me, fresh tears falling down her cheeks. "Why?"

"Because you're *mine*, Maci! You're. Mine."

"You said—"

"I know what I said . . . I was lying. I was scared of what your brothers knew about me, scared of what I could do to you . . . and so I did what I thought would be best for you. But I'm miserable, and I know you are too." I had taken a few steps toward her, but was afraid of pushing her back, so I stopped halfway between her, Sam, and her family.

Maci shook her head, clearly confused. "What you could do to me . . . ? I don't . . . what do they know?"

Turning to look at Dakota and Dylan, I shook my head when I realized and understood what I had to do. I threw my arms out at my sides helplessly when I looked back at Maci.

"I was abused as a child. That's why I'm so protective of Amy. Because she was older, she took my half of the beatings until I was old enough to understand, and made sure that she took as little of them as possible. The guy wasn't even my biological father, but it was my mom's husband, and he was the one who raised us. He almost killed us one night, that's how we met our adoptive parents. My dad was one of the detectives on scene, and he and my mom fought to adopt both Amy and me."

The room had gone completely silent, and Maci stood there staring at me with wide, devastated eyes. Her mouth hanging open as she shook her head back and forth, like she was in denial.

"I've always felt like I had to protect Amy from men. After we were adopted, it took until she met her husband in college for her to trust anyone other than Dad and me. But the problem that your brothers have with us being together is I have my own demons to face from that time in my life. I'm . . . shit, Maci, I'm terrified of turning into him. I have nightmares of being him *to* my future family. I had no idea I'd even told your brothers about all this until they informed me when I approached them about us a couple days ago. Apparently I got wasted one night and told them. I told them that I'd ruin and destroy my future family."

"Connor," she whispered.

"That's why they don't want us together. That's everything I've been keeping from you, and that's why I left you. I thought I was protecting you." Closing the distance between us, I got as close to her as I could without touching her. "Yes, I'm afraid to get angry, because I don't know what I'll do because of the nightmares I constantly have about turning into him. And I know I upset you, but I know that I would never *hurt* you, Maci."

"I—I had no idea. I didn't know. I'm so sorry."

Cupping her face in my hands, it felt like I was taking my first real breath in two days. "You're not the one that's supposed to be sorry. I'm sorry for what I did to you, and I'm sorry I didn't tell you sooner. But, Maci, I can't lose you." Pressing my forehead to hers, I whispered so only she could hear me. "You were so wrong the other night. *You* own *me*. Don't you fucking get that?"

A sound that was half laugh, half sob, left her and she crushed her mouth to mine.

"I'm in love with you Maci," I said against her lips. "God I'm so in love with you."

"Connor."

"What—fuck, Mace!" I wheezed and bent forward when she punched me in the stomach.

"That's for listening to my brothers."

I deserved that. But, shit, that hurt. As soon as I straightened up, Maci threw herself at me; wrapping her legs around my waist as I gripped her body to mine.

"And I love you too." She smiled at me wryly before I captured her lips again.

A few seconds later, someone started clearing their throat. I froze from kissing her, and slowly lowered her back down to the ground before facing her family.

Maci's dad looked around like he was lost. "Well, this has been an interesting vacation so far."

"That's all you have to say?" Dylan asked. "Did you not hear what he just admitted to?"

Mr. Price turned to look at his sons and a sound of disapproval left his chest. "I did, and I must say . . . I'm disappointed in you two for how you've treated him and your sister. Every man has fears that he won't be able to be the perfect husband and father; Connor's are a little different, and for good reason. The fact that you let his fears get in the way of a lifelong friendship and used it against him so he would leave Maci pisses me off about as much as it upsets me to see my little girl cry. Connor just manned up to something he shouldn't have to be ashamed of, and stood up to you all because he's in love with your sister. The two of you could take a lesson."

Dakota and Dylan both stood there staring at the floor with matching expressions of guilt and indecision. Like they couldn't figure out if they wanted to continue fighting their side.

"I think we all need to go to bed so we can sleep on this, and we'll talk about it again tomorrow. No one is level headed enough to continue with this conversation . . . if we can even call it that." Mr. Price turned and walked over to Maci and me, his hand outstretched for me to shake it. "I'm glad it's you, Connor. Really, I am. But if I catch you sleeping with my daughter tonight, I'm likely to change my mind on that. Your room is still free, I'll be sure to check on both you and Maci often tonight."

Gripping his hand firmly, I cracked a smile but looked him directly in the eye. "Understood, sir."

Pulling me in close to pound on my back, he held me there as he said, "You're a good man, and you have nothing to be ashamed of. Wherever this takes you and my daughter, I'd be proud to have you in her life."

I stood there in shock when he stepped back. After everything I'd just said, I wouldn't expect that reaction from any dad, but especially Maci's. He'd always been intimidating . . . which, considering my profession and the kinds of people I dealt with, is saying something.

Maci grabbed my hand, and I looked down to see her smiling up at me.

"Thank you," she said softly, her gray eyes bright with left-over tears.

"For what?"

"Coming back for me."

Cupping her face in my hands, I leaned close and

spoke low, hoping she understood how much I meant every word. "I'm sorry I ever left; I swear it will never happen again."

When she nodded, I pressed my mouth to hers, and savored every second of her lips against mine until her dad grumbled, "Checking your rooms tonight."

Maci laughed, and leaned in to steal another kiss when I quickly pulled away from her. "I'll see you in the morning."

Smiling, I brushed back a few strands of her hair that had fallen forward. "Good night, Maci Price."

With a wink, she turned and waited for Amber to join her before heading downstairs. Once everyone else began dispersing, I glanced over at Dakota and Dylan to see them watching me. Holding back a sigh, I headed downstairs as well and took the room I usually occupied.

Since I hadn't taken the time to pack anything, I put everything on me on one of the nightstands, left my jeans on, and pulled my shirts off before climbing into bed. And for the first time since I'd made Maci cry, sleep came quickly.

JOLTING UP IN BED, I stopped reaching for my gun and blew out a deep breath when I saw Maci shutting and locking my door. The air rushed from my lungs at seeing her standing there, and I had to wonder if I was dreaming for a minute. A residual ache deep in my chest kept the reminder of what I'd done to her . . .

but even through my sleep-fueled haze, I remembered driving up to Mammoth and fighting to get her back.

"Mace, what are you doing?" I asked when she started moving from the door toward my bed.

"I need to be with you . . . I need to know this isn't all a dream."

My lips quirked up on one side, knowing I'd just been thinking the same thing; and even as I grabbed her hand and pulled her down next to me, I shook my head. "Your dad is going to kill me if he finds you in here."

She made a scoffing noise. "He hasn't checked on us once tonight, and he's snoring loud enough that I doubt he'll be up anytime soon."

"Maci . . ." I began in warning, but she moved so she was straddling me, and pressed her fingers against my lips.

"Please, Connor. I need to know I didn't just imagine everything. I need . . . I need to hear you say it again."

Kissing her fingers softly, I removed her hand from my face and gripped the back of her neck to pull her closer so I could look into her eyes. "Hear what? That you own me? That I love you? That I'm a fucking idiot for ever thinking I could live without you, even if it was what's best for you?"

Even in the darkness, I could see the brightness in her eyes from the tears gathering there. When one slipped down her cheek, I used my free hand to wipe it away and searched her face for a long while.

"I'm sorry for ever making you cry," I whispered, "and I'm sorry for taking so damn long to realize what you mean to me. I swear to you I'll spend the next seventy years making up for all the time with you I've lost."

"Seventy?" she asked, her voice thick with emotion even though she was smiling. "You think we'll last that long?"

"I know we will," I vowed.

"We drive each other crazy."

"I like our kind of crazy."

"We're always fighting," she argued.

"As long as it's you I'm fighting with."

"It's only been a month."

"I wouldn't care if it'd only been a week. I need you, Maci. I'll always need you."

A shaky smile crossed her face, and she dropped her head so I couldn't see her eyes anymore. "I've been in love with you for as long as I can remember," she admitted, her eyelids slowly lifting up to see my reaction.

How had I not known? Again, how had I never noticed her before? Knowing that nothing could make up for the years that I was blind to her, I tilted her head back up and kissed her lips gently. "I'm sorry it took me so long."

She shrugged and said simply, "You're here now."

And I had no intentions of going anywhere. Maci now knew the one thing I'd been terrified of telling her, and though I didn't know exactly how she felt about it all, I knew it wasn't going to scare her away. But now that she knew about my past, and my fears, there was one more thing she needed to know.

"I need to tell you about Cassidy."

I felt her body stiffen, and she sat up straighter, her eyes now worried with whatever I was about to tell her. "W-who?"

"Christ, Maci, no. I didn't do anything, I didn't cheat on you," I promised, and waited for her to relax . . . When she didn't, I spoke again. "She lives in Texas with her boyfriend, but she's the reason why I've been so different since this summer. I need to tell you about everything so you'll understand why I was the way I was."

"Okay," she said warily, and started to move off my lap, but I kept her there. I needed her there, needed to feel her touch while I told her.

With a deep breath in, I told Maci everything. Told her about the family-disturbance call that had first led me to Cassidy's parents' house years ago. How I'd believed Cassidy when she told me nothing was happening, and how after her mom burned the house to the ground right before summer started with her and her husband in it, I'd found out that Cassidy had been physically abused by her mom and stepdad every day since she was young. I told Maci about the black eye Cassidy's boyfriend had given her accidentally when Cassidy tried to break up a fight he was involved in, and the day in the coffee shop where I'd told her everything about my life before being adopted. How our similar pasts, and her own fears that had closely matched mine, had left me begging her to be mine, and following her back to Texas after she'd left to be with her boyfriend again. And most importantly, how I'd left when she asked me to, and I'd spent six months trying to feel anything again, and find someone who could evoke any type of emotion in me. How Maci had done that, and more.

When I finished telling her everything, Maci studied my face for a long time before asking, "Do you still feel anything for her?" I shook my head, and began to respond, but she continued talking. "That's a really intense reaction to have to another girl, you can't tell me that after six months of the 'Zombie Connor' that suddenly there's nothing left for her now."

"She wasn't you, Maci. I told you about my fears, and the nightmares that I have. I'd thought that Cassidy was the only one that would understand that and not judge me for it, because I didn't want to put that kind of life on someone who hadn't lived it. As fucked up as that seems . . . but I was wrong. And, if you think what you saw over the last six months was bad, you should have seen me after I made you believe I didn't want you. I'd felt numb after Cassidy . . . but thought I was dying after what I did to you. I didn't think I'd find someone to make me feel anything again after her . . . but didn't know how I was supposed to live without you. Do you see the difference?"

"What if she came back?"

"She won't," I assured her.

"But what if she were to. What would you do?"

I looked into Maci's eyes, and told her honestly, "I would thank her for inadvertently showing me that I deserved the life I want to have with you."

Maci's lips were on me fast and hard, and though I wanted nothing more than to kiss her forever, I forced our mouths apart and waited until she was looking at me again.

"I need to know what you think about everything you know now. My past, my fears for the future, Cassidy . . ." I trailed off.

She thought for a second, her lips pursing as her eyes got a faraway look. "I understand why you have your fears, but I know you and know that you won't turn into him. I will never know what it was like to grow up the way you and Amy did, but I hate it for you and I'm here if you ever need to just talk about it. As for Cassidy . . . I've watched you change completely over the last month. If there were lingering feelings for her, you'd still be a zombie, so I believe you when you say there's not." I kissed her softly, and laughed when she whispered against my mouth, "Besides, if she came back, you really think I wouldn't kick her ass if she tried to take you from me?"

"Nothing will keep me from you again."

"I'm holding you to that," she said softly before pressing her mouth to mine again.

The kiss was slow, but heated. After pulling down the zipper on her hoodie, and pushing it off her, I pulled the strap of her thin shirt over her shoulder, and left a trail of open-mouthed kisses across her collarbone. Her skin was covered in goose bumps, and she shivered against me as her hands went to the jeans I was still wearing.

"Didn't have anything to change into?" she teased.

"Don't, Maci. If your dad walks in, he'll kill me for what I'm already doing to you."

"He won't."

"One of your brothers is in the room next to mine."

Her hands didn't stop as she undid the button and zipper. "Not right now, both Dakota and Dylan went to one of the bars in town to calm down and probably get some girls for a few hours."

"They could be back soon—fuck," I groaned when she freed me from my jeans, and grabbed my length in her hands.

"Stop trying to come up with reasons not to, no one is coming in or going to hear us. And after everything, I need you. *Please*, Connor," she begged in a small voice.

A low growl built up in my chest, and I pulled her off me to lay her down on the bed. Ridding myself the rest of the way of my jeans, I pulled off her sweats and underwear at the same time, and parted her legs as I laid my body on top of hers. "I fucking love it when you beg."

A slow, coy smile spread across her face. "I know."

Shaking my head, I couldn't help but smile before I crushed my mouth to hers, teasing her tongue with mine as I slid inside her. I swallowed her whimper, and pushed in deeper when her fingers dug into my back. I wanted to claim her; I wanted to have to quiet her screams. But the second my lips moved down her neck, and she whispered my name . . . everything changed. My movements slowed, and the air between us went from urgent and needy to something so much more.

Raising up on one elbow, I gently fisted her hair in my hand, and stared into her eyes as I moved slowly inside her. Her breathing was rough, and when it began getting erratic, her eyes fluttered shut.

"Keep them open," I said in a gentle command.

Her heavy lids opened as she tightened around me, seconds before she came with a hushed whimper and breathy exhale. I followed her with my own release, never once taking my eyes off her.

"I love you, Maci," I said into her ear, and kissed her neck as I pulled out of her, rolling us to the side. Her smile was one I hadn't seen before, and I pushed back the hair that had fallen into her face before cupping her cheek with my hand. "What?"

"It's still surreal to hear you say that," she admitted after a few seconds.

"You're gonna have to get used to it, sweetheart. I'm going to be saying it for a long time."

"I'm sure I will eventually." She winked and curled into my arms. "You just promised me seventy years, didn't you?"

"At least."

Seventy years of this. Seventy years of Maci, and our kind of crazy. That sounded like heaven to me.

Epilogue

One year later . . .

Connor

I SAT ON the edge of the bed, letting my hand run through her vibrant red hair, and smiled when she made a little noise of approval in her sleep. She was so beautiful, and waking up early to watch her as she slept was still one of my favorite things.

Once we'd gotten back from the trip to Mammoth last year, everything had changed. Something about not hiding anymore had made my relationship with Maci change in a way I hadn't known was possible. I'd craved her before, and had realized almost too late that I was in love with her. But now I felt like I couldn't breathe without her, and every day there was something new that made me fall in love with her more.

Since she was in love with her apartment, and I

loved using her showerhead on her, I'd moved into her place within a week of getting back, and had continued to pay rent on my apartment until my lease was up two months later.

Dakota, Dylan, and I had talked things out. I'd known they were trying to protect her, but it took us a while for me to get over the feeling of betrayal at how they'd reacted and what I'd let them talk me into . . . and for them to get over their own fear of me hurting her . . . well, and the fact that I was sleeping with their sister.

Honestly, I think the only reason they eventually got over that one was seeing their sister with me. Maci's brothers had always been too overprotective, but in their minds they were watching out for her. Since Maci and I were no longer hiding, her tough exterior with her brothers had started slipping away, and she showed the Maci that I'd fallen in love with. Seeing her happy with me was all they needed to get over the rest.

Don't get me wrong. She was still feisty and didn't put up with anyone's bullshit . . . and I fucking loved it. But she didn't act like she was heartless—or didn't care—anymore, and I think all four of her brothers loved having the *real* Maci around.

Letting my knuckles brush her cheek, I leaned in and kissed her soft lips. "Wake up, Maci."

One eye cracked open before shutting again as she curled her body closer to mine. "Sleep."

"It's Christmas morning, you really want to sleep

right now?" When she nodded her head, I laughed softly and made a trail of lazy kisses down her throat to her chest.

She moaned and turned onto her back, her hands going into my hair as she slowly opened her eyes to watch me. "Mmm, well if I'd known this was what you wanted," she said as her hands traveled down my chest to my drawstring pants.

I wouldn't be able to stop myself if she continued, so I pushed up off her, and laughed against her mouth when she tried to follow me with a growl. "Not right now, baby, I have a fire going upstairs, and no one else is up yet. Besides, I'm not having sex with you when your brother is on the opposite side of this wall."

Her gray eyes were heated, and I almost tore off her clothes when she grabbed my hand, kissed my palm, and then ran it over her throat. "Well then maybe you should make sure I'm kept quiet."

I thought back to the other night when we'd snuck out of the cabin, and I'd taken her right there in the fresh snow, as more snow fell all around us. She'd started getting loud from the combination of me torturing her by getting her as close as possible before backing off, and playing with her nipples and clit with the icy snow. That night I'd had to keep her from making any more noises, and that had just made it hotter for both of us. But that was outside in the middle of the night when everyone was asleep, not in a room next to her brother when everyone would be waking up soon.

I kissed her thoroughly before pulling her off the bed. "Fuck, Maci, you're going to be the death of me, I swear." She started to pout, and I bit down on that perfect bottom lip. "Come on, let's go spend some time together before everyone is up and it gets crazy in here."

After we were upstairs, and I'd pulled her onto my lap in the big chair near the fireplace, she covered us with a blanket and lowered her head onto my chest as we watched the snow fall outside.

"Merry Christmas, Connor," she whispered and played with my hand, which was resting on her stomach. The other was shoved into the side of the chair, feeling the box I'd stashed between the cushion and frame.

"Merry Christmas, sweetheart." I had to swallow a few times before I could speak again. I tried to keep the tremor out of my voice, but I'm sure I failed. "I was thinking that when we get back, we can start packing up right away. We can take things over slowly, or choose a day and just do it all at once."

"Wait, what?" She turned so she was straddling me, her eyebrows pinched together as she looked at me in confusion.

"I'm fine with whichever way you choose, but we'll only have two weeks to get out of the apartment."

"Get out of the apartment? Why? What are you talking about?"

Leaving the box where it was, I pulled my hand out of the cushion and grabbed the chain around my neck that I'd hidden with my sweatshirt, and slowly pulled it off. Maci's eyes widened when she saw the key hanging on the end of it, and I smiled when they began darting between the key and me.

"I think it's time for us to get a place a little bigger, don't you?" I asked with a wink.

"Where does this key go to?" she asked breathlessly.

"Where do you think?" I nipped at her lips, and laughed when she gasped loudly.

"Connor, don't fuck with me right now! Is this to the house I wanted?" I just smiled at her and she shook her head quickly back and forth. "They told us it had already been bought, I thought . . . wait . . . I don't understand!"

"That's because I'd already bought it, sweetheart. Hearing the way you said you'd always loved that house . . . well it wasn't hard to know that you'd want to check into it once we'd actually started looking."

She crushed her mouth to mine, and repeatedly said, "Thank you," over and over as I slipped the chain over her head.

Grabbing the box, I pulled it out of the cushion and slowly worked it open with one hand as I spoke against her lips. "Besides, didn't you always say it had a perfect backyard for a wedding? And I want an actual house for when I carry you over the threshold as my wife, and when we have children."

Maci sat up straight, her gray eyes were wide, and it looked like she was holding her breath.

Once I had the ring between my fingers, I grabbed her left hand and slowly slid it on her ring finger. "Maci Price . . . will you marry me?"

Tears filled her eyes before slowly falling over and down her cheeks. She just sat there on my lap staring at the diamond on her hand before she grabbed my head and fused our mouths together.

"Is that a yes?" I asked when she dropped her head as she cried, and smiled before pressing a soft kiss to her forehead when she just nodded. "I need to hear you say it."

When she looked back up, her eyes were bright with tears, and the most beautiful smile was lighting up her face. "Yes, Connor, I'll marry you." She kissed me again. "And move into that house with you, get married in the backyard, and have kids with you. Yes to all of it. I want it, everything," she cried softly before kissing me harder.

Cupping her face, I pulled back to look in her eyes. "I love you."

"I love you too."

"Does this mean we can start planning the wedding?" A harsh whisper came from behind me, and I rolled my eyes as Maci's head jerked up.

"Yes, Amber, it means we can start planning the wedding now," I answered monotone, but winked at Maci.

"Wait! She knew? And you didn't tell me? You bitch!"

I just shrugged as Amber bounced over to us and

grabbed Maci's left hand. "I needed help picking your ring out."

"Does this mean you already asked her?" a new voice asked behind me.

Maci looked up again as her parents came in the room and she slapped her hands down on my chest. "For fucking real. Did everyone know?"

I smiled as her brothers and sisters-in-law all came out of hiding and confirmed her question. "You mad at me, baby?"

"Yeah, I totally am! I can't believe they all knew before—"

I pulled her to me, and silenced her with my mouth. "No you're not," I whispered and deepened the kiss.

She melted against my chest and smiled lazily. "You're right. I don't think I've ever been happier."

"So you sure you're ready for all this?"

"I'm ready," she whispered and dragged her lips across my jaw. "I want everything with you."

I couldn't agree more. I wanted everything . . . and as long as it was with this girl in my lap, I was ready for it all.

The End

Acknowledgments

As always, thank you to my husband, **Cory**, for being so amazing and helping me out around the house when I was too involved with the story to even notice the dishes needed to be done! Love you, Bear!

Thank you to my amazing editor, **Tessa**, and agent, **Kevan**! Y'all have no idea how much I appreciate everything you do, and your feedback on my stories. I have no clue what I would do without either of you!

Amanda Stone: I love my Sef! I'm pretty sure that says it all, ha! Ah, I love the moments like when we realized we were going to use the same character names and laughed about it, just to start fighting because you didn't like my nickname for the character, and then end on an "I love yewww," all within three minutes. No one else could ever understand us!

Kelly Elliott: As always, I love you like crazy! You

were just at my house for lunch two days ago and already I'm missing my Kel! I don't know what I would do without you, and am so lucky to have you in my life. Mwah!

Bethany and **Adam "Peter" Kalenderian**: Thank you for the simple fact that you are an awesome couple. Adam, I loved that you openly didn't understand your wife's love for books, or her excitement to meet me; which, of course, led to the challenge of putting *Family Guy* in a book. Challenge accepted and met.

To all my **readers**: I spent a couple weeks in the hospital for my back right in the middle of writing this book, and y'all have no idea how much your love, prayers, and support meant to me during that time. I am so blessed to have you all in my life, and my husband and I are so thankful for every one of you. It was hard getting back into the writing groove once I was home and on the mend, but your support for me was what helped me dive back in once I was well. So, thank you, thank you, thank you!

Molly's Mafia girls, and all the **bloggers** and **readers** who help with reveals, teasers, and announcements: I love you all so hard. I am beyond grateful for all the pimping y'all do, and wish I could tackle-hug everyone one of you! True story: you're all amazing.

Want to see where it all began?
Read on for a peek at

FROM ASHES

to see the beginning of Connor's story.

Chapter One

Cassidy

"Do you even know anyone who's going to be there, Ty?"

"Just Gage. But this will be good, this way we'll be able to meet new people right away."

I grumbled to myself. I wasn't the best at making friends; they didn't understand my need to always be near Tyler, and when I'd show up with bruises or stitches, everyone automatically thought I was either hurting myself or Tyler and I were in an abusive relationship. Of course that wasn't their fault; we never responded to them, so the rumors continued to fly.

"Cassi, no one will have any idea about your past, the last of your bruises will be gone in a few weeks, and you're gone from there now. Besides, I hate that you don't have anyone else. Trust me, I understand it, but I hate it for you. You need more people in your life."

"I know." I instinctively wrapped my arms around myself, covering where some of the bruises were. Thank God none were visible right now unless I stripped down to my skivvies, but I couldn't say the same for some of the scars. At least scars were normal on a person, and the worst of them were covered by my clothes, so I just looked like I was accident-prone.

"Hey." Tyler grabbed one of my hands, taking it away from my side. "It's over, it will never happen again. And I'm always here for you, whether you make new friends or not. I'm here. But at least try. This is your chance at starting a new life—isn't that what that favorite bird of yours is all about anyway?"

"The phoenix isn't a real bird, Ty."

"Whatever, it's your favorite. Isn't that what they symbolize? New beginnings?"

"Rebirth and renewal," I muttered.

"Yeah, same thing. They die only to come back and start a new life, right? This is us starting a new life, Cass." He shook his head slightly and his face went completely serious. "But don't spontaneously burst into flames and die. I love you too much and a fire wouldn't be good for the leather seats."

I huffed a laugh and shoved his shoulder with my free hand. "You're such a punk, Ty; way to kill the warm and fuzzy moment you had going there."

He laughed out loud. "In all seriousness"—he kissed my hand, then met and held my gaze for a few seconds before looking back at the road—"new life, Cassi, and it starts right now."

Tyler and I weren't romantically involved, but we had a relationship that even people we'd grown up with didn't understand.

We grew up just a house away from each other, in a country club neighborhood. Both our fathers were doctors; our moms were the kind that stayed home with the kids and spent afternoons at the club gossiping and drinking martinis. On my sixth birthday, my dad died from a heart attack—while he was at work of all places. Now that I'm older, I don't understand how no one was able to save him; he worked in the ER, for crying out loud, and no one was able to save him? But at the time, I just knew my hero was gone.

Dad worked long hours, but I was his princess, and when he was home, it was just the two of us. He'd brave tiaras and boas to have tea parties with me; he knew the names of all of my stuffed animals, talked to them like they would respond; and he would always be the one to tell me stories at night. My mom was amazing, but she knew we had a special relationship, so she always stayed in the door frame, watching and smiling. Whenever I would get hurt, if he was at work, Mom would make a big show of how she couldn't make it better, and I'd have to hang on for dear life until Dad got home. She must have called him, because he would run into the house like I was dying— even though it was almost always just a scratch—pick me up, and place a Band-Aid wherever I was hurt, and miraculously I was all better. Like I said, my dad was my hero. Every little girl needs a dad like that. But now, other than precious memories, all I have left of him is his love for the phoenix. Mom had let Dad have his way with a large outline of a phoenix painted directly above my bed for when I started kindergarten, a painting that's still there today, though Mom constantly threatened to paint over it. And although I tried to keep a ring he'd had all his adult life with a phoenix on it, my mom had found and hidden it not long after he died, and I hadn't seen it since.

My mom started drinking obsessively when he died. Her morning coffee always had rum in it, by ten in the morning she was making margaritas, she'd continue to go to the club for martinis, and by the time I was home from school, she was drinking scotch or vodka straight out of the bottle. She made time for her girlfriends but stopped waking me up for school, stopped making me food, forgot to pick me up from school—pretty much just forgot I even existed. After that first day of being forgotten at school, and the next day not showing up because she wouldn't leave her room, Tyler's mom, Stephanie, started taking me to and from school without a word. She knew my mom was grieving, just not the extent of it.

After a week with no clean clothes and a few rounds of trial and error, I began doing my own laundry, attempted to figure out my homework by myself, and would make peanut butter and jelly sandwiches for both of us, always leaving one outside her bedroom door. Almost a year after Dad's death, Jeff came into the picture. He was rich, ran some big company—his last name was everywhere in Mission Viejo, California—but up until that day I'd never seen or heard of him. One day Stephanie dropped me off and he was just moved in, my mom already married to him.

That night was the first time I'd ever been hit, and it was by my own mother. My sweet, gentle mother who couldn't kill a spider, let alone spank her own daughter when she misbehaved, hit me. I asked who Jeff was and why he was telling me to call him Dad, and my mom hit me across the back with the new scotch bottle she'd been attempting to open. It didn't break, but it left one nasty-looking bruise. From that point on, I never went a day without some kind of injury inflicted by one of them. Usually it was fists or palms, and I began welcoming those, because when they started throwing coffee mugs, drinking glasses, or lamps, or when my mom took off her heels and repeatedly hit me in the head with the tip of her stiletto . . . I didn't know if I would still be alive the next day. About a week after the first hit was when I first got beat with Jeff's socket wrench, and that was the first night I opened my window, popped off the screen, and made my way to Tyler's window. At seven years old, he helped me into his room, gave me some of his pajamas since my nightshirt was covered in blood, and held my hand as we fell asleep in his bed.

Over the last eleven years, Tyler has begged me

to let him tell his parents what was going on, but I couldn't let that happen. If Tyler told them, they would call someone and I knew they would take me away from Tyler. My hero had died, and the mom I loved had disappeared down a bottle; no way was I letting someone take me from Ty too. The only way I had gotten him to agree was agreeing myself that if he ever found me unconscious, all promises were off and he could tell whomever he wanted. But that was just keeping Tyler quiet; we never had factored in the neighbors . . .

After the first three years of the abuse, I stopped sneaking out to Ty's house every night, only doing so on the nights when it was something other than body parts hitting me, but Tyler was always waiting, no matter what. He kept a first aid kit in his room, and would clean up and bandage anything he was able to. We butterfly-bandaged almost all the cuts, but three times he forced me to get stitches. We told his dad I tripped over something while going for a run outside each time. I'm not naïve, I knew his dad didn't believe me—especially since I was not one for running, and the only time I was involved with sports was watching it on Ty's TV—but we were always careful to hide my bruises around him and he never tried to figure out where I actually got the cuts from. I'd sit at their kitchen table and let him sew me up, they'd let me out the front door when they were sure I was okay, and Tyler would be waiting by his open window as soon as I rounded the house. Every night he had something ready for me to sleep in, and every night he would hold my hand and curl his body around mine until we fell asleep.

So when Tyler kissed my forehead, cheek, or hand, it never meant anything romantic. He was just comforting me in the same way he had since we were kids.

"Cassi? Did I lose you?" Tyler waved his hand in front of my face.

"Sorry. Life, starting over. Friends, yeah, this, uh—will be—I need to . . . friends." I'm pretty sure there was English somewhere in that sentence.

Ty barked out a laugh and squeezed my knee, and after a few silent minutes he thankfully changed the subject. "So what do you think about the apartment?"

"It's great. Are you sure you want me to stay with you? I can get my own place, or even sleep on the couch . . ." My own place? That was such a far-fetched idea it was almost funny; I didn't even have a hundred dollars to my name.

"No way, I've shared my bed with you for eleven years, I'm not about to change that now."

"Ty, but what about when you get a girlfriend? Are you really going to want to explain why I live with you? Why we share a dresser, closet, and bed?"

Tyler looked at me for a second before turning his eyes back to the road. His brown eyes had darkened, and his lips were mashed in a tight line. "You're staying with me, Cassi."

I sighed but didn't say anything else. We'd had a version of this argument plenty of times. Every relationship he'd ever had ultimately ended because of me and the fact that we were always together. I hated that I ruined his relationships, and whenever he was dating someone I would even stop coming to his room and answering his calls so he could focus on his girlfriend instead. That never lasted long though; he'd climb through my window, pick me up out of bed, and take me back to his house. We never had to worry about my boyfriends, since I'd never had one. What with Tyler's possessiveness and all, no one even attempted to get close enough to me. Not that it bothered me; the only guy I'd ever had feelings for was too old for me and had only been in my life for a few short minutes. The moment I'd answered the door to see him standing there, my stomach had started fluttering and I felt this weird connection with him I'd never felt with anyone, and even after he was gone I'd dreamed about his cool intensity and mesmerizing blue eyes. Ty didn't know about him though, because what was the point? I'd just barely turned sixteen and he was a cop; I knew I'd never see him again, and I didn't. Besides, other than my real dad and Ty, I had a problem with letting guys get close, strange connection or not. When my already-disturbed world turned completely upside down the minute a new man came into our house . . . trust issues were bound to happen.

Tyler had decided to go to the University of Texas in Austin, where his cousin Gage, who was two years older than us, was currently studying. I'd heard a lot about Gage and his family from Ty over the years, since they were his only cousins, and I was genuinely happy he was going. Gage was like a brother to him and Tyler hadn't seen him in a few years, so their sharing an apartment would be good for Ty. I wasn't sure what I was going to do when Tyler left; the only thing I did know was that I was getting away from the house I grew up in. I just had to make it another month until I turned eighteen and then I was gone. But Tyler, being Tyler, made my future plans for me. He crawled through my window, told me to pack my bag, and just before he could haul me off to his Jeep, he told Mom and Jeff exactly what he thought of them. I didn't have time to worry about the consequences of his telling them off, because before I knew it we were on the freeway and headed for Texas. We made the trip in just over a day, and now, after being here long enough to unpack his Jeep and shower separately, we were headed to some lake for a party to meet up with Gage and his friends.

Gage's family wasn't from Austin; I didn't know where in Texas they lived, but apparently they had a ranch. After hearing that, I'd had to bite the inside of my cheek to keep from asking what Gage was like. I understood we were in Texas now, but already Austin had blown my expectations of dirt roads and tumbleweeds away with its downtown buildings and greenery everywhere. I just didn't know how I'd handle living with a tight-Wranglered, big-belt-buckled, Stetson-wearing cowboy like I'd seen in rodeos and movies. I'd probably burst out laughing every time I saw him.

When we came up to the lake and the group of people, I sucked in a deep breath in a futile attempt to calm my nerves. I wasn't a fan of new people.

Tyler grabbed my hand and gave it a tight squeeze. "New beginning, Cassi. And I'll be right here next to you."

"I know. I can do this." His Jeep stopped and I immediately took that back. *Nope. No, I can't do this.* I had to think quickly of where every bruise was, making sure my clothes were covering them all, even though I'd already gone through this at the apartment. I just didn't want anyone here to know what kind of life I'd had.

I jumped out of Tyler's Jeep, took one more deep breath, and mentally pumped myself up. *New life. I can do this.* I turned and rounded the front and hadn't even made it to Tyler's side when I saw him. I don't know if I made a conscious choice to stop walking or if I was still making my way to Tyler and didn't realize it; all I could focus on or see was the guy standing about ten feet from me. He was tall, taller than Tyler's six-foot frame, and had on loose, dark tan cargo shorts and a white button-up shirt, completely unbuttoned, revealing a tan, toned chest and abs. His arms were covered in muscles, but he didn't look like someone who spent hours in the gym or taking steroids. The only way I can describe them is natural, and labor-made. His jet-black hair had that messy, just-got-out-of-bed look, and my hand twitched just thinking about running my fingers through it. I couldn't see what color eyes he had from here, but they were locked on me, his mouth slightly open. He had a bottle of water in his hand, and it was raised like he had been about to take a drink out of it before he saw me. I had no idea what was happening to me, but my entire body started tingling, and my palms were sweating just looking at him.

I'd seen plenty of attractive guys—Tyler looked like an Abercrombie and Fitch model, for crying out loud. But Mr. New couldn't even be described as something as degrading as *attractive*. He looked like a god. My breath was becoming rougher, and my blood started warming as I took an unconscious step toward him. Just then a tall, leggy blonde bounced over to his side and wrapped her arms around his waist, kissing his strong jaw. It felt like someone punched me in the stomach and I was instantly jealous of whoever this girl was. Shaking my head, I forced my eyes to look away. *What the hell, Cassidy? Calm down.*

"Cassi, you coming?"

I blinked and looked over at Tyler, who had his hand outstretched to me. "Uh, yeah." I glanced back at Mr. New and saw he still hadn't moved. The perky blonde was chatting his ear off, and he didn't even seem to be hearing her. I felt a blush creep up my cheeks from the way he was looking at me, like he'd just seen the sun for the first time, and continued over to Tyler.

Tyler pulled me to his side and whispered in my ear, "You okay?"

"Yeah, I'm fine," I reassured him, trying to slow my heart down for a completely different reason now.

He kissed my cheek and pulled away. "Okay, well let me introduce you to Gage."

Right. Gage. Tyler dropped my hand, only to put his on the small of my back as he led me over to Mr. New and the leggy blonde. *Oh no. No no no no no.*

"'Sup, man?" Tyler slapped him on the back and Mr. New slowly dragged his eyes from me to the guy who'd just hit him.

Gage's eyes went wide when he saw Ty. "Tyler, hey! I didn't realize y'all were here yet."

Oh. Good. God. That voice. Even with that small sentence I could hear the drawl in it. It was deep and gravelly, and easily the sexiest thing I'd ever heard.

"Yeah, we just got here. Cassi, this is my cousin Gage. Gage, this is Cassi."

Gage brought his hand out. "It's a pleasure, Cassi. I'm glad y'all are finally here."

My knees went weak and a jolt of electricity went through me when I shook his hand. From how he glanced down at our hands quickly, he'd felt it too. "It's nice to meet you too." Now that I was up close, I could see his bright green eyes, hidden behind thick black lashes and eyebrows. He was the definition of masculine. From his strong jaw and brow, high cheekbones, defined nose, and perfectly kissable lips, his looks screamed *man*. The only thing offsetting the masculinity were his boyish deep dimples, which had me hooked. Yep, *god* was the only word out there that fit him.

Our hands didn't separate fast enough for the tall blonde, so she thrust her hand forward. "I'm Brynn, Gage's girlfriend." Her eyes narrowed on the last word.

I shouldn't have, but I glanced at Gage again. His brows were pulled down in either confusion or annoyance when he looked at Brynn. *You have got to be kidding me,* I thought. I didn't care if it had been only two seconds since I first saw him, this couldn't be a normal reaction for two people just meeting to have with each other, and he had a freaking girlfriend. It hadn't even felt like this with the cop who came to my door that night, and I'd thought about him for almost two years!

I squared my shoulders and dropped Gage's hand, focusing on Brynn. "It's great to meet you, Brynn!" I hoped my smile looked genuine. I didn't need an enemy yet, especially if she was dating the guy I was going to be living with. But hell, I'm not gonna lie—I was already thinking of ways to get her out of the picture.

Tyler and Brynn shook hands, and she looked back at me, noticing that I was doing everything to keep from looking at her boyfriend. Tyler and Gage were catching up, and every time Gage would speak I had to force myself not to shut my eyes and lose myself in the way his voice caused chills to go through my whole body.

"So, Cassi, what do you say we go introduce you to the rest of the girls?" Brynn finally said sweetly.

Tyler looked elated; this was exactly what he wanted. "Sounds great," I said, and stepped away from the guys. It felt wrong to walk away, but I could feel Gage watching me as I did.

"You and Tyler, huh?" Brynn nudged my shoulder.

"What do you mean?"

"Y'all make such a cute couple." She wasn't complimenting, she was reaching.

"Thanks, but no. Tyler and I are best friends, nothing more."

"You sure about that? I saw the way he was looking at you, and he had his arm around you."

"We're just different like that. We've been best friends our entire lives."

"Right. Are you going to UT too?" she asked, sounding a little too curious.

"Uh, no. I'm not planning on going to school at all."

"So why are you here?" If it hadn't been for the curled-up lip, she would have just simply sounded interested.

"Honestly? I have no idea. Tyler packed my bag and threw me in his Jeep. Apparently Gage didn't care if I lived with them." I smirked and turned to begin the introductions with the girls who were now right next to us.

Gage

WHAT THE HELL *was* that? Nothing like that had ever happened to me. One look at Cassi and it felt like my world stopped. All I could think about was closing the distance between us. I don't know how to describe it, but I needed to go to her. Unfortunately, I was frozen in place, taking in the most beautiful girl I'd ever seen. Her long brown hair was windblown, and those wide honey-colored eyes made me want to get lost in them. She looked so sweet and fragile, I wanted to wrap my arms around her and protect her from seeing anything bad in the world, but something in her eyes told me she knew too well what the world was like and could take care of herself. Which is why it was so damn confusing that she clung to my cousin like he was a lifeline.

Tyler told me he was bringing his friend to live with us, and that she was a girl. I'd remembered hearing her name over the years, but whenever he spoke about her, it seemed like they were only friends, so why did he hold her hand and kiss her damn cheek? I couldn't even stop the growl that came from my throat when I saw it. Then freakin' Brynn. Girlfriend? Really? We'd gone on two god-awful dates last year and I told her before school let out that I didn't want any form of a relationship with her. I thought we'd been clear since she'd avoided me all afternoon until Cassi and Ty showed up.

When Cassi first spoke, I had to force myself to breathe. Her voice was soft and melodic. It fit her perfectly. She was petite and even with how short she was, those legs in those shorts could make any guy fall on his knees and beg. I couldn't stop thinking about how she'd feel in my arms, how she'd look in my truck or on my horse. And yeah, I'm not gonna lie, I'd already pictured her beneath me . . . but one look at her and there was no way not to.

After Brynn guided her away, it took a huge effort to stop watching her, but I didn't want to let on to Tyler that I was already completely taken with her.

"She's mine, Gage. Let's get that clear right now."

Okay, so maybe I'd been a little more obvious than I'd thought. "Thought you said y'all were friends."

"She's my best friend, but you'll see. She's mine."

I nodded and clapped his back, forcing my hand out of a fist. "I got you, man. Come on, let me get you a beer."

As the night wore on, I continued to get closer and closer to where she was. I felt like a creep, trying to be near her, but I couldn't stop it. I wanted to listen to her talk and laugh; I swear she sounded like an angel singing when she laughed. I almost groaned out loud— *Angel singing? What the hell is wrong with me?*

We were all sitting around the bonfire talking and drinking. I was just a few feet from Cassi when she got up to head over to Jackie. If it hadn't been for what happened immediately after, I would have punched Jake in the face for touching her. With one hand he grazed the front of her thigh, and with the other he grabbed her ass, causing her to stumble and fall right into me, her beer soaking my shirt.

Her big eyes got even wider and she sucked in a quick gasp. "Oh God, I'm so sorry!" The sun was setting and it was getting darker, but I could perfectly see her blush. I'm pretty sure Cassi blushing was my new favorite thing.

I laughed and grabbed her small shoulders to steady her, not caring one bit about my shirt. "You all right?"

Her eyes focused on my lips, her teeth lightly sinking into her bottom one. I wanted to replace her teeth with mine and without realizing it, I started to lean forward. She blinked quickly and glanced up, then looked at Jake on my right. "I'm fine. I'm really sorry about your shirt."

Aw hell, this isn't normal. She's said all of two sentences to me tonight and I was about to kiss her? "Don't worry about it," I murmured as she righted herself and continued toward Jackie, only to be quickly pulled away by Tyler as he spoke in her ear, his arms around her.

"Damn, when you said your cousin was bringing a chick, I wasn't expecting her to be so hot," Jake said.

"Jake, touch her again . . . see what fuckin' happens."

"Whoa, got it bad for your cousin's girl already, huh? You gonna try to get with that?"

I eyed Cassi in Ty's arms and shook my head as I brought my beer up to take another long drink. "Nope." *Yes, yes, I am.*

"Well, if you're not, I sure as hell am."

"Jake," I growled.

"All right, all right. Chill, Gage. I won't touch her and you heard her . . . she's fine." Jake leaned forward to grab another beer out of the ice chest and settled back into his chair, his eyes already off Cassi and onto Lanie.

After a quick glance to see Cassi and Tyler still quietly talking, I got up and walked back to where all the trucks were parked. I took my wet shirt off and hung it off the bed of my truck before grabbing a clean one out of the backseat. When I turned around, Tyler was walking up to me.

"I'm real glad you're here, bro," I said.

"Me too." He took a long drink out of his can before setting it down on the tailgate. "We couldn't get here fast enough. Cali was really starting to wear on me; I was ready for someplace new. And hey, I know I've said this, but I appreciate you letting us room with you. I know you could've had anyone share your apartment with you, and he probably wouldn't have brought a girl with him."

"Don't worry about it, you're family. To be honest, I was kinda surprised when you said you were coming to Austin to go to school with me. After you started refusing to come to the ranch with Aunt Steph and Uncle Jim the last few years, I just figured you didn't like us much anymore."

"Nah, it had nothing to do with you. I just hated leaving Cassi behind. Sorry I made you think that though."

I took a deep breath, reminding myself Cassi *had* followed him to Texas. "Really? I don't get it, Ty, you said she was a friend. Then she follows you here, and now you're saying you wouldn't come visit because you didn't want to leave her? How come you never just told me how it really was with y'all?"

"It's complicated; we really were just friends. But she needed me; I couldn't just leave her. And I'm in love with her, man."

Holy hell. I felt like someone had just knocked the air outta me. How was I already so into this girl that it physically hurt to think of her being with Ty? With anyone, for that matter? Seriously. This was not. Fucking. Normal. "What do you mean she needed you?"

Tyler sighed and shook his head. "Like I said, it's complicated."

We both looked up when we heard girls squealing and splashing. Some of the guys were throwing them into the lake, and I couldn't stop myself from going to Jake when he picked Cassi up and threw her over his shoulder. My hands were already balled into fists for when he put her down. Her long hair was hiding her face as she pounded her little hands on his back.

"Put me down! I'm not wearing a suit!" She sounded so determined for a little thing that I almost smiled. Almost. "I'm serious, put me down!"

"Jake, I told you not to touch her. Put her down." I was standing right behind them then. Cassi grabbed the top of his jeans to push herself up and look at me, but Jake turned so he was now facing me. She was trying to kick him as well and his hands high up on her thighs had my hands fisting again.

"Come on, Gage." He sounded annoyed. "All the other girls went in."

"She doesn't want to—" Jake slid her down, causing her shirt to ride up high on her back. I choked on my next words, and at least two other people gasped behind me. *WHAT THE HELL?!*

Tyler grabbed Cassi and started pulling her away. He looked at her sympathetically, and when his eyes met mine they looked worried. Cassi's face was bright red again and her lips were smashed together tight as she let Tyler lead her to his Jeep.

Jake looked at me like I was insane; if it wasn't for the other guys having the same reaction, I woulda felt like it too. I turned and followed Tyler and Cassi to the Jeep, waiting until I was sure no one could hear us. "What the hell did I just see?"

Tyler helped her into the Jeep before going to the driver's side and opening up his own door. Cassi was looking straight ahead, her jaw still clenched.

"Ty, man, what was that?"

"Nothing. We'll see you whenever you get back to the apartment."

"That wasn't nothing!"

He sighed and stepped away from the door, leaning close so she couldn't hear him. "Look, we were trying to avoid something like this, but since you already saw, I'll explain it later. But this is exactly what I was getting her away from, so I'm going to take her back to the apartment now if you don't mind."

I didn't wait for anything else. I practically ran to my truck, grabbed my wet shirt as I put the tailgate up, hopped in, and drove back with them. A million things went through my mind on the way back to the apartment, and each one had me gripping the steering wheel hard. It was dark enough that I couldn't be sure what I'd seen, but it looked like bruises. Lots of them. I'd heard of people with some illnesses who are covered in them. I tried to think of what it could be and thought about her too-small frame. If her face didn't look so healthy, I would have been sure it was that. But the way Tyler talked about not wanting to leave her behind, I couldn't dismiss it either. I refused to think about the obvious; there was no way someone would hurt her. I'd hunt them down if they did.

Why was I so protective of her? I didn't know her from Eve, and we'd barely said anything to each other all night. I was hardly like this when it came to my sisters, and I loved them more than anything. I didn't know what it was about that girl, but she was already completely under my skin. And I wasn't sure if I liked that or not yet.

The drive took forever, and I let out a long sigh when I finally pulled into my spot. When they pulled up next to me, I jogged over to the passenger door and opened it. Cassi's face made me take a step back. There was absolutely no emotion there, and though she wouldn't meet my eyes, hers looked dead. I held my hand out to help her down, but Tyler pushed through me, glaring at me, and helped her out himself. He kept an arm around her as he led her to our place and took her right into his bedroom. I stood in the living room waiting for them to come out, but thirty minutes passed and the door still hadn't opened. With a heavy sigh, I turned and went to my bathroom to take a shower since I still smelled like the beer Cassi'd spilled on me. Thank God I hadn't gotten pulled over on the way home. When I got back to my room, Tyler was sitting on my bed.

"Sorry, Gage, she didn't want to talk to you when we got here."

"Is she sick, Ty?"

Tyler started. "What? No, she's not sick. Why would you—Oh. No. She's not."

Part of me was relieved, but now that I knew that wasn't it, I felt sick knowing what must've happened. "That why you never wanted to leave her?" I asked quietly.

"Yeah, that's why."

"Boyfriend?"

He shook his head.

"Parents?" I gritted my teeth hard when he nodded.

"Hold on a sec." Tyler walked quickly to the other side of the apartment, and I heard his door open and shut twice before he came back to my room, closing the door. "I wanted to make sure she was sleeping; she doesn't want you to know. But since you saw it, I have to tell you—I need to tell someone." He dropped his head into his hands and took a deep breath as his body started shuddering. "I haven't told anyone in eleven years. Do you know what it's been like, knowing what's happening and not being able to say anything?"

"Eleven years?!" I hissed, and made myself lean

back against the wall so I wouldn't go after him. "This has been going on for eleven fucking years and you didn't tell anyone? What the hell is wrong with you?"

"She made me promise I wouldn't! She was terrified they would take her away."

"Did you not see that? Her entire back was black and blue!"

Tyler hung his head again. "That's not the worst it's ever been. She'd come over with concussions; a few times I made her agree to stitches. Swear to God, that girl is tougher than most men I know, because without any pain medication she'd let Dad sew her up right there in the kitchen. Then there were times she couldn't even get off the floor. When she was young, sometimes she'd lie there for hours before she could move; when we got older and got her a phone, she'd have to text me and I'd come get her."

I tried to swallow the throw-up that was rising in my throat. "It got that bad and you never said a word. What would you have done if they killed her one of those times, Ty?"

A sob came from where he sat hunched in on himself. "I hate myself for letting her go through that. But every time I tried to confront them, she'd flip out and make me leave, and when I would, that night or the next day would be one of those days where they'd beat her so hard she wouldn't be able to pick herself up."

"That isn't an excuse, you could have taken her away from them. Uncle Jim could have done something!"

"Look, Gage, you can't make me feel any worse than I already do! I'm the one who had to clean the blood off her, I'm the one who had to bandage her up even during the dozens of times when she should have gotten stitches. I had to buy a mini freezer for my room so I could have ice for when she came over!" He pulled his phone out of his pocket, tapped the screen a few times, and stifled another sob as he handed it over to me.

"What is this?" Whatever these fresh bruises were, they definitely weren't done by hands. The small rectangles looked familiar, but I couldn't place what I thought they were.

"Golf club. I didn't even know about this last time. She just told me about it on the way back here, and I took the pictures before I came in here. She said it happened yesterday morning before I came and packed her bags."

"Are there more pictures?"

He raised his head for a second to nod. "Ever since I got my first phone I've taken pictures every time she came over, and I always transfer them to my new phones so I'll have them. They're all backed up too. She wouldn't let me say anything, but I wanted to have photos in case . . ." His voice trailed off. There wasn't a need for him to finish that sentence anyway; I got the message.

Flipping through some of his pictures, I couldn't believe this was the same sweet Cassi I'd just met a few hours ago. Bruises of all shapes, sizes, and colors covered her body and it was killing me to look at them, but I couldn't stop. You could see all the ones that were fading slowly get covered up by new ones, and other pictures showed her back, arms, and face covered in blood. What killed me was that whenever her face was in the picture, she wore the same expression I'd just seen outside. No emotion, dead eyes, and absolutely no tears.

"What would they do to her?"

"You don't want to know."

Like hell I didn't. I was already planning on going to California with my twelve-gauge. "What. Would. They. Do?"

He was quiet for so long I didn't think he was going to answer. "When it first started, it was *usually* just hitting and kicking. The older she got, the more it turned into whatever they had in their hands or could grab quickly. Once that started, she only came over if it was other objects. She lived for the days when it was only hands."

"So what I saw tonight, you said it isn't the worst?"

"Not even close."

"What was?"

Tyler sighed and looked up at me, tears streaming down his face. "I don't know, there were a few that really stood out, but I couldn't name one that was the worst."

I just kept glaring at him; he needed a beatin' just

for letting this go on for so long. She was seventeen or eighteen now, so she had been six or seven when this all started. And he'd known the entire time.

"A couple years ago, the cops showed up one night—"

"I thought you said she wouldn't let you call?"

"I didn't." He sighed and ran his hands through his hair a few times. "The old lady that lived in between us heard her screaming one night, called the cops."

I shoved off the wall and flung my arms out. "You had a perfect opportunity and you still didn't do anything? *They* didn't do anything?!"

"Gage, I didn't even know the cops were called until she texted me hours after they'd left!"

"What happened?" I demanded, and forced myself back against the wall.

"Cassi opened the door, her mom and stepdad right behind her. None of her bruises were visible then and they all denied the screaming, including Cass."

Seriously? What the fuck?

"When the cops left, her mom took off her high heels, used the pointy heel part to hit her head repeatedly. There was so much blood when I got there, Gage, and she couldn't lay her head even on a pillow for almost a week after that. Another time her stepdad threw a glass of alcohol at her, she ducked, and it shattered against a wall. Since she didn't get hit by it, he grabbed her by the throat, dragged her to where it was, and just kept slicing her forehead, arms, stomach, and back with one of the pieces. She wore a scarf every day 'til the finger marks were gone. That's why she wears her hair with those things, what are they called? Bangs. She got those scars when she was ten and the one on her head isn't very noticeable anymore, but she still tries to hide it. She tries to hide all of them, but some she can't unless she wants to wear jeans and long sleeves in the summer."

I stood there in shock, trying to make the connection between this girl he was telling me about and the girl I'd just met. Even with seeing the pictures it wasn't clicking for me; I couldn't imagine someone touching her, or her being so willing to let it continue. "You're a poor excuse for a man, Tyler." I opened my door and stood next to it, arms crossed over my chest.

He looked like he crumpled in on himself. "You think I don't know that?"

I couldn't say anything else to him. As soon as he was out of my room I slammed the door and fell on my bed. I wanted to make him stay in my room and go to her myself. Hold her and tell her I'd never let anyone else hurt her again. But for whatever reason she wanted him, and we didn't know each other so it would be even creepier than my trying to be close enough to hear her talk tonight.

My whole body shook as I thought about anyone laying a hand on her, let alone sharp objects. Sweet Cassi, she deserved parents and a man who cherished her. Not ones who beat her and a boy who sat back and let it happen. I swallowed back vomit for the third time since I found out what happened and forced myself to stay in my bed.

I closed my eyes and tried to steady my breathing, focusing on her face and honey-colored eyes instead of what I saw on her back and the images that Tyler's phone had seared into my brain. I thought about running my hands through that long, dark hair. Pressing my mouth to her neck, her cheeks, and finally those lips that were full and inviting. *Tyler doesn't deserve her. Not at all.* I thought about taking her in my arms and taking her to the ranch so I could keep her safe for the rest of her life. But she'd already been living a life she didn't choose, so I wouldn't choose for her either; I would wait for her to leave him and come to me.

Chapter Two

Cassidy

WE HADN'T BEEN in Austin for more than six hours before someone saw the bruises. And not just anyone, Tyler's cousin, our new roommate, and the guy who wouldn't leave my every waking thought. I told Tyler not to tell him—let him make his own assumptions— but of course Tyler didn't listen and told him way more than he should have. I couldn't blame him though; I'd made him keep a secret no kid should have to. I know he thought I was sleeping, but even if I had been, Gage yelling at Tyler, or Tyler coming back into our room to hold me and tell me how sorry he was while he cried, would have woken me up. I'd learned long ago that if I cried, I got hit harder until I finally stopped, so I'd become a master at turning off my emotions. But I knew if I had opened my eyes to watch him cry, it definitely would have broken through that wall and I would have been crying right there with him. So I lay completely still, emotions turned off and eyes shut, while Tyler cried himself to sleep.

Once Tyler got in the shower the next morning, I slipped into the kitchen to start some coffee. We'd spent so many nights without sleeping over the years, we'd both started drinking it early on, and I was glad that now he didn't have to sneak an extra cup for me since his parents hadn't exactly known that I stayed the night all those years.

I shut the door quietly and turned to tiptoe across the hardwood floors when I saw Gage, and my heart instantly picked up its pace. He was dressed only in jersey shorts and shoes, his body still glistening with sweat. God, he looked amazing, and my breath caught at how perfect his body and face were. I'd barely caught a glimpse of him without his shirt on last night before Tyler had caught me staring, and now I couldn't make my eyes look away.

"Morning."

My eyes finally snapped up to meet his. In the light and this close, I could see the gold flecks scattered throughout the green of his eyes. They were the most beautiful eyes I'd ever seen. "Good morning, Gage."

"How, uh—how are you today?"

I sighed and walked over to the coffeepot. "I know he talked to you, I could hear you guys last night. I don't want you to be awkward around me now because of what you know."

"Cassi, those things should have never happened to you. He should have told someone."

I turned to find him right in front of me again. "I made him promise he wouldn't."

"Well he shouldn't have listened to you."

"You don't get it, Gage. You weren't there. I couldn't let him."

His eyes narrowed. "No, I wasn't there. But if I had been, something would have been done the first time it ever happened. Why didn't you say anything the night the cops showed?"

I shook my head; there was no point in trying to make him understand.

Gage put a hand on each side of my face and leaned closer. I swear I thought he was about to kiss me, like last night, and it didn't matter that I hardly knew him; I wanted him to. "You didn't deserve that, Cassi, you know that, right?"

"I do."

Before I could realize what he was doing, he brushed my swoop bangs back and traced his thumb over a scar from Jeff's glass. My body instantly stiffened and Gage's eyes turned dark as he looked at it. He slowly tore his gaze from the scar to my eyes and spoke softly. "Didn't deserve any of that."

I took a step back and turned to look at the almost-full pot of coffee.

He reached around me and brought down two mugs before pouring coffee in each one. "I'm sorry if you like cream," he drawled. "I don't have any here."

"That's fine." I breathed a quiet sigh of relief as I walked over to the fridge and grabbed the milk. "I'll go to the store later and get some."

When I was done pouring it in, he put the cap on for me and put it back in the fridge. Walking back over to me, he put a finger under my chin and tilted my head up so I was looking at him. "How often did it happen, Cassi?"

My breaths started coming quicker. What was it about him that made me want to fall into his arms and not ever leave? It took his repeating his question for me to come out of my daydream. I was up against the counter, so I couldn't step back, but I moved my head away from his hand and stared past his shoulder into the living room.

He guessed when he saw I wasn't going to answer. "Every day?"

I still didn't respond; if it was a weekend, it happened at least twice a day. But that was something even Tyler didn't know. My body started involuntarily shaking and I hated that I was showing any sign of weakness in front of him.

"Never again, Cassi," he whispered while he studied my face.

My eyes flew back to meet his and my throat tightened. He sounded like he was in pain just talking about it and I had no idea why. But I'd be lying if I said it didn't make me want his arms wrapped around me. I cleared my throat and forced myself to continue to meet his gaze. "Cassidy."

"What?"

"My name is Cassidy."

"Oh." He looked a little sheepish. "My apologies, I didn't realize."

"No. Um, Tyler doesn't like it. He calls me Cassi. I just wanted to tell you my real name." Really I just wanted to hear it in his gravelly voice.

He smiled softly as he studied me for a minute and took a sip of his black coffee. "I like Cassidy, it fits."

Oh damn . . . yep. I was right in wanting to hear him say that. My arms were covered in goose bumps and I even shivered. Yeah—his voice was *that* sexy.

When I didn't say anything he walked around to the table and held out a chair, waiting for me to sit in it. We sat in silence for a while before I finally looked up at him again.

"This might be rude, but can I ask you something?"

One side of his mouth lifted up in a smile. "I think I already cornered the market on rude questions this morning, so go ahead."

And cue the freaking dimples! I got so lost staring at them I forgot to ask my question and his smirk went to a full-blown Gage smile. At this rate I'd need to start wearing a sleeping mask and earplugs around him in order not to make myself look like an idiot. Though I'd look ridiculous either way. "Well, um, Tyler said you live on a ranch?"

"I do."

"I was kind of thinking you'd look more like a cowboy . . ."

Gage's laugh bounced back off the walls, and I felt my body relax just listening to it. "And how exactly were you expecting me to look?"

"You know, boots, hat, big belt buckle, super-tight bright blue jeans," I replied, a little embarrassed.

"Well I definitely have the boots, and the hats, but I don't think my sisters or Mama would ever let me dress like Dad."

"Oh."

"My dad even has the big mustache, looks like Sam Elliott."

It took me a second to figure out who that was, and then I laughed. "Seriously?"

"Swear, they could be twins."

"I'd love to see that. So where was your hat last night?"

He shrugged. "I leave all that at the ranch."

"What? Why?"

"I don't wear them as a fashion statement, and I definitely don't have any kind of work that would require them here in hippie town."

"Hippie town?" I deadpanned.

"Just wait until we go out anywhere. You'll see."

I nodded. "What kind of work? What kind of ranch do you have?"

"Cattle ranch, and whatever needs to be done that day. Taking care of the animals, moving the cattle to different parts of the ranch, fixing fences, branding . . ." He drifted off. "Just depends."

"How many cows do you have?"

"About sixteen."

Okay, I understand I don't know a thing about ranches, but I figured you'd need more than sixteen cows to make it a cattle ranch. "You have sixteen cows?"

He huffed a laugh and smiled wide at me. "Hundred. Sixteen hundred."

"Dear Lord, that's a lot of cows."

He shrugged. "We'll be getting more soon, we have the land."

"How many acres is the ranch?"

"Twenty."

"Hundred?"

"Thousand."

"Twenty thousand acres?!" My jaw dropped. Why on earth would anyone need or want that much land?

"Yes, ma'am." He spun his mug around on the table.

" 'Ma'am'? Really?"

One of his eyebrows raised. "What?"

"I'm not some grandma—I'm younger than you."

Gage rolled his eyes. "I didn't mean you're old, it's respectful." When he looked at my expression he shook his head and chuckled. "Yankees."

"Uh, get a clue, cowboy . . . I'm not from the North."

"You're not from the South either. Yankee." He smirked, and if I thought that was going to melt me, when he added a wink I knew I was done for.

"Are you going on about Yankees again, bro?" Tyler asked, walking into the kitchen.

Gage just shrugged and his green eyes met mine from under those dark brows again. "She didn't like that I called her 'ma'am.'"

"Get used to it, Cassi, we may be in the city, but it's different here."

I grumbled to myself and Gage laughed.

"So what are you guys talking about?" Tyler sat in the seat on my other side.

"Their huge ranch with too many cows," I answered.

"She's right about that, there are way too many cows there," Tyler said between sips of his coffee.

"You'd like it." Gage looked at me with an odd expression.

"Hell no, she wouldn't! Cassi doesn't like getting dirty, and she hates bugs. Your ranch would be the worst place for her."

Gage flicked a quick glare at his cousin, then looked back to me. "We have horses."

I gasped. "You do? I've never been on a horse!"

"Eight Arabians. I'll teach you to ride when you come to visit." He sat back in his chair and folded his arms, smirking at Tyler like he'd just won something.

Tyler and I both got quiet. My dad told me he was going to let me start taking riding lessons for my sixth birthday and buy me a horse for my seventh. Obviously those things never happened. Not that we didn't have the money, but my mom wouldn't even cook for me; no way she would let me do those things. It didn't help that even though I still loved horses, whenever I saw them I couldn't stop thinking about my dad.

"Did I say something wrong?" Gage looked confused but kept his eyes on Tyler.

"No," I said with a soft smile. "I'd like that."

After a few awkward minutes, Gage stood up and put his mug in the dishwasher before walking toward his room, "Well, I'm gonna take a shower. If there's anything y'all wanna do today, let me know."

Tyler scooted my chair closer to him. "You okay, Cassi? Is it because of your dad?"

"No, it's fine. I mean, I was thinking about him. But I just can't believe he's been gone for almost twelve years. I feel like I should be over it, I was so young when it happened, but I don't think I was ever allowed to grieve, and that's why it's still hard. I'm not looking forward to this birthday. I always thought when I got away from Mom and Jeff, I would finally enjoy my birthdays again, but I'm looking forward to it less than ever. I think we need to give me a new birthday, Ty." I huffed a light laugh. "No one wants a birthday on the anniversary of their father's death."

He pulled me onto his lap and held me loosely so he wouldn't hurt my back. "He was a great dad; you aren't supposed to get over him, Cassi, you'll always miss him. And no new birthdays, you're keeping the one you have and I'll make sure they get better and better every year."

I let him hold me for a few minutes before speaking again. "Thanks, Ty, I love you."

"Love you too, Cassi."

Gage

OH MY GOD, her dad died on her birthday? What else has happened to this girl? Okay, I'll admit I left the bathroom door cracked for a few minutes before shutting it and starting my shower. But the way they'd both got so quiet there at the end, I knew I'd said something I shouldn't have, and I figured Tyler would bring it up as soon as I was gone. I knew she'd be hooked as soon as I mentioned the horses, and she was; I just didn't know telling her I'd teach her to ride would take them back down memory lane to her dad, who was obviously nothing like her mom or stepdad.

Sitting there talking to her before Tyler had come in was the best morning I think I'd ever had, and it didn't even last ten minutes. She smiled so much it made my heart swell each time, and God, that laugh. I was right; it sounded just like freakin' angels. I wanted to die every time she'd start to relax into the chair. Her eyes would go wide for a split second and she'd sit right back up like she'd forgotten about the bruises on her back for a minute. I didn't have to ask her to know she was in pain; there was no way she could have been comfortable with what I'd seen last night. But even with that, her smile never faltered, and that may have killed me even more. She should have been depressed or crying or something. What kind of person goes through that kind of life, as recent as two days ago, and still finds reasons to smile?

When I walked out of the bathroom, she was still curled up on Tyler's lap and I blew out a frustrated sigh. I needed to get over her soon, or living there with them was going to be a challenge.

"Hey, Gage?" Tyler called before I could shut my door.

"What?"

"You up to showing us around the city today?"

No. I want to show Cassidy the city, I want you to go the hell back to California. "Sure."

I shut the door behind me and had just finished getting my jeans on when Tyler walked in.

"You okay, man? We don't have to go out today, I was just asking. Or Cassi and I could go by ourselves. It's not a big deal either way, I just figured since you knew the area . . ."

I never asked Cassidy why Tyler didn't like her name. It was so perfect for her, and why would he even tell her he didn't like it? Seriously, how were we related? "No, it's fine, I just have a lot on my mind. I'll be ready in a minute, we can go whenever."

"All right, well I'm sure she wants to shower. So it'll probably be a while," he called as he walked back out of my room.

I grabbed a shirt and headed out to the living room. Tyler wasn't there, but Cassidy was sitting at the kitchen table, staring intently at her hands. "You okay, Cassidy?"

She jumped and looked up at me, her brows pulled together in confusion and hurt. She didn't say anything, just studied my face for a minute, before blowing out a deep sigh and standing up to walk toward their room.

"I'm sorry for reminding you about your dad. I didn't know." I still didn't know. What did horses have to do with her dad?

Cassidy stopped walking and looked over her shoulder at me for a second, then continued to the door.

I stood there staring at the door, feeling like an ass, even after Tyler walked out of the room and started hooking a gaming system to the TV. Did telling Cassidy I'd teach her to ride really hurt her so much that the girl who asked why I didn't dress like a cowboy just disappeared? Everything in me screamed to go to her and talk to her, but the shower started, so I turned back to the living room. I told Tyler I'd watch him play and flopped onto the couch. I tried not to picture Cassidy in the shower while I listened to the water running, but that was damn hard, so I focused as much of my attention as I could on Tyler shooting people and tried not to think about her and the hard-on I was trying to cover with a pillow.

When Cassidy came out less than an hour later, her hair was wild and slightly wavy, and she had less makeup on than last night too. She looked beautiful. Without all that dark stuff around her eyes and stuff on her face, her honey-colored eyes looked even brighter and you could see a splatter of very light freckles on her nose. Not saying she hadn't looked gorgeous last night, because she had. She took my breath away. But I preferred this almost completely natural look. She was wearing green Chucks, jeans with the bottoms rolled up to her calves, and a worn black Boston concert shirt. *Boston. This girl is perfect.*

"Ty, I'm ready."

She still had yet to look at me since she walked in the room, and though I wanted her to, I was enjoying being able to take her in. I noticed her bottom lip was a little too full for her top lip, and her nose couldn't have been more perfect if she'd chosen it herself. Her eyes flitted over to me quickly, then right back to Tyler; her cheeks got red and I couldn't help but grin. *There's no way she doesn't feel this too.* She started biting her bottom lip, and again I thought about what it would feel like to kiss those lips. I'd never wanted to kiss a girl this damn bad.

"Tyler!" She tapped his leg with her foot and he looked at her, then back at the screen.

"What's up?"

"I'm ready, are we going or not?"

"Yeah, just let me finish this match and we can go. Like eight minutes."

I had already sat up when she entered the room so she could sit on the couch with me, and she was eyeing it now, but instead turned and went into the bedroom. She stayed in there while Tyler played two more matches and didn't come out until he went to get her.

I took them all over Austin that afternoon, and

while she was polite and would respond whenever I asked her a question, she wouldn't hold a conversation with me and made sure she was always by Tyler's side, farthest away from me. Maybe I was wrong about her feeling whatever this connection was, because she definitely didn't seem like she was having a hard time not touching me. It was all I could do not to grab her hand and keep her by my side.

When we were on the way back, she asked if we could stop by the grocery store, and we let her take over the shopping after her third eye-roll at our food choices.

"Don't worry," Tyler whispered as she compared packages of ground beef, "she's been cooking for herself since she was six; she's better than my mom."

I hadn't been worried, and now that added just one more thing I wished I could have protected her from. Because my dad and I worked from sunup to sundown most days, I was only ever in the kitchen to help with dishes. I thanked Mom and my sisters daily for making the food, but I couldn't imagine having to do it on my own when I was just a little kid. I'd have to thank them again.

Other than letting us carry the groceries in for her, she wouldn't let us help put them away and immediately started on cooking dinner for the three of us. I lay down on the couch just watching her move around the kitchen while Tyler played his game again. At one point it looked like she started dancing for a few seconds before she stopped herself, and God, if that wasn't the cutest thing I'd ever seen. When Ty was fully engrossed in the game, I got up and wandered into the kitchen, stepping right up behind her.

"Do you need help with anything?"

Her body tensed for a moment, and once it relaxed she turned her head up to look at me. "No, I'm fine. Thanks though."

"Could I help anyway?"

She continued to watch me with that same hurt and confused look from that morning. "Yeah, sure. You can make the salad." She grabbed a few things out of the fridge and brought them over to me before grabbing a couple more items that she'd bought at the store out of a bowl on the counter. "Dice these, and— wait, do you even like avocados?"

"I'll eat anything, darlin'."

Her mouth tilted up at the corners and her cheeks got red; I smiled to myself and made a mental note to call her that more often. "Well, if you don't like them, I can just put them in my bowl."

I grabbed the avocado from her and looked at it, a little confused. "Like I said, I'll eat anything. But how do you cut this thing?"

She laughed lightly and took it from my hand, sliding the cucumber and tomato in front of me. "Dice these first, then I'll show you how to cut the avocado." She handed me a knife and turned back to the stove.

I was flat-out awful at dicing those vegetables,

but being in the kitchen with her had me smiling the entire time, and whatever she was cooking smelled damn good. "I think I did it right."

"There's really no way to mess up dicing veggies for a salad." She turned and looked. "You did it just fine. Haven't you ever diced something before?" I shook my head and she grinned at me. "Really? Well you did great. Let me show you how to do these."

She grabbed both avocados and handed me one of them before picking up her own knife. I'm not gonna lie, I purposefully kept messing up getting the seed out so that she finally had to reach over and grab my hands to show me what to do. I heard her intake of breath as soon as our hands touched, and I had to look away so she wouldn't see how wide I was smiling.

Hell. Yeah.

She finished showing me how to cut up the avocado and had me grab bowls and plates while she finished up whatever was on the stove. Every time I looked at it, she'd turn me away and say I wasn't allowed to see her secrets. I didn't know what was going on all day, but she was now acting just like she had that morning. Every smile and every touch had me falling for her that much more.

I touched her arm so she'd look up at me and I almost forgot what I was gonna ask as soon as her eyes met mine. "Uh, did I upset you this morning? I swear I didn't mean to. I had no idea about your dad."

She looked down, then back at the stove. "I didn't

expect you to know about him. And what were you thinking upset me?"

"When I told you I'd teach you how to ride."

Cassidy huffed and shook her head once. "No, Gage, that didn't upset me. I would really like to learn how to ride, if you ever want to show me."

Did she think I would offer if I didn't want to? And would it be bad if I asked what those two things had to do with each other? "Of course I will. I mean, I heard what Tyler said, but I do think you'd like the ranch. I can't wait to take you there." Ah, too much. Too much.

"Sounds great." She picked up a spoon, then set it right back down and put both her hands on the counter before looking back at me. Her mouth opened and her eyebrows pulled together, then she looked into the living room at Tyler and back at me. "Dinner is about ready," she said softly. "Would you mind putting the salad on the table?"

When I turned around with the bowls, I saw Tyler staring at us and held back a sigh. I was gonna get crap for this later.

Cassidy had made crispy chicken fettuccine Alfredo, and all I could say was damn. I had to agree with Tyler that it was better than Aunt Steph's, and it rivaled Mama's cooking.

I stood up to help when she started clearing the dishes, but Tyler stepped in front of me before I got far. "I'm serious, man, she's mine."

"I heard you the first time."

"You sure about that?"

I glanced back at Cassidy. "Yeah, I'm sure. But you're the one who brought her here; you can't expect me to never talk to her, or offer my help when she's making us food. If we're all gonna live together, you need to get over the fact that I'm gonna be friends with her."

He remained quiet and smiled, waiting for Cassidy to return to the kitchen. "I couldn't care less if you're friends with her. Just don't forget that I'm the one who's been there for her every day for the last eleven years. Not you. I still see how you're looking at her, I'm not fucking blind, Gage."

Cassidy

"I'M KIND OF TIRED, I'm going to bed. Thanks for showing us around today, Gage."

Tyler stood and walked over to me. "Want me to come with you?"

I shot a quick glance behind Ty to Gage, who was openly glaring at his cousin. "No, you guys need to catch up, I'll see you later."

"Sleep well, Cassidy," Gage said.

I smiled and waved like an idiot. "Night."

Tyler hugged me and Gage winked when I looked over Ty's shoulder at him. Seriously, this guy was so confusing! I walked to the bathroom I shared with

Tyler to wash my face and brush my teeth before slipping into some pajamas and crawling into bed. I could hear the boys talking and Gage started laughing, warming my entire body. I sighed and flipped onto my side. I didn't understand him at all. First, he had a girlfriend, then he'd almost kissed me last night, and this morning I could have sworn he was flirting with me. Then he got upset when we wanted to go out this morning and Tyler told me that when he went to talk to him about it, Gage said he didn't want me living here, but tonight in the kitchen he kept finding a reason to touch me and wouldn't stop smiling at me. What the heck? I didn't know how to even act around him.

I must have fallen asleep, because I felt a little groggy when Tyler slipped into the bed later that night.

"Sorry, I didn't mean to wake you," he said softly.

"It's fine, I meant to wait up for you. I guess I was more tired than I realized."

He pulled me close to his body and wrapped his arms around me. "You've had a long last three days, you needed to sleep."

"True. Did you guys have fun talking?"

"Yeah, it's good to see him again. It's been a long time since we hung out."

"I'm sorry I'm ruining that; you really shouldn't have brought me, Ty."

He leaned back a little so he could see my face. "Cassi, I'll take you with me everywhere I go. And don't worry about Gage, he'll get over it eventually.

I'm sure it's not you that he doesn't like, he just said it's going to mess up his relationship with Brynn having a girl live with him."

"I don't want to do that." *Yes, yes, I do.* I'd never experienced jealousy until I met Gage last night, and it was one ugly feeling. "When I turn eighteen, I'll get my own place, Ty."

"No, you won't. He'll get over it, and I want you with me, okay?"

I curled into his chest and nodded. "Love you."

Tyler leaned back again and tilted my face up to his. "I love you too, Cassi." His lips fell onto mine and I scrambled back, pushing against his chest as hard as I could.

"What the hell, Tyler?!" We slept in bed with each other, but we'd never actually kissed before.

"I'm sorry! I thought you wanted me to."

"What? Why would I want you to?" *Oh my God, seriously, what the hell just happened?!*

He sighed and relaxed his hold on me. "I don't—I don't know what got into me. I'm sorry, that was really stupid."

"Is that why you brought me to Texas with you?"

"No, it's not, I swear. You're my best friend, I would have never left you there. I'm sorry, like I said, that was really stupid."

I crawled off the bed and grabbed my pillow. "Maybe I should sleep on the couch tonight."

"No! Cassi, come on, don't do that. I'm sorry."

"It's fine, it hasn't just been a long three days for

me. It's been even longer for you. I think we're both too tired and we aren't thinking clearly."

"Cass." He sighed and got out of the bed as well. "I'm sorry, I don't know what I was thinking doing that." He hugged me loosely and stepped back. "Please get back in bed."

"It's all right, I promise. I'm just going to sleep out there tonight—I think it would be best for us. I'll be back in here tomorrow, okay?"

"I'll go out there, you can stay in the bed."

I put my hand on his chest and pushed him onto the bed. "I'm way shorter than you; that couch was practically made for me. Good night, Ty, see you in the morning."

Want more Molly McAdams? Check out

FORGIVING LIES

Available now

Chapter One

Rachel

"CANDICE, YOU NEED to focus. You have got to pass this final or they aren't going to let you coach this summer."

She snorted and her eyes went wide as she leaned even closer to the mirror and tried to re-create her snort. "Oh my God! Why didn't you tell me how ugly I look when I do that!?"

I face-planted into the pillow and mumbled, "Oh dear Lord, this isn't happening." Lifting my head, I sent her a weak glare. "Snorts aren't meant to be cute. Otherwise they wouldn't be called something as awkward as 'snort.'"

"But my—"

"Final, Candice. You need to study for your final."

"I'm waiting on you," she said in a singsong voice. "You're supposed to be quizzing me."

I loved Candice. I really did. Even though I currently wanted to wring her neck. She wasn't just my best friend; she was like a sister to me and was the closest thing to family I had left. On the first day of kindergarten, a boy with glasses pushed me down on the playground. While he was still laughing at me, Candice grabbed his glasses and smashed them on the ground. That's playground love. And since then we've never spent more than a handful of days apart.

By the time we started thinking about college, it was just assumed we would go away together. But then my parents died right before my senior year of high school started, and nothing seemed to matter anymore. They had gone on a weekend getaway with two partners from my dad's law firm and their wives and were on their way home when the company jet's engine failed and went down near Shaver Lake.

Candice's family took me in without a second thought since the only relatives I had lived across the country and I hardly knew them; if it weren't for them I don't know how I would have made it through that time. They made sure I continued going to school, kept my grades up, and attempted to live as normal a life as possible. I no longer cared about graduating or going away to college, but because of them, I followed through with my plans of getting away and making my own life. I would forever be grateful to the Jenkins family.

I applied to every college Candice did and let her decide where we were going. She'd been a cheerleader for as long as I could remember, so it shouldn't have surprised me when she decided on a university based on the football team and school spirit. And granted, she was given an amazing scholarship. But Texas? Really? She chose the University of Texas at Austin and started buying everything she found in that god-awful burnt-orange color. I wasn't exactly thrilled to be a "Longhorn," but whatever got me away from my hometown was fine by me . . . and I guess the University of Texas accomplished that.

When we first arrived I remember it felt like walking into a sauna, it was so hot and humid; of course the first thing Candice said was, "What am I going to do with my *hair*?!" Her hair had already begun frizzing, and not more than five minutes later she was rocking a fro. We got used to the humidity and crazy weather changes soon enough though, and to my surprise, I *loved* Texas. I had been expecting dirt roads, tumbleweeds, and cowboys—let me tell you, I had never been so happy to be wrong. Downtown Austin's buildings reminded me of Los Angeles, and the city was unbelievably green everywhere and had lakes and rivers perfect for hanging out with friends. Oh, and I'd only seen a couple of cowboys in the almost three years we'd been there, not that I was complaining when I did. I had also worried when we arrived that with Candice's new burnt-orange fetish, people were going to be able to spot us like Asian tourists at

Disneyland. Thankfully, the majority of Austin was packed with UT Longhorn gear, and it was common to see a burnt-orange truck on the road.

Now we were a little less than two weeks away from finishing our junior year and I couldn't wait for the time off. Normally we went to California to see Candice's family during the winter and summer breaks, but she was working at a cheer camp for elementary-school girls that summer, so we were getting an apartment that we planned to keep as we finished our senior year.

That is, if we ever got Candice to pass this damn final.

Before I could even ask my first question, Candice gasped loudly. "Oh my God, the pores on my nose are huge."

Grabbing the pillow under me, I launched it at her and failed miserably at hitting anything, including her. At least it got her attention. Her mouth snapped shut, she turned to look at the pillow lying a few feet from her, then she turned around with a huff to walk back to her desk.

Finally. "Okay, what is—"

"So are you ever going to go on a date with Blake?"

"Candice!"

"What?" She shot me an innocent look. "He's been asking you out for a year!"

"This—you need—forget it." I slammed the book shut and rolled off my bed, stretching quickly before going to drop the heavy book on my desk. "Forget it, we'll just see if we can get our deposit on the apartment back. I swear to God, it's like trying to study with a five-year-old."

"You never answered my question."

"What question?"

"Are you going to go on a date with Blake?"

I sighed and fell into the chair at my desk. "One, he's your *cousin*. Two, he works for UT now; that's just . . . kinda weird. Three, no."

"It's not like he's your professor! He isn't even a professor, period. And do you realize that if you marry him, we'll actually be family?"

"Marry? Candice— Wait . . . how do you even jump from me going on a date with him to marrying him? I'm not going to marry your cousin; sorry. And I don't care if he's a professor or not, it doesn't change the fact that he works for the school. Besides, he's not even my type."

"Not your type?" she said, deadpan, and one perfect blond eyebrow shot straight up. "I seem to remember you having the *biggest* crush on him when we were growing up. And I know he's family, but I can still say that he's gorgeous. I'm pretty sure he's everyone's type."

I had to agree with her on that. Blake West was tall, blond, and blue eyed and had a body like a god's. One of these days he was going to show up on a Calvin Klein billboard. "I had a crush on him when we were thirteen. That was eight years ago."

"But you had a crush on him for years. Years. You were devastated when he moved away."

"And like I said, I was thirteen. I was ridiculous."

Blake was five years older than Candice and me, but even so, all of my childhood memories included him. He was always at Candice's house to hang out with her older brother, Eli, and we followed them everywhere. I'd viewed both Eli and Blake as awesome older brothers until the day Blake saved my life.

Okay, that's a little dramatic. He didn't actually save my life.

I was nine at the time; we'd been playing on a rope swing and jumping into a little lake not far from our houses. When I'd gone to jump, my foot slipped into the foot hole and I ended up swinging back toward land headfirst, screaming the whole way. Blake was standing on the bank and caught me, swinging me into his arms before I could make the trip back toward the water.

In that moment, he became my hero, and I fell in love. Or at least my nine-year-old version of love. My infatuation with him grew over the next few years, but he never saw me as anything other than his "little cousin's best friend." I'm sure if I'd been older, that would have been a blow to my ego, but I just kept following him around like I'd always done. When he graduated from high school, he immediately joined the air force and moved away from me. I remember throwing a few "my life is over" fits to Candice, but then I got boobs and hips and the other boys my age started noticing me. And then it was something along the lines of, "Blake who?"

He'd been out of the air force for four years now and had pretty much been off the grid until last fall, when he'd moved to Austin and started working at UT. Candice had flipped out over having her cousin near her again. And I'd just straight flipped out. But then I saw him. He looked like freakin' Adonis standing there in his godlike, too-beautiful-for-his-own-good glory. Every straight female within a mile radius seemed to flock to him, and he loved every second of it.

That is why I refused to go on a date with him.

"Rachel," Candice snapped.

I turned my wide gaze to her.

"Did you even hear me?"

"Not unless we're done talking about Blake."

"We are if you've decided to say yes to him."

I rolled my eyes. "Why is it so important to you if I go on a date with him or not?"

"Because he's been asking you out all year! He's my cousin and you're my best friend and I love you both and I want to see you two together."

"Well, I'm pretty sure you and Blake are the only two who feel that way. I have absolutely no desire to date a guy who has women literally hanging on him all the time." *Stupid air force, turning him into sex on a stick.*

Suddenly she was sporting her signature pouty face. "Rach? How much do you love me?"

"Nope. No, I'm not going."

"Are you saying you don't love me?" I was already shaking my head to say no when she turned on the puppy eyes and continued. "So will you please do this for me? Pleeeeaaasse? I thought you were my best friend."

I can't even believe we're doing this right now! "If I go on *one* date with him, will you drop this forever?"

She squeaked and did a happy clap. "Thank you, I love you, you're the best!"

"I didn't say I would, I said *if*."

"But I know you'll go."

"He works for the school!" I whined, going back to my original argument. Even though he wasn't a professor at UT, he did work there as a personal trainer and helped out in the athletics department. Since I was majoring in athletic training and Candice in kinesiology and health ed, we saw him almost daily in classroom-type settings. That just . . . didn't sit right with me.

"Rachel." She twisted back around to face me. "Seriously, that is getting old. He already checked it out and it's a nonissue. Stop acting like you don't want to date him."

"I don't! Who wants to date a man-whore?"

"He isn't a—well . . . eh." She made a face. "Well, yeah."

"Exactly!" Blake was rumored to be screwing most of the females he trained as well as . . . well . . . he was rumored to be screwing pretty much any female he passed. Whether the rumors were true or not was up for debate. But seeing as he didn't try to squash them and the horde of bimbos was never far from him, I was leaning toward their being true.

"You haven't dated anyone since Daniel. You need to get back out there."

"Yes I have. Candi, just because I'm not constantly seen with a guy, like you are, doesn't mean I don't date."

I had gotten kind of serious with Daniel at the beginning of our second year at UT. But apparently six months was too long to make him wait to have sex and he ended up cheating on me. I found out two days after I'd given him my virginity.

Asshole.

After him I'd gone out with a few guys, but they didn't last much longer than a date or two and an "I'll call you later." Not that there was anything wrong with those guys, I was just more interested in being done with school and Texas than getting my "MRS degree" or risking catching a disease.

I sighed to myself and headed toward our door.

"Are you going to find Blake?!" Candice was bouncing in her seat and her face was all lit up like a kid's on Christmas morning.

"What—Candice, no. It's after midnight! I'm just done talking about this. I'm going to wash my face so I can go to sleep. And I'm not gonna hunt him down either; *if* he asks me out again, then I'll say yes." I grabbed my face wash and was reaching for the knob when someone knocked on the door. I don't know who I was expecting it to be, but I wouldn't have thought Blake West would be the one standing there in all his cocky glory. From the look on his face, there was no doubting he'd heard part, if not all, of our conversation. What the eff was he doing in our dorm?

He pulled one long-stemmed red rose—that was unexpected—from behind his back and looked over my shoulder, and his cocky expression went completely serious. "Hey, Candi. Do you mind if I steal Rachel for a few minutes?"

I turned around to look at her and she was grinning like the Cheshire Cat. *Traitor.* I looked back at Blake and he let out a short laugh at my question-mark expression.

"That is, unless you're busy or don't want to. It looks like you were headed somewhere." He looked pointedly at the hand that wasn't holding on to the door.

It took me a few seconds to look down at my hand and realize he was looking at my face wash. "Oh . . . um, not. No. I mean. Busy. Not busy. I'm not busy." *Wow, that was brilliant.*

Blake's lips twitched and his head fell down and to the side to hide the grin he was failing at keeping back.

Trying not to continue looking like a complete idiot, I took a deep breath in and actually thought about my next question two different times before asking it. Okay, fine, I thought about it four times. "So, what can I do for you?" Yeah, I know. Now you understand why that required a lot of thought.

"I was wondering if I could talk to you for a few minutes."

"Uh, you do realize it's almost one in the morning, right?"

His head lifted and he looked sheepish. That look on this man was so different from anything I'd ever seen, and I almost didn't know how to respond to it. "Yeah, sorry. I think I fought with myself for so long on whether or not I should actually come up here and talk to you, it got a lot later than I realized." He jerked the rose up in front of him like he'd just remembered it was there. "This is for you, by the way."

"And here I was thinking you just walk around holding roses all the time." I awkwardly took the rose from him, looked at it for a few seconds, then let it hang from the tips of my fingers. "So, Blake . . ." I trailed off and searched his eyes for a second before he took a step back.

"Can I talk to you out here for just a minute? I promise I won't keep you long."

Yeah, well, the fact that I've turned you down for the amount of time it takes to make a baby and now you're standing at my dorm room door at one in the morning is kind of creepy. But of course we have history, you're incredibly hot now, and I'm thinking about as clearly as Candice does. So, sure. Why the hell not? I followed him out into the hall and shut the door behind us but stayed pressed up against it.

"Rachel . . ." He ran a nervous hand through his hair and paused for a second, as if trying to figure out what to say. "The school year is about to end and you'll be going back to Cali over the summer. I feel like I'm about to miss any chance with you I may have. And I don't want to. I know you liked me when we were growing up. But, Rach, you were way too young back then."

"I'm still five years younger; that hasn't changed."

He smirked. "You and I both know a relationship between a thirteen-year-old and eighteen-year-old, and a twenty-one- and twenty-six-year-old are completely different."

So? That doesn't help my argument right now. "Well, you and I have both changed over the last eight years. Feelings change—"

"Yes." He cut me off and his blue eyes darkened as he gave me a once-over. "They do."

I hated that my body was responding to his look. But honestly, I think it'd have been impossible for anyone not to respond to him. Like I said. Adonis. "Uh, Blake. Up here." He smiled wryly, and dear Lord, that smile was way too perfect. "Look, honestly? I have an issue with the fact that you're constantly surrounded by very eager and willing females. It's not like I'd put some claim on you if we went on a couple dates, but you ask me out *while* these girls are touching you and drooling all over you. It's insulting that you would ask me out while your next lay is already practically stripping for you."

His expression darkened and he tilted his head to the side. "You think I'm fucking them like everyone else?"

Ah, frick. Um, yes? "If you are, then that's your business. I shouldn't have said that, I'm sorry. But whether you are or not, you don't even attempt to push them away. Since you moved here, I've never seen you with less than two women touching you. You don't find that weird?" Was I *really* the only person who found this odd?

Suddenly pushing off the wall he'd been leaning against, he took the two steps toward me and I tried to mold myself to the door. A heart-stopping smile and bright blue eyes now replaced his darkened features as he completely invaded my personal space. If he weren't so damn beautiful I'd have karate-chopped him and reminded him of personal bubbles. Or gone all Stuart from *MADtv* on him and told him he was a stranger and to stay away from my danger. Instead, I tried to control my breathing and swallow through the dryness in my mouth.

"No, Rachel. What I find weird is that you don't seem to realize that I don't even notice those other women or what they're doing because all I see is you. I look forward to seeing you every day. I don't think you realize you are the best part of my weekdays. I moved here for this job before I even knew you and Candice were going to school here, and seeing you again for the first time in years—God, Rachel, you were so beautiful and I had no idea that it was you. You literally stopped me in my tracks and I couldn't do anything but watch you.

"And you have this way about you that draws people to you . . . always have. It has nothing to do with how devastatingly beautiful you are—though that doesn't hurt . . ." He smirked and searched my face. "But you have this personality that is rare. And it bursts from you. You're sweet and caring, you're genuinely happy, and it makes people around you happy. And you have a smile and laugh that is contagious."

Only men like Blake West could get away with saying things like that and still have my heart racing instead of making me laugh in their faces.

"You're not like other women. Even though these are the years for it, you don't seem like the type of girl to just have flings, and I can assure you, that's not what I'm into, nor what I'm looking for with you. So I don't see those other women; all I'm seeing is you. Do you understand that now?"

Holy shit. He was serious?

"Rachel?"

I nodded and he smiled.

"So, will you please let me take you out this weekend?"

For the first time since he'd come back into my life, he actually looked unsure of himself. I was still in complete shock, but I somehow managed to nod again and mumble, "Sure, where do you want to go?"

He smiled wide and exhaled in relief. "It's a surprise."

I frowned. How did he have a surprise planned if he hadn't even known I was going to say yes? "And by 'surprise,' do you mean you have no clue?"

"No, it's just a surprise."

I started to turn into Candice and whine that I wouldn't know what to wear but was interrupted by my own huge yawn, which made me sound more like Chewbacca. I covered as much of my face as possible with the hand that wasn't holding the rose and laughed awkwardly. "Oh my word, that's embarrassing."

His laugh was deep and rich. "It's late and I stopped you from going to sleep. If for some reason I don't see you for the rest of the week, I'll pick you up at seven on Friday. That sound all right?"

"That sounds perfect. I'll see you then, and, uh, thanks for my rose." Before he could say anything else, I turned the doorknob, gave him a small smile, backed up into the room, and shut the door in his still-smirking face. "Holy hell," I whispered, and let my forehead fall against the door.

"Tell. Me. *Everything!*" Candice practically shrieked, and I turned to narrow my eyes at her.

Like she hadn't been listening.

"We're going on a date Friday. That's about it."

"That is *so* not all that was said, Rachel! Ohmigod, did you swoon when he said all he's seeing is you?"

"Swoon, Candice? Really? This isn't one of your romance novels." And yeah . . . I did kind of swoon. "And that's exactly why I'm not telling you. You eavesdrop anyway, so what's the point in going over it all again?"

"Because I want details of how he looked at you and how you reacted to him."

Oh dear God, this was going to be a long night.

WHY BLAKE THOUGHT we wouldn't see each other the rest of the week was beyond me, because sure enough he was the first person I saw when I walked into the athletic center the next afternoon. And surprise, surprise . . . he only had four girls around him that day. That wasn't including the one he was stretching out on the ground.

Candice's constant talking faded out as I watched him explaining why he was stretching those particular muscles. But I knew the girl wasn't paying attention; all she could care about was that he was practically in between her legs.

The girl on the ground said something I couldn't hear, and the runway-beautiful, mocha-skinned girl standing closest to me practically purred as she reached for his forearm, "Well, that's just because Blake's so good with his . . . *hands.*" The other four girls started giggling and I wanted to gag.

Blake's head shot up and I realized I must have actually gagged out loud. *Whoops.* Our eyes locked for a few seconds before he quickly looked at the girls surrounding him and his position with the one on the floor. When he looked back at me, his blue eyes were pleading, but I just shook my head and walked off toward the back to get my out-of-the-classroom part of my course over with.

"Hey." Candice nudged me. "Don't get upset about that. They aren't the ones who have a date with him on Friday."

"I'm not upset about that." I was upset about the fact that *that* pissed me off. What, did I expect him to change overnight just because we were going to go on one date? Or did his words last night really have me thinking I'd imagined his robot bimbo herd all year? And sheesh, why did I care at all? I didn't even want to go on a date with him! Not really . . .

An hour and a half later, I'd successfully avoided his gaze, which I could feel like a laser on my back. But when I turned to put some equipment away, he was right there and there was no way I could avoid Blake in all his real-life Calvin Klein model–ness.

"You're mad," he said, and began taking the equipment out of my arms and putting it in the closet.

"Um . . . not? And I can put this away myself."

"Rachel, I told you. I only see you."

"Yeah, no, I heard you." As soon as everything was put up, I turned away, only to quickly turn back around and face him. "Look, Blake, I don't think Friday is a good idea."

"Why isn't it?"

"Well, it's—you know . . . it's just not. So thank you for your offer. But once again, and hopefully for the last time, I'm not going to go on a date with you.

If you ever move back to California, I really hope this doesn't make family dinners awkward."

The corners of his lips turned up slightly. "All right. You done for the day?"

This was the first rejection he'd taken well, and it threw me off for a moment. "Um, yes?"

"Let's go then."

"Whoa, wait. Go where? Its Wednesday, not Friday. And I said no anyway."

"You said no to a date with me. The date was on Friday. So we aren't going on a date. We're just going to go walk, hang out, whatever you want. But it's not a date." He stepped close enough that we were sharing the same air and his voice got low and husky. "If you want to call it something, we can call it exercising or seeing Austin. You can hardly count that as a date, Rach."

I was momentarily stunned by the effect his voice and blue eyes had on me. "Um . . . ." I blinked rapidly and looked down to clear my head. "I've lived here almost three years, I don't need to see the sights."

"Perfect, I don't get out much other than to come to work, so I do. You can be my tour guide."

"Blake—"

"Come on, Rachel."

Not giving me an option, he grabbed on to my arm and began towing me out of the building. I caught sight of Candice and she waved excitedly as she watched us leave.

Why was she smiling? I sure as hell wasn't smiling, and Blake was practically dragging me away! He could have been hauling me off to slaughter me and leave my remains on a pig farm for all she knew, and Candice was just going to sit there and wave like a lunatic? Playground. Love. Over. Best-friend card officially revoked.

As soon as we were outside, I yanked my arm free and continued to follow Blake as he made his way off campus. Well, at least he was right about one thing: I couldn't count this as a date. No way would I have worn baggy sweats cut off at my calves and a tight tank on a date.

"Are you still mad?"

I glanced up to see his stupid smirk, which I kind of hated right now. "Why would I be mad? I was just dragged out of a building to go *walk* with a guy I turned down for a date."

His smirk turned into a full-blown smile. "Still mad," he said, and looked ahead. "Although I always did find your temper adorable, let me know when you're not."

Thirty minutes later I was getting tired of following him around. Tour guide my nonexistent ass. He wasn't looking at anything. He was walking with a purpose and hadn't looked back at me since he'd asked if I was mad.

"So, this has been awesome and all. Are you going to tell me where we're going now?"

"Are you going to tell me what you're mad about?"

"I'm not mad!"

He slowed his pace so he was directly next to me and I was surprised to see him looking at me completely seriously. "Yes you are, Rach. If you didn't want to go on the date on Friday, you would have never agreed, and you wouldn't be following me right now." I opened my mouth but he cut me off. "You would have gone back to your dorm and you know it. I was two steps ahead of you the entire time; you could have turned back if you were really mad at me."

"You didn't even give me an option to say no!" He raised an eyebrow and I huffed, "All right. Fine. Maybe I am mad."

"And you're mad at me."

"Yeah, Blake, I am."

"But not because I pulled you out of the building."

Oh my word, he was so infuriating! "Uh, yeah, I'm pretty sure that's why I'm mad. Are you going to start telling me I'm not hungry either? Since you all of a sudden seem to know me so well?"

He pulled me to a stop and moved to stand directly in front of me, tipping my head back with his fingers under my chin. "You're mad because of the girls around me when you walked in this afternoon."

"I—"

"And I told you I only see you. I'll tell you that over and over again until you understand that. They mean nothing, nor do I notice anything other than the fact that they talk like they're in middle school."

"I don't care about them the way you think I do. When I saw it, it just reminded me why I never wanted to go on a date with you in the first place. Nothing more, nothing less."

"You're lying, Rachel." I could smell the mint from his gum and feel his breath on my lips, and suddenly I was wondering if I *was* lying. There must have been something in his gum that put me in a daze. "It's fine to admit you were getting jealous. I hate seeing the way Aaron looks at you, and you work with him every day."

I was so not getting jeal— Wait. What?! Aaron's gay. I leaned away from his nearness and started to tell him when I realized we were on top of a bridge surrounded by a bunch of people just standing there looking toward the side like they were waiting for something. I pointed toward the people. "Uh . . . am I missing something?"

Blake looked a little smug as he glanced at his watch, then the sky. "Nope, give it a couple minutes. We got here just in time."

Aaron, his sexuality, and the fact that Blake had gotten jealous over my flaming gay friend completely forgotten, I looked at the sky, then pulled out my phone to check the time. There was nothing special about the time from what I could tell. As for the sky, it was nearly dusk, and although it was beautiful I didn't know why that was anything worth noting either. Glancing at the people and the street around us, I turned and saw the street sign and did a double take. We were on Congress Avenue.

"Oh no. No, no, no, no, no!" I started backing up

but ended up against Blake's chest. His arms circled around me, effectively keeping me there. I felt his silent laughter.

"I take it you know about this then. Ever seen it?"

"No, and there's a reason. I'm terrified of—" Just then, close to a million bats took flight from underneath the bridge. A small shriek escaped my lips and I clamped my hands over my mouth, like my sound would attract the bats to me.

There was nothing silent about his next laugh. Blake tightened his arms around me and I leaned into him more. I'd like to say it was purely because my biggest fear was flying out around me, but I'd be lying if I said his musky cologne, strong arms, and chest had nothing to do with it either. This was something I'd wanted for years, and I almost couldn't believe that I was finally there, in his arms.

I continued to watch in utter horror and slight fascination as the stream of bats, which seemed to never end, continued to leave the shelter of the bridge and fly out into the slowly darkening sky.

Minutes later, Blake leaned in and put his lips up against my ear. "Was that really so bad?"

Forcing my hand from my mouth, I exhaled shakily and shook my head. "Not as bad as I'd imagined. Doesn't change the fact that they are ugly and easily the grossest thing I've ever seen."

"But now you can say you've faced one of your fears."

"The biggest."

"See?" He let go of me and started walking again in the direction we'd come from. "You up for a drink?"

I realized I was still shaking so I nodded my head and followed him. "Just one though."

We walked for well over half an hour while Blake tried to re-create my shriek at seeing the bats and I accused him of doing that with every girl so he'd have an excuse to put his arms around her. The air between us was much more relaxed this time as he asked about my life after he'd joined the air force. I told him all about the end of middle school and high school but never once mentioned my parents. I wasn't sure if he knew about them or not, but there was no point in bringing up that hurt. Besides, if he had known, he hadn't even come back for the funeral. Just as we were passing the school, Blake slid his hand down my arm and intertwined our fingers.

"Rachel, why did you finally agree to go out with me?"

When I looked up, I was surprised at his somber expression. I would have expected something a little more taunting. "Do you want me to answer that honestly?"

"I'd appreciate it. I've asked you out for . . . shit. I don't know, nine months now? No matter what I said, your answer was always no. Until last night."

"Well . . ." I looked down at the sidewalk passing beneath our feet.

"You can tell me, it's fine. You never were one to hide your feelings. And your hate for me lately has been a little more than apparent. I'm already expecting the worst."

"I don't hate you. I just don't exactly like you . . . anymore." I squinted up at him and nudged his side with the arm he still had a firm grip on.

He gave a little grunt with a forced smile.

"Um, Candice is always bugging me for turning you down. She said she would stop if I agreed to one date with you." I know, I know, I could have made something up that wasn't so harsh. But I didn't. If I hadn't looked back down, I probably would have missed the pause in his step.

"Figures." We walked for a few more minutes before he paused and turned to me. "I'm not going to make you go out with me."

"You aren't. I said I'd go."

He raised an eyebrow, making it disappear under his shaggy hair. "You also told me earlier today that we weren't going anymore. I'm just letting you know I'll stop. All of it. Asking you all the time, what I did today. And I'll talk to Candice."

"Blake—"

"No, Rach, I should have stopped a long time ago. I'm sorry you felt pressured into it last night. I want you to *want* to go on a date with me. I don't want you to go just so she'll drop it or because you want me to quit asking. Which I will." I couldn't tell if he looked more embarrassed or hurt.

Is it ridiculous that I want to comfort him? "I want to go."

"No, you don't."

Okay, still somewhat true. "I didn't . . . before." *Ugh, who am I kidding. He knows I'm lying anyway.* "Look, I don't know what you want me to say. You can't exactly blame me for not wanting to go out with you." He looked as if I'd slapped him. I hurried on before I could chicken out on the rest. "I mean, come on, Blake, you were rumored to be screwing all these students, coworkers, and faculty. And not once did you try to shut down those rumors. Add to that, the Blake I grew up with is completely gone; now you're usually kind of a douche. Why *would* I want to go out with someone like that?"

"Rumors are going to spread no matter what I do. The more I try to stop them, the guiltier I look. Trust me. As for you thinking I'm a douche . . ." His voice trailed off and he ran a hand through his hair. "Try seeing it from my side. The only girl I've wanted for years now and can't get out of my head no matter what I do repeatedly blows me off like I'm nothing."

Did he say years?

Letting go of my hand, he turned away from me and ran a hand agitatedly through his hair. "Come on, I'll walk you back to your dorm."

"What about drinks?"

"I'm not going to make you do this, Rachel."

"Blake, why can't you just be like this all the time? If how you were growing up, last night, and the last hour was how you always were . . . I probably wouldn't have ever turned you down."

He huffed a sad laugh. "Yeah, well . . . obviously I've already fucked that up."

I watched him begin walking in the direction of the dorms and squeezed my eyes shut as I called after him, "You know, you kinda traumatized me tonight. I feel like you owe me a beer." Peeking through my eyelashes, I saw him stop but not turn around. "And maybe dinner on Friday night?"

When Blake turned to face me, his smile was wide and breathtaking.

Chapter Two

Rachel

DRINKS WITH BLAKE had actually been more fun than I would have thought, and we'd ended up spending Thursday afternoon and evening together as well. He seemed to slip back into the Blake that Candice and I had spent years following around. On Friday, when I stepped into the athletic center, I was met with three red roses and a heart-stopping grin. He'd said that regardless of his reasoning on Wednesday afternoon, he was counting the bats and bar on Wednesday, and movies on the couch in my dorm room on Thursday, as dates. So Friday night would be our third and deserved three roses.

I'm not gonna lie, I totally did the *aww, you're so sweet* girly thing as I took the roses from him and kissed his cheek in front of the circle of girls he was doing pretty well at fully ignoring. When Candice dragged me out of the center not even an hour later to go get a pedicure and have me start getting ready for the date, she pressed me for every single detail of my time with Blake thus far. She was really rooting for this whole actually-being-related thing.

He was sweet, attentive, and completely down-to-earth. But I was glad he was still giving me my space. Even being alone in the dorm room with me for three movies, he never once tried to pull me into his arms and had yet to try to kiss me. Which Candice was taking as a bad sign. I rolled my eyes at that assumption. Now that Blake was finally getting his dates, he was letting me take this at the speed I wanted, and I couldn't have been more thankful.

But then Friday night was just . . . odd.

Blake picked me up in his silver Lexus convertible and took me to the Oasis, a restaurant sitting on the lake with the most amazing view as the sun set, which it began to do just after we'd arrived. I honestly don't think I'd ever seen anything more beautiful, and just as I began to tell Blake that, our waiter arrived to take our drink order. Without a word, Blake handed him both menus and placed our order for our food and drinks. I hadn't even looked at the menu yet. The food was just as he said it would be, to die for. But from the way he continued to treat me I was expecting him to cut my meat and feed me himself by the time our food got there.

Conversation was at a standstill until we were back in his car.

"Want to go for drinks again?" he asked suddenly, halfway back to campus.

Obviously he had missed how awkward the last hour had been. "Two margaritas are more than enough for me. I'm good."

His laugh boomed throughout the small car as his hand fell onto my upper thigh and gave a little squeeze. "Okay, no drinks. Anything else you want to do?"

"Um . . ."

"Do you like horses?"

"Horses?" That wasn't something I'd been expecting. "Of course I like horses."

"So how about we go for a carriage ride down Sixth Street before I take you home? Sound good?"

"I don't know."

"Rachel, did I do something? I feel like we've gone back a few steps."

"No, I'm sorry . . . I'm just tired. I've felt off all day. Is it okay if you take me back?"

"Of course there's always tomorrow!"

I stifled a groan and smashed myself as close to the side of the car as possible. The entire way back he kept his hand on my thigh and continued to rub his thumb back and forth. In an effort to not smack it away, I crossed my arms under my chest and resorted to burning imaginary holes in his hand with my eyes. After we got to campus he walked me all the way to my room before trapping me against the door frame and leaning in. I turned my head away at the last minute but that didn't seem to faze him. Grabbing my hips and pressing his body closer to mine, he started kissing a line down my neck, and I swear he smelled my hair before groaning. I tried not to gag.

"Blake, please? Can we not do this?"

He pulled back and his blue eyes flared. "Fine." The way he looked at me from under his eyelashes caused a chill to run down my spine. And not a good one. "I'll see you later." Without another word he pushed off me, turned, and stalked down the hallway.

"RACH, WAKE UP and tell. Me. *Everything*!"

Cracking my eyes open the next morning, I looked at a too-perky Candice and groaned. "Where were you when I got back last night?"

"With Jeff." She dismissed his name with a wave of her hand. "Now, tell me about your date!"

"Wow, Jeff too, huh? Nice, Candi."

"Don't stall!"

Pulling myself up so I was resting on my elbows, I didn't even feel like sugarcoating the prior night. "It was awful."

Her eyes went wide. "What do you mean? What'd you do?"

Bitch. "Why is it that I had to do something?"

"Um, let's see." She started counting on her fingers.

"One, you didn't want to go out with him in the first place. Two, unlike Wednesday and Thursday, Blake didn't text me after to tell me about your time together. Three, you didn't want to go out with him in the first place."

"You already said that."

"Exactly, that's a big enough one that it counts for two! So what happened?"

I sighed and flopped onto my bed. "It was just weird. It's like we had nothing to talk about. Which was crazy because we talked the entire time we were together on Wednesday and Thursday. And he didn't even let me see a menu; he ordered for me. Like I was a three-year-old or something."

"Is that all?"

"Well, yeah. Oh! And when we were on our way back he just started acting like the night had been completely normal and not awkward in any way. Then when we got back, he pushed me up against the door and started kissing my neck. I kind of asked him to stop and he got weird. Like creepy, scary weird . . . and then he just up and left. I don't know, the whole night was just a bust."

Candice didn't say anything; she just sat there staring at me.

"What?"

"Are you insane? You told him to stop kissing you?!"

Really? That was all she got from what I told her? "Yeah, we had a bad date; why would I want him to kiss me? Maybe if it had gone something like the first two nights I wouldn't have—"

"No, no. Rachel. Oh my God. We need to fix this. I can't believe you still managed to mess up the date after everything I went over with you yesterday!"

"Wow." I shook my head and let my arms give out so I face-planted into my pillow again. I was so dumbfounded I didn't even know what to say anymore.

After running to a café to grab a quick breakfast, we made our way back to *hopefully* study for finals, which were next week. But from the way Candice had tried to lecture me on all I probably had done wrong on the date during breakfast, I doubted much studying would take place if it involved her.

Not even two minutes after getting back into our room, there was a knock on the door. And surprise freaking surprise. Blake West. With *four* red roses.

"You do realize it's not even nine on a Saturday," I said. And yes, I laid the California-bitch tone on thick.

Blake didn't miss a beat, and his smirk didn't falter. "Morning, Rach. Can I take you out to breakfast?"

"Oh, we just ate!" *Darn.* I didn't even try to sound disappointed.

Candice gave me a look that I pretended not to notice.

"Well, that's okay." His smile was full of easy confidence. "How about we go grab some coffee instead?"

"I actually need to start studying for my finals."

"All the more reason for coffee now; it'll keep you awake."

Dear Lord, what is it with him and Candice? Do they not get hints? Must come from her mom's side of the family. "Sure, why don't we all go? Candice, you want to get coffee?"

"Nah, I'm good. I just texted Eric to come over in a few to help me, um, study."

Traitor. I glanced back at a victorious-looking Blake. "Could you give me a couple minutes?"

"See you down there." He handed me the four roses, winked, and walked down the hall.

"Eric today, huh? I'm sure you two will get tons of studying done. Maybe I should stay and help you; you can't afford to fail this thing."

"You better go!" She looked me over and raised an annoyed eyebrow. "Please tell me you're going to change."

I looked down at my yoga pants and off-the-shoulder Iron Maiden concert shirt. "Ha! No, definitely not. It's early in the morning, and we're just getting coffee. Which means I get to stay skanked up."

"You do not stay skanked up when you're trying to get the man of your dreams to fall in love with you! You stay skanked up if no one is going to see you! You know this, Rachel."

Love? God, this whole dating-her-cousin thing was making her more dramatic than usual. I threw my long, dark hair up into a cute messy bun, grabbed my purse, and sighed heavily. "See you later."

Blake didn't say a word to me as I slid into the passenger seat of his car, and he continued to stay silent as we drove to one of the Starbucks near campus. The only acknowledgment he made of my presence was to put his hand high up on my thigh again and hold tight. Too tight. And not much changed once we were finally in the shop. Conversation didn't happen, his hand was back on my thigh, and we had four different stare-downs.

I only won one of those.

At least he let me order my own coffee. That was honestly the only good part of this morning.

I was barely able to hold in my sigh of relief when my phone chimed.

"Who is that?" Blake's eyebrows were pulled down, and he seemed more than a little annoyed.

Only checking the text preview on the lock screen, I shrugged. "Oh, it's just a friend, he wants to get a study group together tonight." I started to put my phone back in my purse when his hand shot out and grabbed on to my arm, effectively keeping it suspended above my purse.

"Well, it's rude to keep him waiting. Aren't you going to answer him?" He looked like he was struggling to keep himself in check.

I tried to pull my arm back and he finally released it. Sheesh, what was his problem? It was just a text. "Sure, I guess."

"Just let him know you can't go."

"Excuse me?"

He leaned forward and his eyes narrowed. "I'd prefer that you study with Candice."

Now I was getting mad. He didn't own me, he definitely wasn't my boyfriend, and this was Aaron. The same gay guy that Blake didn't like "looking at me." "And since when do you get to decide who I hang out with? Look, maybe I've been giving you the wrong impression over the last few days, but we aren't together. You have no say in what I do."

Like a switch had been flipped, his face went back to its usual smooth, sexy expression. "You're right. Actually I think it's a good idea for you to study with some other people besides Candice; I'm sure you wouldn't get anywhere with her."

Wait. What? The sudden change in his mood made me almost feel dizzy. It was like I had my own personal Dr. Jekyll and Mr. Hyde sitting next to me.

When I could finally get my mouth to stop opening and shutting like a fish, I shook my head and exhaled roughly. "Speaking of, I really need to get back to campus." I stood to leave without giving him the chance to say no.

Without another word, Blake followed me out to the car. We didn't say anything on the drive back but he put his hand on my thigh again. Was I imagining how tight he was holding it? When we arrived at the dorm, he parked in one of the spaces rather than letting me out in front. I grabbed the handle to open the door and he pushed down on my thigh, gripping it tighter. I turned to look at him and was surprised to see he still looked light and easygoing.

"I'll get the door for you. Wait here for just a second."

Crap, I hope he isn't going to walk me to my room. I bet Candice still has Eric in there with the door locked. As soon as he released me, my thigh throbbed from the relief of the pressure he'd put on it and I almost wished I was wearing shorts so I could look at the damage I was making myself believe he'd done. The passenger door opened and I stepped out without looking up at him. We walked without saying anything and I made sure to put some distance between us. I was relieved when he began to slow down as we reached the main entrance of the dorm.

"Well, thanks for the coff—"

He caught me around the waist, pushed me up against the wall, and kissed me roughly, interrupting my good-bye. Before I had time to realize what was happening and push him away, his body left mine and he started backing up toward his car.

"I'll see you later." He winked, then turned away from me.

I have no idea what my face looked like; I couldn't even pin down an emotion. I was disgusted, annoyed, confused, and pissed. It took a second before I was able to compose myself. I shook out my arms and walked up to my room.

I didn't know if I was ready to tell Candice about this, or if I even wanted to. Knowing her, she'd somehow turn it around so that I had done something wrong or I didn't know how to kiss. Needless to say, I was dreading facing her. Luck was on my side. Eric must still have been in there, because the door was locked, and on the mini whiteboard attached to our wall in Candice's writing were the words "DON'T come in." I texted Candice, asking her to put my laptop and books outside while I went to the bathroom so I wouldn't be subjected to a flushed and rumpled Candice and Eric. After I picked those up, I went back to the common room and pulled out my phone to finally text Aaron back.

Sounds good. What time and where?

AARON: 7p @ Starbucks

Great. Like I wanted to go there again. I sighed, cracked open a book, and tried not to think about Blake.

WITH THE STUDYING I'd done before the group and the five hours with them, I felt fully prepared for this final and was glad it was on Monday. Once that was out of the way, I only had two days left of easy finals and this year would be over.

I was still wired from all the espresso I'd sucked down in the last few hours, and since it was a twenty-four-hour Starbucks, I decided to stay in the café and write in my journal. After my parents' accident, Candice's parents tried everything to get me to talk. I think they were afraid I would never come out of my depression. Her brother, Eli, had been the only one who had known how to handle me—so to speak.

He'd been home from college for the summer when
the accident happened, and unlike his first few years
away, he came back every weekend to see me once
school started up again. He would hold me while I
stared off into space and never spoke a word. Eli's
form of healing was my favorite, since it was silent,
but we all knew he couldn't be there for me forever.
One night when I got home from school there was a
journal on my bed with a note from Candice's dad,
George. He suggested using the journal to write to my
parents like they were still here. At first it freaked me
out, but I told him I would try, and I'm glad I did.
Even I could see the difference in myself. I wrote to
them every day, even if it was just a few lines. But
I viewed it as a way of continuing our family time.
Every night after dinner while I was growing up, we'd
pile on the couches, turn on the TV, and talk about
our day while watching whatever shows were on that
night. So that's what I did. I just told them what was
going on in my life like I would have if they were still
there.

When I finished a couple hours later, I put everything in my purse and called out good-byes to the too-
awake baristas. As soon as I pushed open the door
and walked out into the muggy night air, my phone
went off and the words on the screen caused me to
stumble and a chill to shoot through my body.

BLAKE: You look beautiful tonight.

Instead of bolting for my car like any sane person would have, I looked around until I found him. Well, running to my car wouldn't have helped much; he was parked right next to it and leaning against the driver's door of his shiny little Lexus.

How did he know I was here? If he didn't know I was here, what is he doing here at two in the morning? Oh my word, he's been following me! No, that's ridiculous; come on, Rachel, get a grip. He is not following you. Frick, I really need to stop thinking the world and everyone in it revolves around me. He just happened to be here and saw your car. That's all. Right? Right.

I took a few steps closer to the cars and took a deep breath as I dropped my phone back into my purse, trying to calm myself down. "Hi, Blake."

"I was starting to think you would never leave. I've been out here for hours."

Oh God, he has been waiting for me! Those words were creepy enough, but paired with the sexy, innocent smile they seemed even worse. I meant for my voice to sound strong and annoyed but it was barely a whisper. "Why are you following me?"

"Following you? I'm not following you. Candice told me you were waiting for me to pick you up from the study group. Jesus, Rachel, you look like you've just seen a ghost; are you all right?"

"Candice said what? No, I was definitely not waiting for you; I drove myself here. That should be obvious, since you're parked next to my Jeep." I didn't know what was going on, but I wanted to get out of there and away from him. Now.

"Yeah, but your car isn't starting. Which is why I'm here." He said every word slowly, like I was a child or something. "Don't you remember, Rachel? You called her almost three hours ago, but she was busy, so you told her to call me. Are you feeling okay? Come on, get in the car. I'll get you back to your room."

"I am *not* getting in your car, I'll drive myself back!" With that I took the last few steps to my car, got in, locked the door, and put the key in the ignition. I turned it but nothing happened. There wasn't even a click. What had happened to my car? I knew I hadn't called Candice. And even then, if I'd wanted Blake to pick me up I would have called him myself. Someone tapped on the window and even though I knew who it was, I still jumped.

"Come on, Rach, this is dumb. Just get in the car and I'll take you back. I'll get your car towed in a couple hours."

There was no point in trying to call someone else. It was two in the morning, everyone was asleep, and I definitely couldn't walk back at this hour. I grimaced and opened the door.

"That's my girl. Come on, let's go." He helped me into his car, then got in beside me. This time he didn't put his hand on my thigh.

The short drive to the dorm seemed to take forever, and besides his asking me a few times if I was feeling all right, there was no conversation. Blake seemed genuinely concerned about me. Had I called Candice? Did I just forget about everything while I was writing to my parents? Is that why I went in to write to them in the first place? Maybe all the studying mixed with my caffeine high, which was turning into a major crash, had my mind all jumbled. I must have just forgotten. It would have been easy to grab my phone and check the recent call history, but something inside me tightened and I knew it would be the wrong thing to do. We finally reached the dorm, and just like that morning, Blake parked in the lot. Aces.

"Are you sure you're feeling okay?" he asked for the fifth time since we'd gotten in the car. "You freaked when you saw me."

"I'm fine, really, don't worry about me. I probably just forgot and lost track of time in there." I tried to make my smile convincing; I didn't want him to walk me to my room. I got out of the car, ducked my head back in to thank him, and saw he was getting out too. Crap.

"You don't really think I'm going to let you walk up there by yourself, do you?"

"Of course not," I muttered. "I was just trying to be polite. It's late and you've already been waiting on me for hours . . . apparently."

He just laughed as he walked toward me, put his arm around my waist, and led me to my room. When we got there he reached out to open the door for me; at least the good-bye would be quick. But my happiness was short-lived; he walked me into the empty room and then turned to shut and lock the door behind us.

"Where's Candice?" I couldn't stop my voice from shaking. How weird that just Thursday I'd spent hours alone with him in this room and had felt comfortable and enjoyed my time with him. But now, being in here with him felt . . . wrong.

"She didn't tell you when you talked? All she told me was she was busy," he said a little too innocently.

I turned to face the room again to see if her cell was around; if it wasn't I was going to call her immediately. Before I could find—or hopefully *not* find—her phone, Blake came up behind me and began kissing the back of my neck.

"Uh, Blake? Can you not do that right now? I need to find out where Candice is."

Instead of stopping, he turned me around, pushed me up against my wardrobe, and resumed his place on my neck. I tried pushing him back, but it was useless. The guy was a rock and he wasn't budging.

"She'll be back when she's ready to come back," he breathed between kisses and little bites.

Well, I wasn't about to wait for that to happen. I wanted him out of my room *now*. "Okay, I'm really ti—"

He quickly moved up to my lips, shutting me up, and his kisses became rough and possessive. Just as they'd been that morning, only these weren't lasting three seconds. We were close enough to the door that he reached out to flip off the lights and caught me around my waist again before I could take advantage of the break in his strong hold. He started backing me up toward the bed, and I pushed as hard as I could against the hand holding my head in place. His only response was to push against me harder. My bed was high enough that it hit at the small of my back and helped me stay standing when he tried to push me down. When I didn't immediately fall onto the bed, he pulled my head back to look at me, giving me the break I needed.

"You need to leave. Now!" My arms had been caught between us, but with the new space I put them against his chest and tried to push him back farther. Instead of moving away, he got a smile that turned my body to ice and my arms to Jell-O. This is what I imagined a crazy person looked like.

"You don't mean that," he growled as he pulled my face back to his.

Did he really think I was just playing hard to get? I wanted him off me! He let go of my waist and began searching for the bottom of my shirt, but even though my waist was free I still couldn't move; I was caught between him and the bed. When he found it he didn't waste time traveling up to grab my chest. I could feel him getting excited and it made me want to throw up. His lips moved back to my neck.

"Please. Stop." I hated how small my voice sounded.

"This would be over sooner if you'd just lie down and shut up."

Grabbing both sides of my waist, he lifted me

onto the bed, pushed me down, and climbed on top of me. I tried to tell him to stop again, but nothing was coming out except for my rapid breathing. My body was shaking violently and I was dangerously close to hyperventilating. He bit my bottom lip, causing me to gasp enough that he could slide his tongue into my mouth. Blake's knees were pinning my legs to the bed and I bucked my hips and pushed against his shoulders, but he still didn't move. He gathered both my wrists in one hand and pinned them above my head. Tears pricked at the back of my eyes. I tried to move my head to the side so I could scream for help but he moved with me as he thrust his tongue in my mouth over and over again. I froze for all of five seconds before biting down on his tongue as hard as I could. He flew back with a pained cry and I tasted blood in my mouth. I was going to throw up. Before I could scream, his free hand slammed down on my throat and his face was directly above mine again. He growled as his blue eyes turned to ice and he just stared at me as I gasped for air.

"You're going to regret doing that, sweetheart." My vision blurred from my tears; the outer edges were turning black as I struggled to stay conscious.

Blake's breathing deepened and the look that crossed his painfully handsome face terrified me. My mouth opened and shut, but I couldn't pull in any air and I couldn't make a sound. My arms gave up their fight seconds before my bucking hips did the same, and soon I could hardly focus on Blake at all. I prayed that someone would come and save me as the hand that had been holding my hands down on the mattress slid down and cupped me through my thin yoga pants.

I felt his hot breath on my ear. "I'll make sure you never want to fight me again, Rachel."

The hand that was cupping me went up and slid under my pants and underwear. I tried to roll away but it was taking everything in me to stay awake. Tears spilled over and fell down my cheeks. Just as my mind started shutting down, the hand clasped around my throat was gone and I began gasping for air.

Waves of dizziness washed over me, and the blackness slowly faded away. I heard the distinct sound of his zipper over my gasps and sobs and my head shook slowly back and forth. I felt like I was underwater and couldn't find my way to the surface. His hand closed around my throat again and I frantically tried to pull in air and claw at his hand, but it was useless. My arms lost function quickly and the edges of my vision were going black again, and I begged the darkness to come quicker when he began moving inside me. I didn't want to be conscious through what he was doing. I didn't want to remember this. The sweet numbness began claiming me, and at that moment, the most beautiful sound in the world came from outside the door.

Candice's voice.

Blake was off the bed and putting himself back in his shorts in seconds while I wildly tried to take in as much oxygen as possible. He roughly pulled my pants up just as the key could be heard in the lock and took the few steps toward the door to flip the light on before coming back to my side. When the door opened, Blake was standing at the side of my bed looking down at me. The light brush of his fingers over my throat and his solid glare were clearly a warning. But I was still on the verge of fainting, now from trying too roughly to inhale.

Candice said good-bye to whomever she'd been talking to as she shut the door. "Oh, hey, cuz! I didn't mean to—" Blake turned to look at her and Candice's eyes went wide when she saw me. "Oh my God, Rachel, are you okay?!"

She rushed over to me, but Blake touched her arm and pulled her away. "She was attacked by a couple guys outside Starbucks tonight. She called me about half an hour ago. She's in shock but she'll be okay."

"What?!" Candice screamed, and tears instantly filled her eyes.

What? No. No, no, no. My head shook back and forth as I choked on a sob and my breathing got even faster and heavier. I tried to tell her that was wrong, that he was lying, but all that came out was the ragged sound of my breathing.

I could see Candice and Blake's mouths moving, but I couldn't hear anything else. Everything tilted to the side and the blackness came back full force. I reached out for Candice but missed her arm as the dark claimed me.

About the Author

MOLLY McADAMS grew up in California but now lives in the oh-so-amazing state of Texas with her husband and furry daughters. Her hobbies include hiking, snowboarding, traveling, and long walks on the beach . . . which roughly translates to being a homebody with her hubby and dishing out movie quotes. She has a weakness for crude-humored movies and fried pickles, and loves curling up in a fluffy comforter during a thunderstorm . . . or under one in a bathtub if there are tornados. That way she can pretend they aren't really happening.

Visit www.AuthorTracker.com for exclusive information on your favorite HarperCollins authors.